Ellen Anderson Gholson Glasgow

The Descendant

A Novel

Ellen Anderson Gholson Glasgow

The Descendant
A Novel

ISBN/EAN: 9783337001056

Printed in Europe, USA, Canada, Australia, Japan

Cover: Foto ©Andreas Hilbeck / pixelio.de

More available books at **www.hansebooks.com**

THE DESCENDANT

A Novel

"Man is not above Nature, but in Nature"

HAECKEL

NEW YORK

HARPER & BROTHERS PUBLISHERS

1897

TO

G. W. McC.

BOOK I

VARIATION FROM TYPE

OMNE VIVUM EX OVO

THE DESCENDANT

CHAPTER I

THE child sat upon the roadside. A stiff wind was rising westward, blowing over stretches of meadow-land that had long since run to waste, a scarlet tangle of sumac and sassafras. In the remote West, from whose heart the wind had risen, the death-bed of the Sun showed bloody after the carnage, and nearer at hand naked branches of poplar and sycamore were silhouetted against the shattered horizon, like skeletons of human arms that had withered in the wrath of God.

Over the meadows the amber light of the afterglow fell like rain. It warmed the spectres of dead carrot flowers, and they awoke to reflect its glory; it dabbled in the blood of sumac and pokeberry; and it set its fiery torch to the goldenrod till it ignited and burst into bloom, flashing a subtle flame from field to field, a glorious bonfire from the hand of Nature.

The open road wound lazily along, crossing transversely the level meadow-land and leading from the small town of Plaguesville to somewhere. Nobody—at least nobody thereabouts—knew exactly where, for it was seldom that a native left Plaguesville, and when he did it was only to go to Arlington, a few miles farther on, where the road dropped him, stretching southward.

The child sat restlessly upon the rotten rails that were

once a fence. He was lithe and sinewy, with a sharp brown face and eyes that were narrow and shrewd—a small, wild animal of the wood come out from the underbrush to bask in the shifting sunshine.

Occasionally a laborer passed along the road from his field work, his scythe upon his shoulder, the pail in which his dinner was brought swinging at his side. Once a troop of boys had gone by with a dog, and then a beggar hobbling on his crutch. They were following in the wake of the circus, which was moving to Plaguesville from a neighboring town. The child had seen the caravan go by. He had seen the mustang ponies and the cowboys who rode them; he had seen the picture of the fat lady painted upon the outside of her tent; and he had even seen the elephant as it passed in its casings.

Presently the child rose, stooping to pick the blackberry briers from his bare legs. He wore nankeen trousers somewhat worn in the seat and a nankeen shirt somewhat worn at the elbows. His hand was rough and brier-pricked, his feet stained with the red clay of the cornfield. Then, as he turned to move onward, there was a sound of footsteps, and a man's figure appeared suddenly around a bend in the road, breaking upon the glorified landscape like an ill-omened shadow.

It was the minister from the church near the town. He was a small man with a threadbare coat, a large nose, and no chin to speak of. Indeed, the one attribute of saintliness in which he was found lacking was a chin. An inch the more of chin, and he might have been held as a saint; an inch the less, and he passed as a simpleton. Such is the triumph of Matter over Mind.

"Who is it?" asked the minister. He always inquired for a passport, not that he had any curiosity upon the subject, but that he believed it to be his duty. As yet he had only attained that middle state of sanctity where duty and pleasure are clearly defined. The next stage is the one in which, from excessive cultivation of the senses or atrophy of the imagination, the distinction between the things we ought to do and the things we want to do becomes obliterated.

The child came forward.

"It's me," he said. "Little Mike Akershem, as minds the pigs."

"Ah!" said the minister. "The boy that Farmer Watkins is bringing up. Why, bless my soul, boy, you've been fighting!"

The child whimpered. He drew his shirt sleeve across his eyes.

"I—I warn't doin' nothin'," he wailed. "Leastways, nothin' but mindin' the pigs, when Jake Johnson knocked me down, he did."

"He's a wicked boy," commented the minister, "and should be punished. And what did *you* do when Jake Johnson knocked you down?"

"I—I fell," whimpered the child.

"A praiseworthy spirit, Michael, and I am glad to see it in one so young and with such a heritage. You know the good book says: 'Do good unto them that persecute you and despitefully use you.' Now, you would like to do good unto Jake Johnson, wouldn't you, Michael?"

"I—I'd like to bus' him open," sobbed the child. Tears were streaming from his eyes. When he put up his hand to wipe them away it left dirty smears upon his cheeks.

The minister smiled and then frowned.

"You've forgotten your Catechism, Michael," he said. "I'm afraid you don't study it as you should."

The boy bubbled with mirth. Smiles chased across his face like gleams of sunshine across a cloud.

"I do," he rejoined, righteously. "Jake, he fought me on o'count o' it."

"The Catechism!" exclaimed the minister. "Jake fought you because of the Catechism?"

"It war a word," said the child. "Jake said it war consarnin' me an' I—"

"What word?" the minister demanded. "What did the word mean?"

"It war an ugly word." The boy's eyes were dry. He looked up inquiringly from beneath blinking lids. "It war dam—damni—"

"Ah!" said the minister, in the tone in which he said "Amen" upon a Sabbath, "damnation."

"Air it consarning me?" asked the child with anxious uncertainty.

The minister looked down into the sharp face where the gleams of sunshine had vanished, and only the cloud remained. He saw the wistful eyes beneath the bushy hair, the soiled, sunburned face, the traces of a dirty hand that had wiped tears away—the whole pitiful littleness of the lad. The nervous blinking of the lids dazzled him. They opened and shut like a flame that flickers and revives in a darkened room.

"No," he said, gently, "you have nothing to do with that, so help me God."

Again the boy bubbled with life. Then, with a swift, tremulous change, he grew triumphant. He looked up hopefully, an eager anxiety breaking his voice.

"It might be consarning Jake hisself," he prompted.

But the minister had stretched the mantle of his creed sufficiently.

"Go home," he said; "the pigs are needing their supper. What? Eh? Hold on a bit!" For the boy had leaped off like laughter. "What about the circus? There's to be no gadding into such evil places, I hope."

The boy's face fell. "No, sir," he said. "It's a quarter, an' I 'ain't got it."

"And the other boys?"

"Jake Johnson war looking through a hole in the fence an' he wouldn't let me peep never so little."

"Oh!" said the minister, slowly. He looked down at his boots. The road was dusty and they were quite gray. Then he blushed and looked at the boy. He was thinking of the night when he had welcomed him into the world—a little brown bundle of humanity, unclaimed at the great threshold of life. Then he thought of the mother, an awkward woman of the fields, with a strapping figure and a coarse beauty of face. He thought of the hour when the woman lay dying in the little shanty beyond the mill. Something in the dark, square face startled him. The look in the eyes was not the look of a woman of the fields, the strength in the bulging brow was more than the strength of a peasant.

His code of life was a stern one, and it had fallen upon stern soil. As the chosen ones of Israel beheld in Moab a wash-pot, so he and his people saw in the child only an embodied remnant of Jehovah's wrath.

But beneath the code of righteousness there quivered a germ of human kindness.

"Er—er, that's all," he said, his nose growing larger and his chin shorter. "You may go — but — how much have you? Money, I mean—"

"Eight cents," replied the child; "three for blackberrying, an' five for findin' Deacon Joskins's speckled pig as war lost. Five and three air eight—"

"And seventeen more," added the minister. "Well, here they are. Mind, now, learn your Catechism, and no gadding into evil places, remember that."

And he walked down the road with a blush on his face and a smile in his heart.

The child stood in the white dust of the road. A pale finger of sunshine struggled past him to the ditch beside the way, where a crimson blackberry-vine palpitated like a vein leading to the earth's throbbing heart. About him the glory waned upon the landscape and went out; the goldenrod had burned itself to ashes. A whippoorwill, somewhere upon the rotten fence rails, called out sharply, its cry rising in a low, distressful wail upon the air and losing itself among the brushwood. Then another answered from away in the meadow, and another from the glimmering cornfield.

A mist, heavy and white as foam, was rising with the tide of night and breaking against the foot of the shadowy hills.

The boy shifted upon his bare feet and the dust rose in a tiny cloud about him. Far in the distance shone the lights of the circus. He could almost hear the sound of many fiddles. Behind him, near the turnpike branch, the hungry pigs were rooting in the barnyard. He started, and the minister's money jingled in his pocket. In the circus-tent were the mustang ponies, the elephant, and the fat lady. He shifted restlessly. Perspiration stood in beads upon his forehead; his shirt collar was warm and damp. His eyes emitted a yellow flame in their nervous blinking. There was a sudden patter of feet, and he went spinning along the white dust of the road.

THE circus was over. One by one the lanterns went out; the tight-rope walker wiped the paint and perspiration from his face; the clown laid aside his eternal smile.

From the opening in the tent a thin stream of heated humanity passed into the turnpike, where it divided into little groups, some lingering around stationary wheelbarrows upon which stood buckets of pink lemonade, others turning into the branch roads that led to the farm-houses along the way.

In the midst of them, jostled helplessly from side to side, moved that insignificant combination of brown flesh and blue nankeen known as Michael Akershem. As the crowd dwindled away, his pace quickened until he went trotting at full speed through the shadows that were flung across the deserted road. Upon the face of the moon, as she looked down upon his solitary little figure, there was the derisive smile with which crabbed age regards callow youth and Eternity regards Time.

Perhaps, had he been wise enough to read her face aright, the graven exaltation of his own might have given place to an expression more in keeping with the cynicism of omniscience.

But just then, as he trotted resolutely along, the planet was of less importance in his reverie than one of the tallow candles that illumined the circus-tent.

The night was filled with visions, but among them the solar system held no place. Over the swelling hills, along the shadowy road, in the milky moonlight, trooped the splendid heroes of the circus-ring. His mind was on fire with the light and laughter; and the chastened brilliance of the night, the full sweep of the horizon, the eternal hills themselves seemed but a fitting setting for his tinselled visitants. The rustling of the leaves above his head was the flapping of the elephant's ears; the shimmer upon tufts of goldenrod, the yellow hair of the snake-charmer; and the quiet of the landscape, the breathless suspense of the excited audience.

As he ran, he held his worn straw hat firmly in his hand. His swinging strides impelled his figure from side to side, and before him in the dust his shadow flitted like an embodied energy.

Beneath the pallor of the moonlight the concentration of his face was revealed in grotesque exaggeration. His eyes had screwed themselves almost out of vision, the constant blinking causing them to flicker in shafts of light. Across his forehead a dark vein ran like a seam that had been left unfelled by the hand of Nature.

From the ditch beside the road rose a heavy odor of white thunder-blossom. The croaking of frogs grew louder as, one by one, they trooped to their congress among the rushes. The low chirping of insects began in the hedges, the treble of the cricket piercing shrilly above the base of the jar-fly. Some late glow-worms blazed like golden dewdrops in the fetid undergrowth.

The boy went spinning along the road. With the inconsequence of childhood all the commonplaces of every day seemed to have withered in the light of later events. The farmer and his pigs had passed into the limbo of forgetable things.

With the flickering lights of the cottage where Farmer Watkins lived, a vague uneasiness settled upon him; he felt a half-regret that Providence, in the guise of the minister, had thought fit to beguile him from the unpleasant path of duty. But the regret was fleeting, and as he crawled through a hole in the fence he managed to manipulate his legs as he thought the rope-walker would have done under the circumstances.

From the kitchen window a stream of light issued, falling
upon the gravelled path without. Against the lighted interior he beheld the bulky form of the farmer, and beyond
him the attenuated shadow of the farmer's wife stretching,
a depressing presence, upon the uncarpeted floor.

As the child stepped upon the porch the sound of voices
caused him to pause with abruptness. A lonely turkey,
roosting in the locust-tree beside the house, stirred in its
sleep, and a shower of leaves descended upon the boy's
head. He shook them off impatiently, and they fluttered to
his feet.

The farmer was speaking. He was a man of peace, and
his tone had the deprecatory quality of one who is talking
for the purpose of keeping another silent.

"My father never put his hand to the plough," said the
farmer, and he stooped to knock the ashes from his pipe;
"nor more will I."

He spoke gently, for he was a good man — good, inas-
much as he might have been a bad man, and was not. A
negative character is most often a virtuous one, since to be
wicked necessitates action.

The voice of the farmer's wife flowed on in a querulous
monotone.

"Such comes from harborin' the offspring of harlots and
what-not," she said. "It air a jedgment from the Lord."

The child came forward and stood in the kitchen doorway, scratching his left leg gently with the toes of his right
foot. The sudden passage from moonlight into lamplight
bewildered him, and he stretched out gropingly one wiry
little hand. The exaltation of his mind was chilled suddenly.

For a moment he stood unobserved. The farmer was
cleaning his pipe with the broken blade of an old pruning-
knife, and did not look up. The farmer's wife was knead-
ing dough, and her back was turned. All the bare and sordid aspect of the kitchen, the unpolished walls, the pewter
dishes in the cupboard, the bucket of apple parings in the

corner, struck the child as a blight after the garish color of the circus-ring.   He felt sick and ill at ease.

The monotone of the farmer's wife went relentlessly on. "A jedgment for harborin' the offspring of harlots," she repeated.   "God A'mighty knows what mischief he air workin' to-night.   He air worse than a weasel."

From the child's face all brightness was blotted out. His lips tightened until the red showed in a narrow line, paling from the pressure as a scar pales that is left from an old sabre cut.

The farmer replied soothingly, his hand wandering restlessly through his beard.   "He air a young child," he said, feebly.   "I reckon he air too little to work much."

Then he looked up and saw the shrinking figure in the doorway.   He shook his head slowly, more in weariness than wrath.

"You hadn't ought to done it," he murmured, reproachfully.   "You hadn't ought to done it."

A sob stuck in the boy's throat.   With a terrible revulsion of feeling, his passionate nature leaped into revolt. As the farmer's wife turned, he faced her in sullen defiance.

"I 'ain't never seed nothin' afore," he said, doggedly.   "I 'ain't never seed nothin' afore."

It was the justification he offered to opposing fate.

The woman turned upon him violently.

"You ingrate!" she cried.   "A-leaving me to do your dirty work.   A-sneaking off on meetin' night an' leaving me to tote the slops when I ought to led the choir.   You ingrate!"

The child looked pitifully small and lonely.   He pulled nervously at the worn brim of his straw hat.   Still he sought justification by facts.

"You are been to meetin' every Wednesday night sence I war born," he said, in the same dogged tone, "an' I 'ain't never seed nothin' afore."

Then the impotence of all explanation dawned upon him and his defiance lost its sullen restraint.   He felt the rage within him burst like a thunder cloud. The lamplight trembled in the air. The plank floor, the pewter plates, the chromos pinned upon the wall passed in a giddy whirl before his eyes. All his fire-tinctured blood quickened and leaped through his veins in a fever of scarlet. His face darkened from brown to black like the face of a witch. His thin lips were welded one into the other, and Nature's careless handiwork upon his forehead palpitated like a visible passion.

He sprang forward, striking at vacancy.

"I hate you!" he cried. "Curse you! Curse you!"

Then he turned and rushed blindly out into the night. A moment more and he was speeding away into the meadows. Like a shadow he had fled from the lamplight, like a shadow he had fled from the gravelled walk, and like a shadow he was fleeing along the turnpike.

He was unconscious of all save rage, blinding, blackening rage—a desire to stamp and shriek aloud—to feel his fingers closing upon something and closing and closing until the blood ran down. The old savage instinct to kill fell upon him like a mantle.

A surging of many waters started in his head, growing louder and louder until the waters rose into a torrent, shutting out all lesser sounds. The sob in his throat stifled him, and he gasped and panted in the midst of the moonlit meadows. Suddenly he left the turnpike, dashing across country with the fever of a fox pursued by hounds. Over the swelling hills, where the corn-ricks stood marshalled like a spectre battalion, he fled, spurred by the lash of his passion. Beneath him the valley lay wrapped in a transparent mist; above him a million stars looked down in passionless self-poise.

When he had run until he could run no more, he flung himself face downward upon the earth, beating the dew-drenched weeds into shapeless pulp.

"I hate 'em! I hate 'em!" he cried, choking for speech.

"Damn—damn—damn them all. I wish they war all in

hell. I wish the whole world war in hell—the farmer and the missis, and the minister and little Luly! I wish everybody war in hell—everybody 'cept me and the pigs!"

He ran his hand through his hair, tearing apart the matted waves. His lips quivered and closed together. Then he rolled over on his back and lay looking up to where the sky closed like a spangled vault above him.

"I hate 'em! I hate 'em!" he cried, and his cry fell quiveringly against the relentless hills. "I hate 'em!"

Back the faint echo came, ringing like the answering whisper of a devil, "h-a-t-e 'e-m—e-m—h-a-t-e!"

Above him, beyond the wall of stars, he knew that God had his throne—God sitting in awful majesty before the mouth of hell. He would like to call up to Him—to tell Him of the wickedness of the farmer's wife. He was sure that God would be angry and send her to hell. It was strange that God had overlooked her and allowed such things to be. Then he pictured himself dying all alone out upon the hillside; and the picture was so tragic that he fell to weeping. No; he would not die. He would grow up and become a circus-rider, and wear blue stockinet and gold lace. The farmer's wife and the farmer's ten children, their ten braids all smoothly plaited, would come to watch him ride the mustang ponies, and he would look straight across their heads and bow when the people applauded.

He saw himself standing before the glittering footlights, with the clown and the tight-rope walker beside him, and he saw himself, the most dazzling of the trinity, bowing above the excited heads of the farmer's children.

Yes, that would be a revenge worth having.

He sat up and looked about him. The night was very silent, and a chill breeze came blowing noiselessly across the hills. The moonlight shimmered like a crystalline liquid upon the atmosphere.

His passion was over, and he sat, with swollen eyes and quivering lips, a tiny human figure in the vast amphitheatre of Nature.

Beyond the stretch of pasture the open road gleamed pallid in the distance. The inky shadows through which he had passed some hours ago seemed to have thrilled into the phantoms of departed things. He wondered how he had dared to pass among them. Upon the adjoining hill he could see the slender aspens in the graveyard. They shivered and whitened as he looked at them. At their feet the white tombstones glimmered amid rank periwinkle. In a rocky corner he knew that there was one grave isolated in red clay soil—one outcast from among the righteous dead.

He felt suddenly afraid of the wicked ghost that might arise from that sunken grave. He was afraid of the aspens and the phantoms in the road. With a sob he crouched down upon the hillside, looking upward at the stars. He wondered what they were made of—if they were really holes cut in the sky to let the light of heaven stream through.

The night wind pierced his cotton shirt, and he fell to crying softly; but there was no one to hear.

At last the moon vanished behind a distant hill, a gray line in the east paled into saffron, and the dawn looked down upon him like a veiled face. Presently there was a stir at the farm, and the farmer's wife came from the cow-pen with a pail of frothy milk in her hand.

When she had gone into the house the boy left the hillside and crept homeward. He was sore and stiff, and his clothes were drenched with the morning dew. He felt all alone in a very great world, and the only beings he regarded as companions were the pigs in the barn-yard. His heart reproached him that he had not given them their supper.

The turnpike was chill and lonely as he passed along it. All the phantoms had taken wings unto themselves and flown. Upon the rail-fence the dripping trumpet-vine hung in limp festoons, yellow and bare of bloom. He paused to gather a persimmon that had fallen into the road from a tree beyond the fence, but it set his teeth on edge and he threw it away. A rabbit, sitting on the edge of a clump of brushwood, turned to glance at him with bright, suspicious eyes. Then, as he drew nearer, it darted across the road and between the rails into the pasture. The boy limped painfully along. His joints hurt him when he moved, and his feet felt like hundredweights. He wondered if he was not going to die shortly, and thought regretfully of the blue stockinet and tinsel which he could not carry with him into an eternity of psalm-singing.

Reaching the house, he seated himself upon the step of the porch and looked with miserable eyes at the kitchen window. The smell of steaming coffee floated out to him, and he heard the clinking of cups and saucers. Through the open window he beheld the bustling form of the farmer's wife.

Then, with a cautious movement, the door opened and the farmer came out upon the porch. He glanced hesitatingly around and, upon seeing the boy, vanished precipitately, to reappear bearing a breakfast-plate.

The child caught a glimpse of batter-bread and bacon, and his eyes glistened. He seized it eagerly. The farmer drew a chair near the doorway and seated himself beneath the bunch of red pepper that hung drying from the sash. He turned his eyes upon the boy. They were dull and watery, like the eyes of a codfish.

"You hadn't ought to done it, sonny," he said, slowly. "You hadn't ought to done it."

Then he drew a small quid of tobacco from his pocket and began to unwind the wrapping with laborious care. "It war a fine show, I reckon," he added.

The child nodded with inanimate acquiescence. It all seemed so long ago, the color and the splendor. It might as well have taken place in ancient Rome.

The farmer reached leisurely down into the pocket of his jeans trousers and drew out the old pruning-knife. Then he cut off a small square of tobacco and put it in his mouth.

"Sence it war a fine show," he said, reflectively, "I wish I'd ha' done it myself."

And he fell to chewing with a sigh.

THE child grew apace. He shot upward with the improvident growth of a weed that has sprung in a wheatfield. The changing seasons only served to render his hold upon life more tenacious and his will more indomitable. And, by-and-by, the child became the youth and waxed strong and manly. At nineteen he was lithe and straight as a young pine. Slightly above the average height, he had the look of a sturdy, thickset farmer, but with more than a farmer's breadth of brow. The dark hair still grew in a tangled mat upon his head, his features had roughened, and the lines in his face were deeply hewn. His jaws were strongly marked, and he had thin, flexible lips that quivered with reserve or paled with passion. Beneath the projecting brows his eyes were narrowed by a constant blinking.

Between himself and his little world there was drawn an invisible circle. The shadow that moved before or followed after him was a moral plague spot to the vision of his neighbors. If, with a spasmodic endeavor, they sought occasionally to rescue this stray brand from the burning, the rescue was attempted with gloved hands and a mental pitchfork. In periods of relaxation from personal purification, they played with the boy as children play with fire. It was the only excitement they permitted themselves.

As for the brand himself, he made the mistake of regarding the situation from a personal standpoint. Feeding the flame as he did, he naturally was unable to appreciate the vantage-ground of those who were only singed by it, and consequently in a position to enjoy that thrill of possible danger which is only enjoyable because the danger is

2

not possible at all. Being insensible to any danger, he failed to experience the thrill.

But what he did experience was a silent rage that in the end froze into a silent bitterness. As we all look upon life through the shadows which we ourselves cast upon it, so the facts of organic existence shape themselves in our horizon conformably with the circumstances which have shaped our individual natures. We see large or small, symmetrical or distorted forms, not according to external forces which have played upon external objects, but according to the adjustment of light and shade about our individual lenses. Truth is only truth in its complexity; our convictions are only real in their relativity. But Michael had not learned this. He still believed in his own ability to make plain the crooked ways of his neighbors' consciences. Socrates believed this, and where had arisen a greater than Socrates? Perhaps the one thing which Socrates and Michael had in common was a faith in the power of truth and the impotence of error; but then, Socrates and Michael each followed a different truth. Only the name of their divinity was the same—his face was different.

So Michael saw the village doors close upon him, and laughed. He saw the girls pass him by with averted modesty and turn to look after him, and laughed again. He saw them, one and all, watching with a vulgar interest for the inheritance to creep out and the blood to show—and he sneered outwardly while he raged within.

He was a bright lad. The school-master had said so, and the school-master was right. Easily he outstripped all the hardy farmers' louts in the class, and easily, in the end, he had outstripped the school-master himself. Then the minister had taken him in hand, and before long he had outstripped the minister.

"Here are my books," the minister had said, "make use of them." And he had looked over his shoulder to see that blue-eyed Emily was afar. He was a bright lad, but—well, blood is blood.

And Michael had made use of the books. He had fed upon them and he had laid up a store of capital. One and all, he had read them and absorbed them and pondered over them, and one and all he had disbelieved them.

The minister handed him "The Lives of the Saints," and the next day he had brought it back, throwing it down upon the table.

"A lot of pig-headed idiots," he said, with his lip curling and his grating laugh, "who hadn't enough sense to know whether they were awake or asleep."

The minister shuddered and recoiled.

"Be silent," he said. "If you have no respect for me, at least show some for God and the holy men who represent Him."

"Fiddlesticks!" said Michael. "They were so befuddled that they got God and the devil mixed, that's all."

But he laid the book aside and helped the minister about his copying. He was not without a wayward regard for worth. He was only warm with his fresh young blood and throbbing with vitality. The restless activity of mind could not be checked. The impassioned pursuit of knowledge was sweeping him onward. Self-taught he was and self-made he would be. The genius of endurance was fitting him to struggle, and in the struggle to survive.

So he drew out the minister's dog-eared sermon and set about the copying. He had copied such sermons before, and it was a task he rather enjoyed, given the privilege of making amendments — which the minister good-naturedly granted. As for the minister himself, perhaps he remembered the occasions upon which the boy had written sermons as compositions, and how he had delivered them as substitutes for old ones of his own which had worn threadbare. In his simple-minded search for divine purposes, the cleverness of the lad appeared inexplicable. That the hand of the Almighty should have overreached a flock of his elect to quicken with consuming fire the mind of an Ishmaelite seemed suspiciously like one of those stumb-

ling-stones to faith which we accept as tests of the blind-
ness of our belief.

That Michael knew more philosophy than he, he had acknowledged cheerfully, and now he was fast beginning to
harbor a suspicion that Michael knew more theology as
well.

He heaved a perplexed sigh and went to interview a con-
sumptive concerning his spiritual condition, while Michael
dipped his pen in the inkstand and fell to work.

It was a moment such as he enjoyed, when his intellec-
tual interests were uppermost and his mind eager to seize
an abstract train of thought.   He remembered such exalta-
tions during the long winter nights when he had sat up
with a tallow candle and attacked the problems of political economy.   He had spent plodding hours in mastering
them, but mastered them he had.   The dogged endurance
of mind had perhaps served him better than any natural
quickness.

The remembrance of those winter nights turned the
channel of his thoughts, and from the minister's sermon he
passed to larger premises and wider demonstrations.   Pushing the paper aside, he leaned back against the cushioned
back of the minister's chair and allowed his gaze to wander
from the sheets before him to the flower-beds in the garden
below, and then, past the wood-pile, where the hickory chips
had rotted to mould, to the jagged line of purple mountains.
The landscape was radiant with color.   As the sunlight fell
over them the meadows deepened in opalescent tints, purpling with larkspur, yellowing with dandelion, and whitening
to a silver sweep of life everlasting.

Across Michael's lips a smile passed faintly, like the
ripple of sunlight upon a murky pool.   He put up his hand
and brushed a lock of hair from his brow.   He looked suddenly younger and more boyish.   Then his reverie was
broken by a sound of footsteps.   The lattice door in the
passage opened and shut, and a shadow passed across the
chintz curtain at the window.   He heard voices, at first

broken and indistinct, and then clearer, as his mind left its
cloudy heights and returned to commonplaces.

One was the gentle voice of the minister's wife. "And
if you can help me out with the custard-spoons," it said,
"I'll be mightily obliged. I have a dozen of mother's, to
be sure, but, somehow, I don't just like to use them. If you
can let me have ten, I reckon I can manage to make out
with them and some tin ones Aunt Lucy sent me last
Christmas."

The other voice was sharper and brisker.

"I reckon I can piece out a dozen," it returned, with the
ringing emphasis of one eager to oblige. "If I can't, I'll
just borrow them from old Mrs. Cade without saying what
I want with 'em. And I'll send all the things over by Tim-
othy as soon as I get home—the custard-spoons, and the
salver for the cake, and the parlor lamp. If that glass
stand for butter ain't too badly cracked, I'll send that along
too; and I'll be over in plenty of time to help you set the
tables and fix things."

A murmur of thanks followed in the gentle tones, and
then the brisker ones began.

"You'll have a first-rate evening for the party," they observed. "When I got up this morning the wind was in the
east, but it has shifted round again. Well, I'll send the
things all right."

"I'm mightily obliged," responded the minister's wife, in
her repressed manner. "I hope it warn't any trouble for
you to bake the cake—our stove draws so poorly. It seems
a heap of work to go to, but the minister never can deny
Emily anything; and, after all, a birthday tea ain't much to
do for her. She's a good child."

The other voice chimed in with cordial assent. "If a
little party makes her happy, I reckon you don't begrudge
the work. She won't be sixteen but once, I say, and it's
just as well to do what we can."

"If it makes her happy," added the gentle voice, and
then it sighed softly. "There's always a cloud," it said.

"To be sure, this is a very little one, but, as I told the minister, it was the prophet's little cloud that raised the storm."

It was silent for a moment and then spoke sadly.

"It's about Michael," it said.

The brisker tones drooped.

"That boy!"

"Well, the minister's compassions are great, you know, and he can't feel just easy about not asking him. Of course, we must consider the other young folks, but the minister says it don't seem to him human to leave him out."

"Of course, I ain't as fit to judge as the minister, but I know I shouldn't like to have him around with my Lucy. And it seems to me that it ain't right to encourage him in familiarity—with his birth, too."

"Yes," assented the soft voice, deprecatingly, "but the minister can't feel easy about it. He says he knows Christ would have had him."

The brisk tones rose in an ejaculation.

"But the Lord never lived in such times as these!"

"I can't help its worrying me," continued the minister's wife, "and Emily is just like her father—all tenderness and impulse. It does seem hard—" Then the voice changed suddenly. "Oh, you wanted the nutmeg grater," it said. "I forgot all about it."

And the lattice door opened and shut quickly.

When the minister came in a while later he found Michael standing beside the desk, his clenched hand resting upon the lid. At his feet lay the uncopied sermon. It was crumpled and torn, as if it had been held in a brutal grasp. The boy's lips were pale and a yellow rage flickered in his eyes. As the minister paused, he confronted him.

"I hate these people!" he cried. "I hate them! I hate everybody who has come near this place. I hate my father because he was a villain. I hate my mother because she was a fool."

He said it vehemently, his impassioned glance closing upon the minister. The minister quavered. The genial smile with which he had entered faded from his face. He had faced such storms before and they always stunned him.

"I—I feel for you," he stammered, "but—" and he was silent. The boy stood upon other ground than his, and he could not follow him; he saw with other eyes, and the light blinded him. In his veins the blood of two diverse natures met and mingled, and they formed a third—a mental hybrid. The spirit that walked within him was a dual one—a spirit of toil, a spirit of ease; a spirit of knowledge, a spirit of ignorance; a spirit of improvidence, a spirit of thrift; a spirit of submission, a spirit of revolt.

"I hate them all!" repeated Michael.

His scorching gaze blazed through the open window and seemed to wither the beds of flowering portulacca in the garden. "I hate these people with their creeds and their consciences. They dare to spit upon me, that I am not as clean as they. I hate them all!"

From without the full-throated call of a cat-bird floated into the room. Then it grew fainter and was lost in the graveyard. Michael's face was dark and ugly. All the ingrowing bitterness of his youth was finding an outlet.

"What have I done?" he cried, passionately. "What have I done? Is it my fault that the laws of nature do not wait upon marriage banns? Is it my—" He paused suddenly.

"I—I am sure that you misjudge them," said the minister. "I am sure that—"

The door opened, and his own pretty Emily, her blue eyes all alight, darted into the room. Michael's eyes fell upon her, and, unconsciously to himself, they softened.

The minister saw the softening, and he stammered and grew confused. He fell back as if to shelter the girl from the look, pushing her hastily into an adjoining room.

"Go—go, my dear—your mother wants you, I am sure of

it." Then he turned and took up his speech. "I — I am—" and his conscience stung him and he blushed and stammered again. Michael laughed shortly. There was something brutal in the sound of it.

"Your daughter is safe," he said. "I will turn my eyes away.".

And the minister blushed redder than before.

There was something masterful about the boy, and he had the brow of a genius, but—well, girls will be girls, and there's no telling.

Michael walked to the window and stood looking at the flower-beds in the garden. Then he turned and faced the minister, all the bitterness of his warped and sullen nature in his voice.

"I want to get away," he said. "Anywhere that I am not known—anywhere. I can work. I can work my fingers to the bone—but I must get away."

The minister thought for a moment.

"I could help you a little," he said, slowly. "Say, lend you enough to pay your passage to, and a week's board in, New York. Such a bright fellow must find work. And, by-the-by, I've a cousin in the grocery business there; perhaps he could get you a job—"

He said it honestly, for he wished well to the boy; and yet there was a secret satisfaction in the chance of getting rid of him, of losing the responsibility of one stray sheep. God, in his wisdom, might redeem him, but the minister felt that the task was one for omnipotent hands to undertake. It was too difficult for him. If the Lord could unravel the meshes of Satan, he couldn't, and it shouldn't be expected of him.

"I'll go," said Michael. He said it with determination, bringing his quivering hand down upon the table. "I'll go. I'd rather die anywhere else than live here—but I won't die. I'll succeed. I'll live to make you envy me yet."

A sudden flame had kindled in his eyes. It shot fitfully

forth between the twitching lids. He became infused with life—with a passionate vitality, strong to overcome.

"I'll go to-morrow," he said.

He left the minister's house, walking briskly down the narrow path leading to the whitewashed gate. At the gate he paused and looked back. In a patch of vivid sunshine that fell upon an arbor of climbing rose he saw the blue flutter of pretty Emily's skirts. She put back the hair from her eyes and stood gazing after him, an expression of childish curiosity upon her face. All the joy of life at that moment seemed filtered through the sunlight upon her head.

He sighed and passed onward. Upon the steps of the farmer's cottage sat a plump child in a soiled pinafore. It was little Luly, the youngest of the farmer's ten children. As he entered the house she rose and trotted after him on her plump little legs.

In the doorway he was met by the farmer's wife. She held a pan of watermelon rinds in her hand. "Take these here rinds to the pig-pen," she said, "an' then you kin draw some water fur dinner. There ain't none left in the water-bucket." The boy looked at her silently. He was debating in his mind the words in which he would renounce her service. He had often enacted the scene in imagination, and in such visions he had beheld himself rising in righteous wrath and defying the farmer's wife with dramatic gestures. Now, somehow, it all seemed very stale and flat, and he couldn't think of just what to say. The woman was harder to confront in real life than she had been in his dreams. He wished he had gone away without saying anything to anybody.

At last he spoke with a labored emphasis.

"I won't feed the pigs," he said, and his voice sounded half apologetic, "and I won't draw the water; I am going away."

At the dinner-table the farmer was sitting before a plate of cabbage. He removed his knife slowly from his mouth and regarded the boy with mild amazement.

"An' the crops ain't in," he murmured, reproachfully.

The farmer's wife set the pan on the table and wiped her face upon the corner of her gingham apron.

"You ain't goin' fur good, I reckon?" she suggested.

Michael stood awkwardly before her. He had expected vituperation, and when it did not come he felt curiously ashamed of his resolve.

"Yes," he said, with a long pause between his words, "yes; I am going for good—I am not coming back ever any more. I am going for good."

A stifled wail broke from little Luly. "An' you 'ain't made my water-wheel," she cried. "You 'ain't made my—"

Her mother silenced her, and then looked at Michael in rising anger.

"You kin go as fast as you please," she said. "It'll be a good riddance. I won't hev my children mixin' with the offspring of har—"

But Michael had flung himself out of the room.

THE *Old Dominion* steamed slowly into the New York wharf, and her passengers made a precipitate rush for the gangway. Among those who left the third-class cabin there was an awkward youth in an ill-fitting suit of clothes and a cheap straw hat. From his right hand was suspended a small bundle which held all his earthly possessions of a tangible quality. His capital he carried in his brain.

As he stepped from the gangway to the wharf he hesitated and fell back, confused by the din of traffic.

" Step lively there !" called some one from behind, and the young man collected himself with a shake and started down the long wharf amidst a medley of boxes, trucks, and horses' feet.

" If you air looking for New York I guess you won't find it in that direction," remarked a laborer who was winding a coil of rope at some little distance.

Michael turned, his face reddening, and retraced his steps to his starting-point, from whence he made a fresh venture.

The tumult bewildered him. He was feeling strangely homesick, and there was a curious weakness in the pit of his stomach. It was as if he were passing to a scaffold of his own erecting. He wondered how so many people could ever have come to New York. Surely, if he had known what it was like, he would have remained where his lines had fallen until death had readjusted them. He had never heard so much noise in his life, not even in Arlington on court day.

But when at last the shipping district lay behind him and he turned into Sixth Avenue, his youth and energy combined to reassure him, and a flush of excitement revived something of his dominant bearing. Even the knowledge that his trousers bagged hopelessly, which dawned upon him like a revelation, was not sufficient to check the rising exaltation of spirit. It was like being born again to start upon life with no ties in the past to bind one — with no past, only a future. His second birth would be free from the curse that had descended upon his first. He would make himself, let the weathercock of circumstances veer beneath ill-winds as it would. Circumstances crumble before a determined mind.

Yes; with two hands and a brain to guide them he would create a new Michael Akershem, as God had created a new Adam. He had the power—there was nothing beyond him —nothing.

With a vigorous gesture he threw back his head and surveyed his surroundings. He regarded them with the curiosity with which a thinking infant might regard the universe as it sprang into existence.

Several points about the city impressed him, fresh from his primitive environments; first the size, secondly the ugliness, and thirdly the indifference. No one noticed him, no one turned to look after him, and when he jostled anybody they accepted his apology without seeing him or knowing what he meant. In the beginning it was refreshing, and he thrilled with the knowledge of freedom. Here, his right was unquestioned, his identity ignored; he was but one atom moving in its given line amidst many thousands. Then the denseness of population oppressed him, humanity jammed into a writhing mass, like maggots in a cheese. The tenements, with their smoke-stained windows —their air of dignified squalor—seemed to cut off all means of ventilation. He examined them curiously, pausing on the sidewalk to look upward, dazed by their height and by the number of their tenants. He laughed at the fire-escapes, spindling from the roof, at the inevitable geranium in its tomato-can, stunted and bare of bloom, the burlesque of a living flower.

On the Bowery he found a cheap restaurant with a sign reading, "Corned-beef & Onions, 10 cents," and he went inside and got breakfast at the counter. Then he came out and set about making his fortune.

That was the first day, and on that day he went into twelve offices seeking employment. Upon the second day he went into twenty-four; upon the third, fifty. At the end of the third day his courage faltered, at the end of the fourth it failed, and at the end of the fifth it oozed rapidly away.

He wandered restlessly about the streets. He no longer feared the crowd, he no longer feared anything. He was desperate and hungry, like an untamed animal. Corned-beef and onions at ten cents are cheap, but when one has not the ten cents they might as well be twenty.

"I want work," he said to the foreman of some machine shops.

"Work!" repeated the man. "Why, there are a thousand men outside wanting work as hard as you, and as little likely to get it."

"It's my right," cried Michael, hotly; "the world owes me a living and I'll have it."

"The world owes you a living, very probably," said the man, "but you'll find it deuced hard to collect. The world's a bad debtor."

He had gone out with an impotent curse upon the destiny that held his leading-strings. It was unjust! It was damnable!

The sunshine blinded him. He was young and strong and vibrating with energy, and yet, in the prodigal waste of Nature, this strength and energy were held of less account than the blowing of the wind. The former exultation of mind recoiled upon him in a wave of bitterness and dwindled to a slough of despond.

In the beginning he had sought only for a situation in which there might chance a rise. He had taken his brain into consideration, and in imagination he had allowed his ambition full play. Now, in the delirium of apparent failure, he cried out that for manual labor alone he was fitted, and that his dream of mental power was but the self-deception of a fool. Then it was that he went to the wharf at which he had landed, and asked for a job at the trucking.

It was given him, a substitute being needed in place of one of the employés who had been injured.

For a week Michael worked at the wharf among the common laborers. He stood shoulder to shoulder with negro hands and swung freight across the gang-plank. It was the roughest work that he had ever done, and his hands grew redder and more knotted and his shoulders lost their uprightness.

With the loading of the vessels frenzy seized upon him, and he worked at the high-pressure of insanity. Then, in the hours of leisure, the vultures of disappointed hopes preyed upon his vitals, and he faced life as Prometheus faced Jove. In all the years that came, the scars that those days wrought were not obliterated.

When the injured man returned the job was lost, and he went from the shipping-port with brutal inconsequence.

But Fate had not wearied of her puppet. He was yet to know the worst.

Night and day he walked the streets, hungry and defiant. During the day he watched the world in its fevered haste, during the night he watched it in its restless sleep. He stood upon the corners looking over the blackness of closed tenements, or, walking to the arch of Brooklyn Bridge, watched the swelling tide of water, the flickering of the lights around the city, the islands dotting here and there the dusk.

Among the tramps that thronged the bridge he loitered, as desperate as they.

And at this time his mind and his life were forming. Circumstances were busy making the man; the man was busy cursing circumstances. A rage that years could not cool consumed him. He looked with blood-shot eyes for the cause of such a ghastly condition—and, finding it, lifted against it the full force of his impassioned mind. It was not the man, but the system! It was the system that he hated—the system that suffered such things to be—that protected oppression in the name of liberty, and injustice in the name of law.

With the altered direction of his wrath, the early hatred for his parents melted away. He had found something vaster upon which to vent his undisciplined passion; and with the larger hate the old childish one seemed dwarfed and lifeless. He saw in his parents now but victims to the existing order—a machine which ground out millions of sentient beings and ground them into nothingness again. He even felt a half-tenderness for his mother and thought regretfully of the grave in the overgrown churchyard, with its red clay soil bare of bloom. He wondered how he could have thought of her save as wretched and bruised like himself, reviling the system that hemmed her down. He forgot, in his awakened sympathy, that she was but a woman of the fields, coarse and of great ignorance, into whose comprehension no system could have entered.

On the eleventh evening he fainted in a public square, and a woman of the street laid his head upon her lap and bathed his brow. He had come to life to see her bending over him, the street light flickering about her, revealing the paint upon her face and the dye upon her hair.

But he had not known. He knew nothing of women and little of life. She seemed only kind and helpful to him, and as he staggered to his feet he thanked her.

"You are good," he said. And the woman had been touched and turned to look at him. She saw his ignorance, which was innocence, and all the charity buried beneath a ruined virtue responded to his words.

"You're starving," she said. And she slipped something into his hand and went her way, her harsh laughter softened for a span. A man beside him had called after her a ribald jest, and Michael staggered up to him.

"Do you know that lady?" he asked.

And the man laughed—a coarse, loud laugh that pained his ears.

Like a flash Michael understood, and he shook and quivered, red with humiliation.

He turned away, stumbling blindly to his room. As one dazed by a sudden blow, he stood staring with hollow eyes at vacancy. For the first time he knew himself for what he was—an outcast, and, with it all, he felt blindly his own impotence—the quagmire in which he was floundering—the depths to which his ambitions had sunk.

And like a prophecy it broke upon him that it was a depth from which no man riseth.

The hour of his degradation was complete.

"To-day will end it," he said, and with calmness he went out to make his last throw—to take his last chance at the hands of Fate.

He bought an ounce of laudanum from a druggist at the corner. "How much do you want?" the man asked, and Michael answered:

"Oh, enough to kill a dog." The man looked at him curiously as he handed him the phial.

Across the street was the sign, " Corned-beef and onions," and, going over, he spent his last dime at the counter.

"I'll eat heartily," he thought; "enough to live on or—to die on."

Leaving the restaurant, he walked aimlessly to his left. The crowd passed hurriedly around him. A woman let her bundle fall at his feet and he stooped to pick it up. Afterwards, in the midst of her stitching, she remembered the bitterness of his look.

A group of bareheaded children darted in front of him, their arms interlaced. He looked at them attentively, noting the red curls of one, the plaid frock of another. He felt calmer than he had felt for days. The struggle was over, he had thrown up the game, and, when the end came, could resign from the competition. It mattered little. One nameless, homeless cur the less, that was all—one clod the less to deter the footsteps of the coming generation, nothing more.

And then he looked up and his eye fell upon a sign posted upon a building across the way. He halted and read it:

"MEN WANTED."

Then he re-read it. It was not the first of such signs that he had seen. Others had meant failure, why not this? Well, never matter.

He crossed the street and went in at the office door. After waiting awhile a man came out and spoke to him. Yes, he might see the manager, he was within. And in the next room he found a jovial gentleman with a philanthropic cast of features, who put on his spectacles and asked him his name.

"Michael Akershem."

"Occupation?"

"None."

"No trade?"

"No, sir; I have just left the country."

"What part?"

"Virginia."

"Why did you leave?"

"I wanted to make my way."

The gentleman smiled. He was of a philanthropic cast of mind as well as cast of countenance. Only that morning he had donated a check of some thousands to be invested in missionaries and other religious matter for the development of the Hottentots. His charity was universal. If it did not begin at home, at least it ended there, and his interest in his employés was only second to his interest in the natives of Damaraland.

3

"Respectable people?" inquired the gentleman.

Michael winced.

"I don't know," he answered. "My mother died when I was born."

"Your father?"

"I—I don't know anything about him except—" and the old childish spite overcame all his new-found theories, "except that he was a—scoundrel."

"Ah!" The gentleman tapped his spectacle-case reflectively. "Bad blood," he muttered. "Bad blood." Then he looked at the man before him, strong of brow and of eye.

"You see," he said, "we want only skilled workmen—mechanics."

"I can learn."

"Yes, but unfortunately we cannot undertake to teach you. I'm sorry, Mr.—Mr. Akershin—"

Michael's hand had closed over the phial in his pocket. So this was how it must end. He had left the room when the gentleman called after him.

"Hello!" he said. Michael turned. "You're an educated man, aren't you?"

"Yes."

"Why don't you use your head? There's a new paper— *The Iconoclast*—across the way. It has capital and it wants brains. Try that." And Michael tried. He looked for the sign, went into the office, and hesitated a moment before the city editor's door.

"Come in!" said a voice. The editor put aside a paper, took his feet from his desk, and turned towards him. "What can I do for you?" he asked.

"Give me work."

"Oh, indeed!"

"I was sent here," said Michael, "by a man across the way. He said you wanted brains—"

"Oh, indeed!" said the editor. He was a tall man with shrewd eyes. The eyes twinkled.

" And you think you can supply my lack ?" he asked.

" Yes."

The editor looked up at him, saw the purpose in his face, caught the light of the eyes between their nervous blinking. There was power in the man, and he saw it.

"We want bright heads," he said, "very bright ones. We want some one to take the existing order in hand and show it up. This is a free-thinking journal, you know. We endeavor to correct abuses—"

" Begin with the universe," said Michael.

" And to throttle injustice—"

" Begin with humanity."

" In short, to furnish an independent, readable, and as original a paper as is to be found on the market. As I tell you, we need bright heads—"

Then he looked up and caught the impassioned glance. " I'll try you," he said. " Walk into the next room; you'll find the foreman."

And Michael walked in.

BOOK II

THE INDIVIDUAL

" Every man takes the limits of his own field of vision for the limits of the world."—*Schopenhauer.*

CHAPTER I

A MAN passed along South Fifth Avenue and entered the *Chat Noir.* Finding the tables filled, he frowned impatiently and fell back against the door. Then, as a waiter passed, with a tray in his hand, he spoke. "Put me anywhere," he said; "I'm in a hurry."

The waiter looked up, recognized him, and nodded. "Good-evening, sir," he said. "In a moment." He led him down the room to a platform at the rear end, and ascending the steps gave him a seat at one of the tables.

As the man sat down several persons turned to look at him. He was lithe and squarely built, with a maze of rough, dark hair, a prominent brow, and nervous eyes.

"There are brains for you," said an artist in a threadbare coat to his companion. "Look at his brow. That man has the head of a genius."

"And the hair as well," answered his companion, who was fair and florid. "On the principle that 'a genius his hair never combs.' Is that the fact from which you generalize?"

"Pish!" retorted the other. "Read his leaders and you'll see. He has created an epoch in journalism. Why, the man has the power of an Ibsen and the audacity as well. He leaves nothing unassailed. He has a genius for destroying. If he has a sentiment, one needs a microscope to find it. His lectures on Social Lies, you know, fairly set society ablaze. By Jove, it's genius, and, what's better, it pays, which, I happen to know, all genius doesn't do. I'd change places with him to-night, hair and all, damn me if I wouldn't! It's better than painting landscapes at ten dollars a gross and no demand."

"Waiter!" his companion was saying, "chops for one! Mind you, I didn't say one chop, I said chops for one. Be quick, please. Oh, your man! Yes, as you say, painting doesn't pay. I've 'A Pair of Loves' at my studio for which I asked five hundred a year ago, and, by Jove, I'd knock it off for fifty to-night if I got the chance. The age of art has gone by, the age of action has commenced."

"It's an age of small things," admitted the first, sadly. He was gazing pensively at the frieze of black cats around the ceiling. "I'm profoundly convinced that it is an age of small things. From the age of dollars I have passed to the age of cents, from the age of chicken to the age of chops—"

"Be warned by a poor devil and stop before you arrive at the singular," said the other. "In me behold one who has reached an age of chop—or, to be exact, an age of quarter ounce mutton, two ounce bone— The devil! Your man's mad!"

The man in question had turned sharply to speak to some one who was leaning over his chair. His face had paled and a deep vein across his forehead was swollen and livid.

"And, if I did write it," he demanded, "does it concern you, sir?"

"Only in this," said the other, soothingly, "that I can't understand how a man of your judgment can wilfully give expression to such a—a string—of falsehoods."

"Ah, is that all?" The man turned slowly away, filling his glass with white wine. "Really, I can't be made responsible for your lack of understanding," he said. "Waiter! oysters, please."

He went quietly on with his dinner. A girl across the room was smiling at him between the spoonfuls of her soup, but he did not notice. He ate his oysters slowly, with deliberation, his gaze abstracted, one hand playing nervously with the crackers beside his plate. Once he paused to stroke the black cat that rubbed against his knee.

The threadbare artist and his companion had gone out.

A gentleman in a gray shooting-jacket had taken their places, accompanied by a lady with beautiful glistening hair. She moved with a slow Delsartean action, as actresses do before they have become artists.

"Yes, it has been a trying day," said the lady, speaking with a strong Southern accent. "I did not dream that an actress's life could be such drudgery. And the hardest lesson one has to learn, harder than all the lines, is how to be an actress and a lady, too. Really, it takes all one's time. And one is thrown with such common people, too; it is so —so—"

"So humiliating," suggested the gentleman.

"Yes, it is quite humiliating. And that dreadful manager! Why, I saw him, with my own eyes, kiss a chorus girl behind the scenes last night. If I had dreamed of such outrageous things, I'm sure I should never have left home. I mightn't have been famous, but I should, at least, have been respectable—and I am getting to believe that the two are opposed. No! no wine, thank you!"

"So you regret your step?"

"Well, hardly that, but I regret that I don't regret it." The lady sighed, putting up her hand to smooth her beautiful hair. Presently her gaze wandered over the room and she spoke more rapidly, her eyes growing bright and wide. "Why," she said, "isn't that the editor of *The Iconoclast?* There—over there in the corner?"

The gentleman followed the direction of her glance. "So it is," he said. "Akershem, you know, created quite a stir, hasn't he?"

"Indeed, yes," assented the lady, drawing on her long gloves. "But don't you think him rather wicked? Think of the things he has said about society and religion and marriage."

"Brilliant fellow, though," suggested the gentleman.

"Brilliant? Yes, I suppose so. But I haven't read his articles. I wouldn't for anything. I fear he's one of the powers for evil."

"For pleasure?" asked Michael, with a laugh.

"Yes, for pleasure. I tell you I haven't been bored a day since I took up reform." Then he seemed to gather all his enthusiasm, bringing it to a focus. It was as if he lashed himself into fanaticism for the pleasure of it. "We shall accomplish a great work," he said. "Watch the progress. Society shall shiver, shall totter, shall come down with a crash. We will erect a new one upon the ashes of the old. We will make freedom the watchword and equality the law. *Liberté! Égalité! Fraternité!* We shall win a great victory. Our children and our children's children shall live to see the triumph of our cause, and, in the midst of their prosperity, shall rise up and call us blessed."

Michael was listening, his face flushed, all traces of bitterness gone. His lips were apart, his head thrown back in the old childish fashion. His breath came quickly; the glare of his nervous eyes was almost blinding. "We will do it," he said. "Society is a fetich, upon whose altar human beings are sacrificed. We will tear it down."

"In time," said the other. "Give us time. We will prove that liberty—glorious liberty—is the only birthright worth possessing, and that it is the equal birthright of all. Sweep away poverty and you have swept away crime. Make men happy and you make them holy. Oh, humanity will become a fine thing yet—no more class robbery, no more drudgery of women and children—no more laws binding two human beings together for all time—no more room for immorality and injustice. A man shall have equal opportunity as the son of a millionaire or a mechanic—" He stopped suddenly, the enthusiasm dying from his fair, flushed face, the strained fanaticism in the eyes giving place to the habitual gleam of good-humor. "But, enough of this," he said; "tell me about yourself. How long have you been in the editor's chair?"

"Two years."

"And with the paper seven. Ah, you've done well. You're young yet, however, and you may temper down.

Half the conservatives of to-day were reformers in their youth. You may change."

"Never!" said Michael, and he said it hotly, fixing upon the other his blinking eyes.

"Oh, well," said Semple, "time will show. But how's your staff? A good one, I suppose. And Driscoll, the former editor; where's he?"

Akershem's face brightened. "He gave it up," he answered. "It was a great loss. His health gave out and he grew conservative. He said the profession of sensationalism wrecked his nerves. He got tired of pie and civilization. One, he said, had given him dyspepsia, the other blue devils. So he went to try a state of simple nature in Florida, on an orange farm. I haven't heard from him lately. I guess the freeze down there brought him to his senses."

"He was a fine fellow—that man."

"Fine! He was the only man I ever knew worth bowing to."

Semple laughed good-naturedly. "Cynicism is a sure sign of youth," he said.

"Not cynicism," returned Michael. "I've passed that. "Life is like an apple. It has three stages, first, the rind, which is sour—cynicism; next, the pulp, which is sweet— optimism; and thirdly, the core, which is rotten — pessimism. Well I've tried the first. I skipped the second, and I'm pretty well into the third."

The room was less crowded. Some of the tables were vacant. At the one across from them a girl was sitting alone. She wore a loose artist's blouse of black cloth with a rolling collar of white and a small cap of some rough material. In her hand she held a drawing-block and a pencil.

"There's a woman of the time," said Semple, suddenly, nodding his head in her direction. "As independent a young person as is to be found in New York—Miss Gavin; do you know her?"

The man had unbuttoned his coat and his loose tennis blouse, open at the throat, was visible. The tables were crowded now. In the centre of the room and about the door a line had formed waiting for vacated seats. Near the door a group of merry young fellows were gathered about a table. They were laughing and passing wine with boyish good-humor.

"Here's to to-morrow," said one, "and the evil it doesn't bring."

"Here's to the job it does bring," added another.

"How many goes to-day, Bob?" asked a third.

"Eight in all. Began with *The Herald* and ended with— By Jove! I've forgotten the name."

"There's Debbins over there," said one. "He's on *The World*, they say."

"And there's Akershem of *The Iconoclast*—there's your chance. Go it, Bob."

"And get my nose bitten off for my pains. He's about as amiable as the devil's wife on a wash day."

"I heard a jolly story about him the other day," said a young fellow with a snub-nose. "Symonds went to him for work. You know Symonds, the fellow with the grandfather who did something of some sort. Well, Symonds was hauling out his recommendations. 'I'm of first-rate people, sir,' he said. 'My grandfather was—' and Akershem broke in with: 'What in thunder have I to do with your grandfather? He may have been the devil, for aught I care. I don't want to adopt you,' and he didn't give him the job, either. 'I've no doubt many papers would be glad to get you, Mr. Symonds,' he said, 'on your grandfather's account,' and he ushered him out."

"He's a temper of his own," said the first one, "and a head, too; but that Billy Summers on his staff worships the ground he walks on. He says Akershem raised him from the gutter to glory."

And Akershem went quietly on with his dinner, his gaze abstracted, his square, beardless face bent over his plate.

He was young, not more than six-and-twenty. He was old, for he had lived much during those six-and-twenty years.

Suddenly he paused, looked up, and bowed in response to a gentleman who had seated himself across from him. He was a stout man of some forty odd years, with thin, fair hair and clear-cut features. His eyes rested upon Michael and their pupils contracted in puzzled scrutiny. They were humorous eyes, light and clear of vision. "I beg your pardon," he began, then hesitated. "Are you Mr. Michael Akershem of *The Iconoclast?*"

"I am." There was an aggressive defiance in Akershem's retort.

"And I am Semple—Hedley Semple—you have heard of me?"

"Heard of you!" A smile passed over his face like gleams of sunshine across a cloud. "Heard of you? Why, I've *heard* you a dozen times, but I thought you were lecturing abroad."

"So I was; but 'he who fights and runs away,' you know. I talked the German public mad in a month, the English in a week, and the French in exactly two hours and forty minutes. The American public, being a gigantic mongrel, I expect to have it hooting at my heels before the month's up. But you're doing a great reform work. Read your leaders this morning. So marriage is not a failure, but a fake, is it? Oh, but I wished for you across the water! I'd a poor chance of fight sometimes, but on social reform I got the people, the aristocracy sitting by and kicking its heels."

Michael laughed. "That's all it is good for," he said. "An aristocrat is a man who sits down to think about what his grandfather has done while other men are doing something themselves."

"Oh, but it's a great work," said Semple. "It infuses an interest into a man. One need never fear *ennui* when one has a purpose to serve. A man who hasn't a cause to fight for should invent one."

"No! I don't like women."

"She is a type."

"I detest types of women. I never saw but one, and that was the fool type."

"Fie! shame on you! Well, she's a genius, they say. Had some fine things at the Oil Exhibition last spring. Took the medal. She has made a god of her art, I'm told. An interesting woman and a strange one."

"A strange one indeed." Michael had turned and was looking across at her. She was of medium height, slight, but with broad, straight shoulders and an independent, half-audacious carriage of the head. The cap had slipped to one side, showing the backward wave of the dark hair that was coiled low on the nape of the neck, and giving her a slightly defiant appearance. Her face was oval and somewhat sallow, with a firm chin, and a nose squarely cut at the tip. Her eyes were gray, deeply set in the sockets, and with a black shadow thrown across them by the lashes—but gray most decidedly—a clear, deep gray like the mountains when a storm is near. They were eyes that suggested the possibility of a smile. When grave, her face was set and strongly marked, without a trace of color except the thin line of the lips, and almost overshadowed by the straight black eyebrows.

She was feeding the cat with bits of partridge from her plate, stroking its head with one large, ungloved hand.

"A strange woman, indeed," Michael had said.

"I'll wager she'll make a success of whatever she undertakes," said Semple. "If art, so much the better ; if love, so much the worse." Then he started. "By Jove," he said, "she's sketching you. It can't be me— No! it's you."

The girl had rested her block upon the table, and was busily applying her pencil to it, her gaze passing from the paper to Michael and back to the paper again.

"Cool!" he muttered, "but she's welcome to it. May it do her more good than it's done me."

Semple rose. "It's a pity to disappoint the young woman," he said, "but wounded vanity pricks, and, since she's
selected you, I'm off. I've an engagement in twenty minutes. I'll look in at the office to-morrow. By-the-bye, I
want you to meet my wife."

"Your wife?" said Michael. He recoiled as though some
one had struck him between the eyes. He felt dazed.
"Your wife?" he repeated, "why, I—I thought you—you
were an opponent of marriage."

"Oh! that's different. I *am* of marriage—of marriage
in general, you know. But my wife—she's such a fine woman—such a deuced fine woman. You must meet her. Good-
bye."

He had gone, and Michael pushed his glass aside and
rose. He felt a crushing sense of disappointment. Here
was a man who held publicly the most advanced views of
the day, and who privately— Was it lack of principle or
lack of policy?

Then his gaze fell on the girl across from him, and he
went boldly over to where she sat, his brilliant glance fixing her like magnetism.

"You are sketching me," he said.

The girl looked up and frowned. Then the corners of
her mouth went up, the lines about her eyes dimpled, and
her straight brows arched. She was provokingly mirthful.
"A study if you please," she said, "for John the Baptist—
as he left the wilderness, of course." The promise of her
smile was fulfilled. Then her lips fell and grew prim, a
gray cloud hid the stars in her eyes, the dimples from the
corners fled. She frowned.

Michael looked gravely down upon her. He was always grave. There was a certain interest in watching the
changes in her mobile face, the quick play of thought
across her sensitive features. He wanted to make her
angry and see the flash come out in her eyes. There was
a delicious danger in playing with the fire of her glance.
He desired and feared to meet its level brilliance.

"You might have asked my permission," he said; "but since you didn't, I'll grant it anyway. Turn about is fair play. I'll walk home with you." Then he drew slightly back and looked at her, waiting with a cynical amusement to see the effect of his words.

The girl rose quietly, gathered up her wraps, found her gloves, and paused to turn the fingers right side out. She picked up her drawing-block from the table. Very deliberately she tore off the outer leaf, and, tearing it in half, let it fall lightly to the floor. Then she raised her eyes to his face. The corners of her lips curved upward in their delicious way, showing all the sharp, white teeth. With a provoking air of bravado she passed him, looking back over her shoulder to throw a humorous glance.

"St. John was hardly worth it," she said. "I'm as much as I can look after, thank you," and she passed away from him and out into the street.

CHAPTER II

AND this was Michael Akershem!

As he passed along under the glimmer of the electric light, he almost laughed to himself at the thought—laughed impersonally as a stranger might have done.

This was Michael Akershem.

This the bare-footed child in Virginia, chasing the pigs from the cornfield, submitting to the harsh railings of the farmer's wife, choking with suppressed rage and gnawing bitterness. This the lad growing up under the minister's eye, pried after by the village women, badgered by the village boys. This the man who walked these same streets seven years ago, hungry, sore, and homeless, asking only the hire of a common laborer, ready to toil in the shops or in the foundery, passionate, alert, and spurred onward by the lash of unsatisfied ambition.

And to-day *this* was Michael Akershem. Strong, fearless, and fired by an unfaltering will. His hand against every man still, and every man's hand against him, but the single hand—no mere wavering fist of a farmer's hireling—but a hand, powerful and heavy of grasp, mighty and sure to wound. The years of labor had set their mark upon him, had stamped the lines of self-sufficiency upon his brow, as they had graven the expression of habitual bitterness about his mouth. He owed the world nothing. His success he had earned by the sweat of his brow, with a brain which had ached like a madman's and yet toiled on. The bread which he ate was the bread of independence, the bread of his own plodding youth, the bread which separated him from all claim from his fellows. The world and he were at odds. He had gained nothing from it that it had

4

not begrudged him, and had he his will it should gain nothing from him until it gained his dust to enrich the earth.

As for men and women, they were but moving atoms— burlesques of what might have been had Nature been less of a niggard. For him they had only distrust; for them he had only jeers. They could distrust; well, he could afford to despise. They could upbraid; well, he could sneer. It was all one to him; he had known nothing else from his birth, and he expected to know nothing else until his death. The sins of men must have scapegoats. He was a scapegoat; but he could rebel, and rebel he did.

The force of his wrath he spent upon the one vulnerable point. His genius for invective was expended where its effects were most sweeping. He could not reach *one* man, thousands he could. He could not assail the individual, the system he could.

Like a torrent he bore down upon the objects of his resentment. The genius which might have created was exerted to destroy. The brilliancy which might have won love was given in hate. The strength which might have ennobled could only embitter. He had suffered, and against the things whereby he had suffered his voice was lifted. Had his life been otherwise, the strength might have been welded to gentleness, the courage to humanity. But otherwise it had not been. Circumstances are mighty and man is weak. The wheel of the potter grinds on and the clay is moulded into symmetry or distorted by mishap. If it is misshapen by the mishap and regains not its rounded form, is it the fault of the potter or of the clay?

And Michael rallied. Brilliant, bitter, hated and hating, stirred by a restless, untempered energy which sought ceaselessly its outlet. With swift, fire-tinctured blood and a nature never at peace, he carried on his impotent revolt.

He walked briskly along with swinging strides, passing under the shifting shadows cast by the electric light. He was thinking, his fevered, over-active brain bearing down upon the past and dissecting it as with a microscope. Sort-

ing the years, one by one, and throwing some aside to a
mental rubbish heap, and labelling some and laying them
away, and fastening upon some his keen regard as for the
moment's use.

With all the salient irregularity of face and figure, it was
more as a personality that he impressed one than as a person; more as a mind than as a man; more as a will than
as a body. A subtle, illusive, yet trenchant quality which
enforced submission or inspired resistance. The friction of
an abnormal nature against normal ones. And in the friction the emphasis of his personality was made manifest;
the conscious predominance of the psychical existence.
Reaching the office, he let himself in with a latch-key, lighted the lamp, and began his night's work. He was preparing the sheets for the morning press.

He worked steadily with that unwearied, absorbed application which is the surest warrant of success. Occasionally
he would glance up, his brilliant gaze abstracted, his brow
ruffled. Then the thought would be run down and captured
and he would work on with his restless pen. At two o'clock
he rose, put out the lamp, let himself out, and went home.

For seven years he had done such work.

The next day while Akershem worked at his desk a rap
sounded at the office door. He glanced up sharply. The
door was labelled "private," and was supposed to be so.
He detested interruptions.

"Come in," he said, curtly.

The door swung open and a man entered, a tall man with
heavy brows and delightful eyes—light, shrewd, quick-sighted eyes, with twinkles in their pupils.

Like a flash Michael was upon him.

"Why, Driscoll, old man, it's too good to be true! When
did you come? Where did you come from? Are you back
for good?"

"Hold on, Shem—you don't mind, Shem, do you?—it's so
convenient—wait a minute and I'll take you down in order.
First, when did I come? Answer, exactly nineteen and

one-half minutes ago by the Pennsylvania Railroad. Secondly, where did I come from? Answer, from a place known to the natives as the Sunny South—South literally, Sunny by courtesy. Thirdly, am I back for good? Answer, dubious, judging from the state of my pocketbook; I fear I'm back for bad."

He had taken Michael's vacated seat, swinging his feet upon the desk with a leisurely action. As he did so he displaced the papers upon which Akershem had been working.

" Pick them up, Shem," he said, "there's a good fellow. You haven't been to Florida and gotten rheumatism. This is a confounded habit of mine, I know, but it's inherited. I got it from my father, who contracted it in South America when he lived in a tent with some centipedes. But go on, my young fanatic. What have you been doing? What, I mean, besides coveting your neighbor's goods? Aren't you tired of using society as a football? Why don't you give it up? Get out of the profession of sensationalism, or turn conservative. In these degenerate days it's the only party in which a man doesn't get his brains jammed into jelly with all the rest! We'll bring out a respectable paper of some kind, with domestic advice to dutiful wives and a column for correspondents and recipes for plum-pudding and gooseberry jam. I'll even offer to take the correspondence off your hands; think of that—"

"But, Driscoll, what about the orange farm?"

"My dear Shem, I can tell you a lot about the farm. Walked that over in two days, but I know deuced little about the oranges. There was a rumor up here to the effect that there was a grove on the place, but I didn't see it, though I examined every shrub through field-glasses.

" Well, a freeze came and it took my neighbors' oranges, and, in default of oranges, it took me. I contracted rheumatism, so here I am. By Jove, I used to get bored down there. There was no fishing, and the only sport I had was hunting in the pond for tadpoles, chasing them under a rotten log and catching them by the tails. There was a small darky who used to join me. We got sixty-nine one day, and didn't let one get away. Then I read your diatribes and saw that you needed the check rein, so I came back. My dear Shem, you are making the mistake of being in earnest. Nobody should be in earnest, it is bad form. Theories are meant for playthings; if you use them as weapons, they go to pieces and cut you."

Akershem laughed.

"That's a fact, Shem; the only successful reformer is the one who never attempts to put his reforms into practice. They're the men the world goes mad over while it stones their tools."

"I was born to be stoned."

"Nonsense! don't give Fate a chance to rile you. Providence has to be hoodwinked. If you want to get anything in this world, turn to wanting something else, and ten chances to one the first will come — only you won't want it."

"Any more moralizing at my expense?"

"Lots. You need it. You have gone and made society a bugbear, and now you're trying to bully it. Let it alone. People aren't half as big fools as they look, and, anyway, it's no concern of yours. If men choose to erect idols in the market-place, why should you trouble to tear them down? A sensible man doesn't do that—a sensible man is wild, wicked, stupid, if you will, but he is never in earnest. He knows that if society is rotten he can't purify it by poking and prying, but will only succeed in soiling his hands in the filth. Let the world alone and it'll let you alone."

"But it hasn't let me alone and I won't let it. I'll protest against it with my dying breath. I was talking to Semple last night—"

"Semple!" said Driscoll, "Hedley Semple! He's a man who is playing with edged tools. I tell you what is play to him is death to you. He talks his views, but you live yours. That's wrong. Theories have nothing to do with life; they are to be talked about, that's all. Make it play, Shem, don't—"

Then he broke off with a laugh.

"I'm getting in earnest myself," he said, "which I don't do on principle. My state of simple nature, you see, has cultivated in me the simplicity of primitive man. It is the only life worth leading, after all. This vast machine of nervous energy called civilization is demoralizing. It keeps the brain at fever heat and produces vertigo. It destroys individuality. Quit it, my dear Shem; you need rest. Leave politics, the tariff, the currency, and all the other fruits of perdition alone. The currency is the devil's own institution for making maniacs of men. I recognize his stamp."

"Don't be an ass, Driscoll. I know what I'm doing."

"The deuce you do! I never saw a reformer who did. They might be classified as a distinct species having eyes in the back of their heads."

"You've managed to readjust yours, I see."

"Ah, well, a young sinner makes an old Solomon. There is nothing so profitable to a philosopher as the sins of his youth."

"Or so confoundedly pedantic as the repentance of his age."

"Quit it, Shem! Run down to Florida for a bit. Six weeks spent with that delightfully uncivilized small darky will raise your respect for humanity exactly twenty degrees. It did for me. I assure you, when I left here I was inclined to look upon mankind as an unmitigated failure. After my first introduction to him I began to think that it wasn't such a bad case, after all. And when I saw him sitting in a watermelon patch, eating out of the rind quite like the natural man, I felt that, take the high pressure of civilization away, humanity might be a first-rate thing. Then he taught me to fish for tadpoles, and, by Jove—" He rose suddenly and lounged over to the window. "It makes me homesick," he said, "such a bully day for the sport, too. I shouldn't be surprised to hear that he'd caught the can full." Then he picked up his hat and was making off. "Come out with me, Shem. I've half promised to look in at the water-color exhibition. Nevins wants me to stand sponsor for his 'Mother's Plague' or some such nonsense. Come!"

Michael yielded. He seldom withstood Driscoll. "The work may go," he said. "It's your work, anyway. But for you I shouldn't be in the world to-day," he added, awkwardly.

Driscoll laughed as he swung open the door. "Spare me, my good fellow," he said, "don't — don't shove such a responsibility upon me. So I am the unconscious instrument of your evil fate?"

At the Academy Michael loitered about while Driscoll went in pursuit of "The Mother's Plague" and its creator. Presently he came back. "Confound it," he said, "I can't find the thing. What does a man want to make such a fool of himself, anyway, as to paint plagues. There're enough of them in real life. By-the-bye, have you seen the gem of the exhibition? It's that gray thing over there by Rachel Gavin—a study of dawn. Ah! there is Miss Gavin herself before it."

Michael turned. It was the girl of the evening before, flannel blouse, yachting-cap, and all. The same prominent, sensitive features, the same wide mouth with its long curling upper-lip, the same eyes with the purple shadows under them as though worked in with India-ink. The same impassioned, brooding, concentrated expression. The same evanescent passage of thought across the mouth and eyes. She was alone, her drawing-block under her arm, her pencil in her ungloved hand.

As Michael looked she knelt before a picture which had been hung near the floor.

"When she gets up," said Driscoll, "she will know how every stroke was put in. Nothing escapes her. It's pluck that girl has, and to spare. For man or woman it is no joke to work ten hours a day at an easel, but she has done it. If you'll wait a moment I'll speak to her."

He crossed the room, and Michael saw him bend above the kneeling figure.

"At your shrine, as usual, Miss Gavin," he said. The girl glanced up, rose, and held out her hand. She spoke, but Michael did not catch her words.

Presently Driscoll came back.

"I asked her about the 'Plague,'" he said, "and she says she'll look out for it. By-the-bye—" He stopped, for the girl was at his elbow. "Oh, Mr. Driscoll," she said, "I've found it. It's over there in the corner, behind the 'Peachtree.'"

She spoke rapidly, gliding over her vowels with a soft, Southern accent.

"And since you've discovered it," said Driscoll, "will you kindly unfold to me its merits or demerits? By-the-bye, you won't mind knowing Akershem, Miss Gavin. He is simply dying to meet you. He hasn't said so, but he has looked it. You have much in common, I've no doubt. You paint, and he—well, he would like to if he could, only he can't, you know."

"Oh! 'The Mother's Plague.' Now, really, will you tell me if that chest of drawers is well done or if it is not? I'm not asking out of idle curiosity, mind you. I have to write an article about it and I want to know."

Up went the sensitive corners of the girl's mouth, and the fine lines about the eyes came into play. Michael thought he had never seen anything so delightful as the way in which these irregular little eye dimples came and went. She put up her hand and brushed a stray lock of hair from her temple, fastening it by means of a tiny hairpin into the dark coil behind. "That depends," she said. "Do you speak of Art or Nature? For Nature I should consider it somewhat too ethereal. In fact, a chest of drawers liable to become absorbed in the surrounding atmosphere. For Art—well, it is a conscientious sacrifice of form to color."

"Well," said Driscoll, "that shows the use of an inquiring mind. Now, if I hadn't asked your opinion I should have strongly suspected my friend Nevins of being guilty of a daub."

"It is well hung," said Michael, hastily. "It has an excellent foil in those bananas to your right."

Then he became conscious of having said an awkward thing, for a young fellow near him blushed hotly and shambled off.

The girl frowned, with an imperious wrinkling of her brow. Then she slipped past him in bold pursuit of the departing figure of the young man. "Oh, Mr. Buttons!" she called. He turned and came eagerly towards her.

"I have just noticed your fruit!" she said. "Do come and tell me how you worked in those shadows. I am dying to know."

The young fellow grew radiant, then flushed scarlet, and together they leaned over the picture. Driscoll drew back and laughed.

"That is like her," he said. "She wouldn't hurt the lad for worlds. He is as sensitive as a baby. I remember her cutting him upon the street one day and then running a block to apologize. I reminded her at the time that she had cut Stetherson as well, and she laughed and said, 'Oh, that is different. That doesn't matter; he has left off painting bananas, you know.'"

"It is like me, too," said Michael, gloomily. "I never had a trace of manners in my life, and, what's more, I never expect to have any; and, what's more, I don't care a—a —a—"

"Don't excite yourself, my dear fellow. It doesn't matter. By to-morrow she will have forgotten all about it, and about you, too. Well, let's be off. By-the-bye, where are you staying now? Old place?"

"No. I have taken apartments in the Templeton. Come up this evening and give me a room-warming. I've just moved in."

"Oh, the Templeton! I believe that's where Miss Gavin is. You're neighbors. Well, I'll dine with you to-night, somewhere. At your rooms?—so much the better."

He swung leisurely across to the avenue, and Michael went back to the office.

PEOPLE said it was a pity that John Driscoll had thrown himself away. John Driscoll said that he might have done something great if he had not preferred doing nothing. However that may be, for greatness is relative, and Driscoll was hardly the best judge, the fact that he had never done anything was indisputable, the theory that he might have done something untenable and easily assailed. As every man who has not written a play, recklessly proving his inability, is convinced that he could write one if he only chose, so every man who has not made desperate throws at success is equally convinced that it is a matter of choice. It is only after one has striven and strewn the path of balked ambition with bloody sweat that the mocking finger of Failure may be pointed and may hurt. He is a wise man who has not fallen because he has not climbed. "As long as it's my own fault that I'm a failure," said Driscoll, "I don't care; if it had been the fault of Providence I'd have been blamed mad."

At college he had been noted for his versatility and his vacillation. He had picked up Latin and Greek as one picks up the alphabet, had plodded away at Sanscrit with marked success; had wearied of the classics and turned to law. In a year he had taken his B. L. and satiety, but, instead of leaving college, he had thrown himself with a feverish zest into natural science, and finally, when he left for a naturalist's voyage to South America, he carried with him the enthusiastic commendations of the faculty and the paternal blessing of the chair of biology.

For several years the promise seemed approaching fulfilment; he was heard from constantly, and the scientific re-

views carried his name.   He brought out a small work upon
South American Sea Urchins, and later another upon *Rudi-
mentary Nervous Systems*.   Then for a time he was lost sight
of, and just as the American biologists were beginning to
look for a more ambitious venture from their promising disciple, there appeared upon the literary market the first volume of what seemed to be a work of widely comprehensive
scope entitled *Ethnic Affinities*.   The book bore the name
of John Driscoll.   Ethnologists applauded and looked eagerly forward to the completion of the survey, but no second
volume was forthcoming, although John Driscoll himself was.
Quite unexpectedly he loomed upon the horizon, interested,
interesting, and alert.

"Oh, my *Ethnic Affinities !* I've given that up long ago,"
he said.   "It is all bosh, you know.   What is the use of
pottering about among pots and kettles and customs?"   He
mingled in society for a while, becoming easily the idol of
the hour; then he arranged and executed an expedition in
the direction of what is supposed to be the North Pole.

At the end of three months he was found and brought
home by a rescuing party, and after a long illness he put
aside science and went into politics.   But he was independent, and independence is often out of place, and always
out of office.   He wrote clever, keen-sighted articles against
the Republican Administration, and voted the Democratic
ticket; then the Democrats came in and he saw their errors
as clearly as he had seen the errors of their opponents.   The
articles against the Democratic Administration were just as
clever and just as keen-sighted, and he voted the Republican ticket.

"Must I blindfold myself because of party principles?"
he asked, and he wrote against them one and all.   He got
disgusted with the government and became a Socialist.   The
Socialists welcomed him with acclamations and triumphant
cheers, but upon nearer inspection he perceived the defects
in the platform and he made clever, sarcastic "copy" out
of them for the magazines.   He wrote for the party, but he

wrote against the party errors, and the party got mad, as was highly proper. They charged him with being a traitor, and a battle ensued.

Then a wealthy syndicate purchased *The Labor Gazette*, rechristened it *The Iconoclast*, backed its success with an array of cool millions, and offered Mr. Driscoll the leadership. Mr. Driscoll accepted. It was a new opening, a chance for some skilful pioneering, difficulties to clear away and a path to hew out. It represented a change, and he liked it. For five years he stuck to it faithfully. At first he infused new life into the journal; he made it clever, humorous, candid; but it held no convictions, it followed no party, it wavered incessantly. For six months it preached the boldest radicalism, when the quick, scrutinizing glance saw the faults upon its own side, the good upon its opponents'. He veered round, and the orthodox party raised a thanksgiving over the conversion. He soon deserted them and followed the Socialists; he took to admonishing the Socialists, and they objected. The end was a combat royal between *The Iconoclast* and all organized parties.

People said that it was lack of principle, but it was not. Too much principle is often more harmful than too little. He had too much honesty to say what he did not believe, a bad thing in political life; and he was too quick-sighted not to perceive a rotten core because he happened to have eaten the apple.

"You have no settled convictions," said a friend to him one day. "A serious fault."

"Confound convictions," retorted Driscoll; "they are always getting in the way of opportunities. The only convictions a man of sense should entertain are those that adjust themselves to circumstances."

"Pshaw!" said his friend. "The opportunities you've thrown away would have made forty men, had they picked them up."

"No doubt," assented Driscoll; "but they would have been deuced bored in the making."

And then, when he had wearied of *The Iconoclast*, and had left it to wither away while he worked out *A Theory of Dynamics*, the door opened and Michael Akershem appeared.

Reckless, energetic, impassioned, ready to throw heart and brain into the cause, Driscoll hailed him as a new and powerful element. As Michael Akershem warmed to the work Driscoll felt the load slipping from his own wearied shoulders.

"Here is the channel," said Driscoll, "for your bitterness and brilliancy. Rail at society. I do not think it can hurt you, and I'm quite sure it will not hurt society. You're the right man in the right place. You aren't cursed with the ability to see both sides. Go ahead."

Michael went ahead, and Driscoll felt the weight lightening upon his shoulders. Then by a skilful manœuvre he had released himself from the editorship and installed Akershem in his place. Akershem was satisfied, the syndicate was satisfied, and Driscoll was more than satisfied.

Seven years ago Michael Akershem, desperate, hungry, malevolent, had come upon John Driscoll as he sat smoking in his office chair. To-day Michael Akershem stood before the world envied, if not applauded; admired, if not esteemed. Between the two estates a wide gulf yawned, and the gulf had been bridged by Driscoll. Behind his success, his independence, his brilliant career, reached forth the sustaining hand, and the hand was Driscoll's. With an impassioned loyalty Akershem recognized and acknowledged the debt. It was the one indissoluble bond that united him to humanity; the one ray of white light shed upon the turbid passion of his soul.

Seven years ago, if Michael Akershem could have looked ahead and seen himself standing as he stood to-day, he would probably have said: "It is well; my ambition is overleaped," and yet to-day that ambition loomed as vast and far off as it had done seven years ago. The fortune that he followed was a chimera, the load-star of a fevered brain. The mirage stretched like an unconquered world before him; he went forward, and, as he moved, it flitted onward—never any nearer—always blue and satisfying and beyond.

There is no state of satisfaction, because to himself no man is a success. Let the public shower laudations as it will, a man who has planted his foot upon the steep beholds the summit, upon the summit beholds the heaven. At every step he treads the unending circle of ambition, the undiscovered height in the distance looming higher, higher.

A couple of years after Michael Akershem came to New York Driscoll initiated him, so to speak, into the ceremonies of society.

"Mrs. Stuyvesant-Smyth means to take you up," he said, one day, tossing a card across the table. "I'm to dine there next week, and she desires me to bring my 'dreadful friend, Mr. Akershem.'"

"Who is Mrs. Smyth?" asked Michael.

"Mrs. Stuyvesant-Smyth: man, if you have to drop one don't let it be the Stuyvesant. Well, she holds the golden key to society, and no one questions her right of way; but if that does not satisfy you, she is second-cousin to my unworthy self."

"Is she like you?"

"The Driscoll nose, I believe, a misfortune which drew us together. However, she calls hers the Randolph, as her grandmother married a Randolph of Virginia, and mine didn't; but calling a nose a Randolph doesn't make it straight."

"But I shouldn't know what to say," remonstrated Michael, "or how to behave."

"Oh, nobody behaves nowadays, it is not good form; we leave that to the lower classes. Look as though I had dragged you there by the hair of your head and that your worst anticipations were realized. When she asks you to her 'at home,' say, 'So kind of you; charmed, I'm sure'; and look as much like a liar as possible. If you tread on her gown, as you probably will, don't blush and don't stammer—"

"And you think I'd better go?"

"Oh," said Driscoll, "it's her fault, so she can't blame anybody. I told her you weren't her style and that you'd be the deuce in society, but she insisted. She's just like all women, running mad over something new, especially if it's a man with hair like a brush fence and no reputation to speak of."

"Driscoll!"

"Well, the hair speaks for itself, and the world speaks for the reputation, you know. I don't mean that you deserve it, my dear Shem; a man's reputation has nothing whatever to do with what a man is. A virtuous man is simply a man whom nobody knows anything about; a vicious man, one whom somebody has been clever enough to find out. Why, look at Hedley Semple! there is not a better man, morally, in New York; but he has been discovered, as it were, and the women who won't notice Semple on the street will fawn over Madison Lyons, who hasn't a shred of honor to his back. You see it is wiser to be conventionally immoral than unconventionally moral. It isn't the immorality they object to, but the originality."

And Michael went.

When entering Mrs. Stuyvesant - Smyth's rooms he was all but blinded by the glare of light; when taking Mrs. Stuyvesant-Smyth's hand, he was dazzled by her diamonds and her beauty. He felt helpless and ill at ease; he was conscious of himself, of his twenty - one years, and of his feet and hands.

Down to dinner he carried a lady with a chin, who talked shrilly and asked him his opinion of the President's private character at the top of her voice. She was a new woman, but Michael did not recognize the species. Concerning the President, he had no opinion and he gave none; he only looked at his plate and wondered which fork to use and which glass to drink out of. When the hock was passed he allowed it to be poured into his champagne glass, and then, realizing that he had committed a breach of etiquette, blushed and was as miserable as if it had been a breach of honor—perhaps more so. He glanced desperately across at Driscoll and found the shrewd, quick-sighted eyes fixed upon him. Then, as the hock was brought to Driscoll, he pushed forward his champagne glass.

"A habit I got into in South America," he said, carelessly, meeting the eyes of his hostess; "a connoisseur never changes his wine-glasses."

Mrs. Stuyvesant-Smyth had beamed upon him as every one beamed upon Driscoll, and Michael had thrown him a glance of passionate gratitude, which Driscoll ignored with his easy smile. Looking back across all the years of generosity and friendship, Michael knew that all else that Driscoll had done for him was found wanting when weighed in the balance with that one small act of social courtesy. From that moment he had loved John Driscoll as a man loves a man, and with a love which passeth the love of woman for woman.

"I shall never go to another dinner, so help me Providence!" Michael had said as they walked homeward. "What's the use of all that confounded ceremony, anyway? This isn't an Oriental monarchy."

Driscoll stopped to light a cigar, puffing leisurely away.

"It *was* funny," he assented, "to hear you apologizing to Miss La Mode for spoiling her pinafore."

"She didn't have any to spare," said Michael; and then he added, "How beautiful Mrs. Stuyvesant-Smyth is! I never saw such color in my life."

Driscoll threw back his head and laughed. "Nor ever will in *life*," he said. "My dear Shem, your innocence shall become proverbial. I shouldn't mention it if she weren't my relation, but she is the most palpably made-up woman in New York."

"I don't see the use in it all," said Michael. "If that is society, society seems to me a deuced unhealthy thing. I've done with it."

5

"A wise decision, since, most probably, society has done with you. I told Alicia you'd be the deuce at a dinner, and now she knows it. Taking Mrs. Stuyvesant-Smyth as the incarnation of society's creed, the world will forgive you sooner for breaking your choice of the ten commandments, provided, of course, you do it elegantly, than for, let us say, drinking out of your finger-bowl." Then he laughed. "As long as you had to get mixed up, Shem, you might have scored a point by ordering champagne in a goblet. You'd have won social distinction and the reputation of a rake. To an ambitious man the loss of such an opportunity is galling."

"Your story about South America was good," said Michael, still smiling.

"I flatter myself," said Driscoll, complacently flicking the ashes from his cigar, "that nobody can serve a better lie than I when I'm put to it. I don't say that I make lying a specialty, but I do say that a lie to suit my taste must be highly flavored and done to a turn. A clever lie sits no heavier upon the conscience than a stupid one—"

Some hours later when Michael went up to his room, he outlined a set of resolutions as he drew off his coat.

"I've done with people," he said, "and women and— fools. If I ever go to another dinner-party I hope I'll be—" and the light went out.

John Driscoll had gone home, smiling to himself. "Akershem's a queer fellow," he thought; "a deuced queer fellow." He felt a certain uneasiness, despite his flippant bearing. In a sense he had stood sponsor to Michael's career, and the responsibility of the office began to manifest itself. It was as if he himself had served to impel the boy upon his headlong course, for had it not been for his own instability and the need of *The Iconoclast*, he felt that circumstances must have tempered the fire of Akershem's spirit. A graver lesson might have been taught him by labor and experience. Lacking the power to give vent to his intolerance, it must at last have burned itself to smoke. But with no surer knowledge of life than a child that has been fed upon fairy tales, he had hurled like thunderbolts his curses upon conventions. Sustained by the brilliancy that gave them utterance, the curses had not fallen to earth, but were still reverberating through the air.

A check must be put upon Akershem. This Driscoll knew, and he also knew that his hand alone must apply the brake. If Michael would not hearken to him, to whom would he hearken? "Bless me, but I feel like cutting," said Driscoll. "I'd like to make off for the wilds of Africa," and he added, "only I'm tired of savages."

But some days later he relented; for one evening about dusk he was called to Akershem, who lay with a broken leg in Bellevue Hospital. It had been for a dirty little waif, the nurse told him, a crippled newsboy, who had fallen under a cable-car. The gentleman had been by, and the gentleman had gone to his help. It was a brave deed, and all for a dirty little newsboy with a crippled back.

Michael smiled as Driscoll bent over him.

"This *is* uncomfortable," he said, "and it will keep me laid up for months. What a bore!"

"Shem," said Driscoll, looking down upon the strong figure, the helpless, splintered limb; seeing with a fresh sense of wonderment the bitter mouth, the nervous, blinking eyes, "Shem, it might have meant death. An accident saved you. Why did you do it?"

Akershem laughed weakly; his hand was clenched upon the sheet, his face was pallid with self-restraint. He looked like the wreck of the hardy, fearless fellow of yesterday.

And yet, John Driscoll, looking down upon him, started and fell back, wonder-stricken by the evanescent light upon his face. All the good deeds he might have done, all the pure thoughts he might have thought, seemed to circle in a humanized radiance about his head. A fleeting look, and yet John Driscoll felt a sudden chill of regret, for that one moment had shown him the man, not as he was, but as he might have been had not the corroding grasp of shame fastened upon his soul—had the sins of the fathers passed in honor the head of the child.

But Akershem laughed.

"If it had been any one else," he said, "perhaps I shouldn't; but, you see, he was such a poor little cuss, I couldn't help it."

All impulse and emotion! The best as well as the worst in him was the result of those swift, spasmodic changes. He was neither wholly good nor wholly bad; it was a question of chance; right was up, impetuous, supreme; in a flash rose wrong and checkmated it. The elements of his nature warred one with another. Apart they might have formed a wholesome simplicity; meeting they mixed a poisonous complexity. It was as impossible to stem the force of his will as to change the current of the wind, which bloweth where it listeth.

John Driscoll shook his head and went away.

"Akershem," he said, "is in-com-pre-hen-si-ble."

CHAPTER IV

AND Rachel Gavin?

An English art critic, seeing her at this time, had written home to one of the London dailies: "Among the younger American painters, the work of two women gives unquestionably the highest promise. The one a Bostonian, Claude Munro, and the other a Southerner, Rachel Gavin. At present, Miss Munro's work exhibits greater knowledge of technique, Miss Gavin's more original power, the crudity it presents resulting from a triumph of idea over execution. We shall follow with interest their respective careers. . . . In appearance," he added, "one is impressed by the dissimilarity — Miss Munro possesses a beauty which is at once noticeable, Miss Gavin is at first disappointing, afterwards satisfying."

And yesterday the critic paused in the *salon* before a picture of Claude Munro's and wondered what had become of the other, the young Southerner, with her unconscious spontaneity of manner and her exuberant ambition. "It's a pity," he said to himself; "she might have done great things. Married, I suppose, and expending her genius in the nursing of hiccoughy babies. And yet they expect to make women sensible!" and then he forgot all about her.

As for Rachel herself, she had laughed over the criticism, one of her rippling, mirthful laughs.

"Do I resemble a pumpkin pie?" she asked. "Is it in shape or complexion? For we have the happy quality in common that has both disappointed and satisfied Mr. A——'s critical taste. Is it original with the pumpkin or with me?"

And she went about her work with unabated energy.

What if she paused to pat the heads of the street urchins along the way, or lingered at the flower stalls to banter words with a rheumatic old woman, who had ten children, and six of them down with the grippe? She went about her work, nevertheless, and the ten hours daily were spent before her easel.

She was a wholesome young person, with a well-regulated nervous system and a great power of self-absorption. When she expended herself she expended herself utterly. There had been no half-measures in her concentration. Her work had demanded her time, and she had yielded it; it demanded her vitality, and she yielded that as well.

An earnest little thing she was, good at times and bad at times, like the rest of us. Merry at times and sad at times, with an effervescent font of animal spirits which overflowed in laughter or in tears, in anger or in jollity, as the case might be. She had read much in books and little in life, being wise in theories and ignorant in facts, and possessing a good deal of that ignorance which is mistermed innocence. Her clear glance had swept over nature, and had found all things pure and nothing common.

Some twenty odd years ago, when she was a great-eyed slip of a girl in a blue pinafore, she had sketched, in her rash, impulsive way, her philosophy of life. "If you is good, like mamma," she said, "you don't have any fun, an' if you're mean like Aunt Sue nobody loves you. So I reckon I won't be neither; I'll be good at first till people love me so they can't stop, an' then I'll go to work an' have some fun." In those days she was rather inclined to be naughty than otherwise, with a pinafore that was always soiled in front and stockings that were continually slipping over her knees and having to be pulled up with a jerk. She had grown up upon an old plantation, making mud pies in the ditch or climbing on the lap of old Uncle Zeke.

Uncle Zeke· was black and ugly, with only one leg with which to walk and only one eye with which to see. Nobody loved him but Rachel, and Rachel adored him. "It's a mystery," her mother had said; "I don't understand. Why, Uncle Zeke is the most worthless darky on the place." And she had said to the child, "I believe Rachel loves Uncle Zeke more than mamma."

The child leaned her small white face upon her clasped hands and looked away into space. "No!" she said; "I reckon I loves mamma best, but I feels sorrier for Uncle Zeke."

And she had gone through life upon the same great principle.

"I like interesting people better," she said, "but I feel sorrier for the bores. There are so many of them, you know, and they must have such a tiresome time among themselves."

But her redundant vitality served her well, and the surplus energy was worked off in little sparkling outshoots of sympathy. She was seldom bored. "Why, the old woman at the flower stall," she said one day, "is quite diverting. Six of her children have the grippe and they've all taken different prescriptions. And she has given me every one, from castor-oil to sassafras tea."

So she knocked about the world and went unharmed, and scorned nothing, and wept and laughed by turns.

When she came to New York, alone and not quite penniless, with a package of introductory letters in her bag, and a great deal of determination in her brain, she had found that the path of art was not without its allotted share of stumbling-stones. But being an energetic young person, she had set to work to haul the stones out of her way. "Success and society are contradictions with me," she said to herself. "One cannot talk and toil. You can't keep your art and your acquaintances too." So she had chosen the better part, tossed the introductory letters into the fire, bought an outfit of flannel blouses and yachting-caps, brushed all her fine dark hair back from her forehead, and proceeded to follow the path of her choice.

She lived in a suite of rooms consisting of a bedroom and studio on the fifth floor of the Templeton, got her breakfast in the restaurant on the ground floor, brewed her cups of tea at luncheon on the tiny stove behind the Japanese screen in her studio, and took her dinner wherever fate and fortune chanced to favor.

She held out a frank right hand to the world and his wife, from the fat man at breakfast who asked her if she thought that she was descended from the lost tribes of Israel, to the dapper young Frenchman who inquired "if ze negroes ver not quite like ze *human* being?"

To the one she answered, "Oh, I hope so, don't you? I like to think they're found, poor things"; and to the other, "Oh, quite! Almost as good imitations as the French."

So Rachel went on her way. A little woman who lived on the seventh floor had summed up her impending fate in a doleful prophecy. The little woman was a misogamist, as well she might be, having married a foreigner in her youth to repent it in her age. "She's too innocent to come to any good," she said. "In this world innocence is worse than crime." And she had sighed and thought of the foreigner who had smitten her upon the cheek and gone hence. "She'll marry, poor thing," she added, "and she can't do worse unless it be to marry a Frenchman."

But Rachel was unconscious of the prophecy. She had left romance fastidiously alone. Once, it is true, there had been a young Southerner who had pursued her with zeal for the better part of several years. He was convinced that she was in love with him, and endeavored to convince her as well. In the end he had almost succeeded. "This is love!" the girl had said, and she had repeated it to herself at intervals for a whole day. In the afternoon the assertions weakened, and in the evening she confessed her incapacity. "I've been engaged to you a day," she said, "and I feel as if it were a century. Sentiment is *so* wearing. I thought I was in love with you, but I'm afraid I can't be. When one is in love, it doesn't nauseate one to be kissed, does it?"

And the young Southerner had confessed that according to the current creed it did not. "Then you must have mistaken the symptoms," said Rachel. "It was not sentiment, after all. I am sorry you are disappointed." When he had gone, after many tears and more protestations, the girl felt relieved and ten years younger.

"How exhausting is the effort to love!" she sighed. And she had vowed to speak to no man except Dupont, the critic, and Annilt, the picture-dealer, and Chang Lee, who brought her clothes home from the laundry. And all went well. Dupont slapped her upon the shoulder and said, "Go on. You have the heavenly fire." She got into straits and pawned her watch, and got out again and redeemed it. She toiled and shifted and suffered and went without. She laughed and cried and was happy and miserable, like any sensible, well-ordered human being. And then she met Michael Akershem.

She met him and forgot him and met him again. The evening after seeing him at the Academy she came up late from a search for a model and stumbled against him in the elevator.

"Good-evening, St. John."

Michael laughed. "So you haven't forgotten," he said. "Really, won't you take me as a model? Finish this charming little sketch you so wantonly destroyed. See!" He drew a folded paper from his pocket and held it out to her. Then he drew it back.

"No," he said, "you're not to be trusted. But I'll give you permission to make another."

He bent his brilliant glance upon her, the light scintillating between the blinking lids. Rachel laughed merrily. The dimples about her eyes broke forth, away went the corners of her mouth. She gave a little audacious toss of her head.

"No, thank you," she said. "I've taken my feather-duster instead. It answers very well. Thank you for suggesting it to me. It was the striking resemblance that gave me the idea."

The banter was so new to him that he bent his gaze more firmly upon her, his wide brow wrinkling. She was so small, so sensitive, so childlike, that he felt suddenly tender. He had a consciousness that he could crush this white thing by one pressure of his strong arms. He looked down upon her, noticing the slight, full figure, the breadth of the shoulders, the almost childlike slimness of the limbs, the long, straight neck with the unconscious poise of the head.

He felt a strange, new sympathy, a tolerance, nay, a tenderness for a woman—and a young woman at that. Then the elevator stopped and she stepped to the landing. He followed her. He was ignorant of the ways of women, but it seemed to him that she would not bring this good-fellowship to a close.

"Since I may not come as a model," he said, "may I not come as a critic? I am very severe and very just." Then he added, "If not this evening—"

"Oh!" said Rachel, "not this evening. I have only one teaspoonful of tea in the canister and one slice of bread to toast, and I want both myself. But some other time. Not in good light, because I'm always working, but at dusk or by lamplight you may criticise to your heart's content."

And she had given him a deep glance over her shoulder and disappeared behind the curtains of her studio. Michael turned away with a curious feeling of suppressed excitement. He wanted to laugh—to give some forcible expression to his state of mind. He felt as a child feels that has discovered that a doll has hidden springs and can talk. Women were new to him. He had shunned them conscientiously, with a morbid belief that he was cast in a different and rougher mould—that their sensitive edges would shrink from contact with his unpolished exterior. He could marry no woman; of this he had convinced himself, and as yet the possibility of another connection had not suggested itself. He looked upon marriage as the Moloch to which women sacrificed and by which they were sacrificed in turn. That a woman could be found independent enough to hold his views, or, holding them, courageous enough to live up to them, he had not for an instant deemed possible. He held confused and extreme theories concerning the sex, but of practical knowledge he was devoid.

And here, at last, there was thrown in his way — nay, thrust upon him — a woman who was both strong and tender, who was as natural as a child and as innocent of coquetry. It was a fresh experience — something at once convincing and distracting, something which caused a quickening of his pulses and a subtle infusion of tenderness into his heart.

Going to his office, he sat down at the desk and fell to working. It was one of his series of articles upon marriage as an institution, and he found trouble in expressing himself upon paper. His ideas were confused, his words unsuitable.

"Social evolution proves to us," he wrote, "that an institution which is advantageous in a primitive or militant society, which is not without utility in consolidating the interests of men and in protecting the weaker against the encroachments of the stronger, impedes like an incubus the progress of that society when the society has passed from the militant to the industrial state, and— Pshaw!" he said. "Am I a halting idiot?" and he frowned and ran his pen through the lines. Then he began again.

"Like many a custom which has begun as an experiment to end as a fetich, the institution of marriage has not been without a purpose to serve in the course of social evolution. But customs, like garments, wear out and lose their original usefulness, and like garments require to be discarded for a more advanced and more suitable order.

"But, unfortunately, man is less ready to adapt practices to his needs than he is to adapt his needs to practices. Custom, not conscience, maketh cowards of the most of us.

A theory once implanted in the mind of man, be it never so essential to progress in the beginning, in the end is perverted into a fetich, to protect whose altar the blood of human beings will be sacrificed. Truths are not the only things which, to quote Professor Huxley, begin as heresies to end as superstitions. Along with truths a good many falsehoods manage to make a successful struggle for existence, and if we glance about the world to-day I think we shall find that, despite the assertions of our forefathers, truth and falsehood are equally mighty and equally powerful to prevail.

"The majority of men are as able to do good battle under one banner as under another, and, give them time, are quite as ready to swear that the cause for which they did battle was the cause of justice. An inhabitant of the Western world to-day can as obligingly swear to the creed that since 'man is the glory of God, but woman the glory of man,' man should glory in the submission of but one woman, as a native of China can testify that according to revelation and experience he is persuaded that the more glory the merrier. It depends not upon any Heaven-sent revelation concerning the respective glory of the two sexes, but— Pshaw! Am I writing a school-boy's thesis?" And then he drew a long, sweeping line across the page and rose. "I'm all upset," he said. "My brain's in a muddle. Too many cigars."

And he went out for a walk. Meeting Driscoll on the corner, he blurted out with the suddenness of a child :

"Say, Driscoll, what kind of creatures are women, anyway?"

Driscoll took his arm and drew him under the electric light.

"Been drinking, old man?" he inquired. "No; hand cool, pulse not quite even, but will do. Oh, women! Bless me, I give it up. Ask another. They're one of the Almighty's enigmas for proving to men that he knows more than they do. Oh, all women aren't alike, you know.

There 're several patterns. There's the woman with brains and the woman without — last - named variety remarkably plentiful. Then there's the woman of good character and the woman of bad, and the woman who is supposed to have none to speak of. There's the pretty woman and the ugly woman. There's the woman that's worthy of God and the woman that the devil wouldn't take at a bargain."

"Are—are they sensible and thoughtful? Are—are they like men?"

"They're trying to be, my young innocent. But they haven't gotten that far down yet. Give them time, though. Vice is mighty, you know—".

"Nonsense, Driscoll, don't be a fool! Could you—did you—were you ever in love?"

"Could I?—did I?—was I? Well, damn me, I could, and I was, and I did. I wasn't born wise, you know, Shem. I cultivated it."

"You wouldn't marry her because—"

"I'd have been deuced glad to. I couldn't."

"Why not?"

"She wouldn't. Bad taste. I agree with you. She was one of the plentiful type—without brains, you know. She married a missionary."

"Oh!"

When next Michael saw Rachel Gavin it was in her studio. He had gone between lights, when she had just pushed aside her easel and was lolling upon a divan before an open fire. He noticed that she wore a gown that was loose and full and of some dim, nondescript shade. When she lifted her arms the sleeves fell in soft folds back upon the shoulders. It was a dressing-gown, and she had just slipped into it. But Michael did not know. If he had seen her trailing it along Fifth Avenue he would have considered it, had he considered it at all, as entirely suitable and appropriate. He noticed how childlike and pliant her figure was, and how white her small face with the firelight flickering over it. "I'll give you some tea in a moment," said Rachel. And she leaned forward to raise the wick of the tiny stove. "You may pass me the cups. Now take your choice. The pink one is the prettier, but the gold one holds more. Do you know, when you knocked I thought you were poor Madame Laroque, who is continually pursued by the fear of Frenchmen. She lives on the seventh floor, you know, and does linen embroidery for sale. Her husband slapped her and ran away, and ever since madame has lived in hourly dread of his returning to visit the scene of his crime. She says he only slapped her upon one cheek, and she has a presentiment that he will never rest in his grave until he has come back and slapped her upon the other. Dreadful, isn't it? Why, she screams whenever you knock at her door, and she won't let you in until you've given the watchword 'No Frenchman.' And, do you know, when you knocked I thought it sounded as though you were being pursued. Are you afraid of Frenchmen, too? Oh, here is the tea. Beautifully drawn. Give me your cup. One lump—only one, did you say?"

It was delightful. Michael's glance dwelt upon her like one enraptured. She was so frank, he thought, so natural, so free from any shadow of self-consciousness.

She sipped her tea, and then, setting the cup aside, leaned back against the cushions of the divan and threw her arms above her head with a quick, impulsive movement. Her gestures were all quick and impulsive. She was alive to her finger-tips, and warm with the flow of her rich, red blood. He leaned towards her, his eyes narrowing.

"Do you see this?" she asked. "This was sent me as containing proof positive that you were a publican, and to be detested. A correct young man saw me talking to you at the Academy, and this is the result. I read one or two of the articles. They were delightfully funny."

"Funny!" protested Michael. "Abuse them, abhor them, destroy them if you will, but don't laugh at them."

"Oh, but they are so amusingly in earnest—and original,

too. I like originality. There's only one thing I like better, and that is independence."

Michael gave her a quick, radiating glance. He warmed
suddenly. "We've done a good work," he said. "The
circulation of our paper has doubled in a year. At every
meeting of the society—there is a society, you know, composed of persons interested in the journal—stockholders,
journalists, and the like. Why, the meetings are most enthusiastic, or, as Driscoll says, 'most foolastic.' I have an
assistant, a young fellow who has entered body and soul
into the cause. He forms societies among the workmen, and
is the president of dozens of committees for inquiring into
all sorts of abuses. Oh, he's a great help. When my time
is quite taken up with the paper, he goes outside and awak-
ens interest. He has even started a branch among women.
The Twentieth Century Society it is called, and it is quite
in the heart of the most advanced movement of the day."

He was talking rapidly, his face flushed, his eyes blinking, his effulgent glance riveted upon the girl.

The emphasis of his personality became pronounced—a
terrible reserve force within his nature, forever salient and
forever illusive. Some vague, intangible mystery of will
that asserted its dangerous power over man, woman, and
child, stamping even his objective environment with the
impress of a mighty and impassioned personality.

The girl leaned forward, her hands clasped upon her
knees, her deep eyes casting their light upon his face. She
was interested. She became suddenly conscious of the scintillating magnetism of the man.

"But," she said, "I don't quite understand. You aren't
an anarchist—that you deny. You aren't a socialist, for
you laugh at all schemes of socialism. Are you simply advanced? Now, what does it mean to be advanced? Does
it mean to be a little ahead in wickedness of your fellows?"

Michael interrupted her brusquely.

"We do not laugh at socialism," he explained. "We
laugh at the schemes of socialism that have been expound-

ed. They have all failed in the essential principle—that is, in reaching an equilibrium of moral restraint and moral liberty. Socialism and individualism need to coalesce to give us the surest protection to the rights of man with the widest personal liberty. The legal enactments which place unnatural and burdensome conventions upon individuals should be abolished; the freedom which allows the few to possess themselves of the privileges of the many should be restricted. What we need is to place a premium upon individuality, and, at the same time, to protect the individual by giving him an opportunity to prove his capacity for honest labor in the field of his choice, to insure to him the fruits of his labor. We must not allow the stronger in the form of a corporation to crush out the weaker in the form of individual enterprise. Centralization and individualism need to be reconciled, and can be—"

"And you expect to do it," said Rachel, "with one blow of your strong fist? Revolt is fruitless."

"Revolt is the forerunner of all great changes," said Michael. "It's as much a part of evolutionary socialism as the results themselves. The few pioneer and clear the rubbish away, and then the millions follow, like sheep, in their footsteps."

"After having cursed the pioneer," added Rachel, "and most probably stoned him to death, they make a bridge with his bones and pass over."

Then they fell to talking of Michael's work, of Michael's life, and of Michael himself. He told her of his childhood, and then, in a haughty, sensitive way, spoke of his birth.

"I was born under an evil star," he said, "the only kind of star that is absolutely fixed, and that neither rises nor sets. I was formed as a potter forms a pot, and thrown aside into the gutter to be kicked to pieces by strangers. As a child I all but lived in a pigsty. I tended the pigs— No, don't pity me. I sometimes look back now with regret to the long days in the pastures, with only space and weeds and pigs—"

But Rachel was not pitying him. To a woman of her

fearless nature there seemed a certain sublimity in his reck-less defiance. It stirred and thrilled a responsive echo in her own heart. All the latent capacity for hero-worship, that had lain dormant since childhood, awoke with intensity. She adored courage, and perhaps she found a fascination in this moral force that was brave enough to scorn custom, conventions—nay, respectability itself. She looked up at him with a wide, comprehensive glance. She saw all the straight, manly length of him, the heavy brow, the sensitive, quivering mouth. She gloried in the defiance, in the daring that made this man able to face her and say, "I owe no man anything—not even a name." She did not wonder at the inconsistency of his life; did not see that though he defied religion, yet he raged because his own birthright had been without benefit of clergy; that though he opposed marriage, yet he blushed because he himself had been born without the pale.

She was young and impulsive, and she did not see this; if she had seen it, could it have saved her from herself? Perhaps not. And he was sincere enough, God knows. He felt that he had been a victim to adverse circumstances, and so did she. He believed that the hope for future gen-erations lay in sweeping such possible injustice aside, and she—she did not think of future generations at all. She thought only of him.

"I have lived to myself," said Michael, "and I shall die to myself. I have but one friend in the world — a man. As for women, granting that a woman could find aught in me to love—could a woman brave public opinion as I have braved it? Could a woman share my principles and live them as I have lived them? No, don't pity me. I tell you I am not to be pitied."

Rachel looked up at him as he towered above her, alone, miserable, hated, and hating. A sudden rush of sympathy stirred her pulses.

"I don't pity you," she said. "How *dare* you say so? I honor you!"

6

She held out her hand. He took it, and then looked down upon her, and his eyes softened. The hard look died from them, giving place to a gleam of tenderness. He felt a swift desire to lean down and touch the white nape of her neck upon which the dark hair was coiled. And then a swifter and keener desire to take her in his arms— very tenderly, as one takes a child—to feel the pressure of her firm, reliant hands. It was an emotion quite new to him, so new that he felt conscious and half alarmed, fearing to have it fade away.

When he had gone Rachel sat motionless in the flickering firelight, her chin resting upon her clasped hands. Her sympathies had been touched and had responded with all their exuberant force. She was conscious of having been called away from her self-absorption, of having been betrayed into reverencing a man, a man who was leader and pioneer of what the world called a non-moral element, but a man who was strong enough to stand fearlessly alone— ah, that was a man !

She sat there, the firelight flickering over her, casting a rich radiance over her dull gown, shimmering in her wide eyes, and falling like a flash of light across her broad, white brow. Her easel stood beside her. In the corner there was a large unfinished canvas, before which a curtain hung.

"It is my great picture," she had said to Michael—"my great picture, which no one has seen," and she did not lift the curtain. Now she rose and went towards it and drew the hangings aside. It was a half-finished Magdalen, a rough peasant Magdalen, with traces of sinful passion and sinful suffering upon her face. A woman who, having been dragged through the mire and slime, forever carried the stains upon her broken body. It was a great work, as she had said, a work which showed the hand of genius, a hand whose strokes are powerful and falter not.

She let the curtain fall and turned away.

"How strong he is," she said.

CHAPTER V

MISS GAVIN was emancipated, or believed herself to be, which amounts to the same thing.

She had once been heard to remark that she occupied a position in the most advanced flank of the New Woman's Crusade.

"I don't deliver lectures," she said, "nor do I write revolutionary articles for the Sunday papers, but I live the views which most of them only express. They *wish* to be emancipated. I am emancipated."

From all of which it may be inferred that Miss Gavin was as ignorant as the most advanced of her sex. Like them, she was levelling her guns at shadows and making a fierce onslaught upon mere phantom foes. The dust of the conflict was in her eyes, and she was busily aiming her cannon at the inoffensive onlookers, or even the trees along the way, while she clasped her arch-foe to her mistaken breast. She had not learned that the enemy of woman is neither God, man, nor devil, but her own heart.

Some day, in a far distant to-morrow, when the present century is well buried beneath the strata of the earth, when the Quaternary epoch is as far down as the Palæozoic, and our descendants are poking and prying among our relics, as we poke and pry in search of the Ichthyosauri and the Pterodactyls, a wonderful change will have occurred upon the surface of the globe.

While the scientists of the future—mere motory formations of brain matter—are quarrelling as to the degree of barbarity exhibited in our fossils, a more startling discovery will be taking place above their heads.

For woman will have turned upon her real foe, and have

rent the mask apart, and, lo! she will have looked into the face and have seen her own.

From that moment the victory will be gained. Men, manners, and morals will have a rest, and only change fashion in due season, as is highly respectable. And woman will have triumphed.

But that will be to-morrow, and it is of no to-morrow that I write, but of the nineteenth century, somewhere between the years of our Lord "ninety and ninety-five." A momentous period it is, unless I am deceived. A period when we stand with one foot firmly advanced into the twentieth century and our backs turned broadly upon the past. We are progressing finely in these days. The fashions of manners and morals are changing with much rapidity. A new form of vice is in vogue, not the old skilfully draped creature that we of the fifties remember so fondly. Oh no, quite a bold and audacious character, with no covering from her sister virtue, and indeed with no covering at all worth recording. The good old theory of our forefathers that vice was in the naming of it has still a number of adherents; but there is a new school of morality, quite a popular one in its day, and carrying under its banner some of the foremost names of the century—Ibsen, Tolstoï, M. Zola, and many others, who hold that, being done publicly, it is no longer vice but realism. However, that is a distinction in terms, not a difference.

But this is a progressive epoch, let him deny it who will. It dares speak audibly of facts which its forerunners did not whisper, but expressed, as it were by a pantomime, acts without words. Men grow callous to the point of meeting their wives in public, and ladies are able to mention legs in general without the need of smelling-salts. A progressive period, dare you deny it?

But Rachel thought herself emancipated, and was as strong in her conviction as the most of us, before Time has shown us our error.

She believed herself to be emancipated, and yet— She

had behind her a series of grandmothers, from the dear old lady who pottered about her plantation and was bullied by her darkies, to Mistress Eve, who pottered about Paradise and was bullied by Adam. Virtuous women they were, no doubt. As for the old lady on the plantation, I can stake my word, if need, upon her probity, and I do not remember having heard aught derogatory to the honor of Mistress Eve. The devil was the only person likely to inquire into the matter, and, if he knew, he was gentleman enough to keep quiet.

With such irreproachable ancestry Rachel had sprung full armed into existence, since good repute is nine-tenths of morality and the whole of respectability. She was over-shadowed by the virtues of those gentlewomen who were such adepts in the kitchen and the nursery. For the space of some fifty years Miss Gavin's own great-grandmother was held triumphantly up before her long-suffering neighbors as a pattern of modesty and meekness. Her husband, a true gentleman of the old school, knee - breeches, lace ruffles, and all, to say nothing of the sobriety, was heard to speak of her as the ideal of St. Peter, a woman from whose lips fell only "chaste conversation, coupled with fear." Whether the hearing or the patience of the old gentleman gave out was never known, but the benefit of the chaste conversation was usually bestowed upon the slaves for want of other audience. The gentleman of the old school preferred to spend his evenings at the Red Cross Tavern, where a lady was then residing who is nameless in polite society, and whose conversation was hardly held to be an example of chastity. But the virtuous old gentlewoman knew her duty, and, what is quite another thing, she performed it to the best of her ability. When the jolly gentleman staggered home in the wee, small hours of the morning, very red of face, very husky of voice, and very revolting altogether, my lady would be sitting beside her distaff, her powdered hair as unruffled as at noon. She met him thus for fifty years ; she greeted him with a wifely kiss ;

she assisted him to bed, after mixing his night-cap of whiskey and water with her own aristocratic hands. Then she said her prayers, and thanked the Lord that Satan had not beguiled her from the path of duty. Oh, that was a wife worth having !

In the natural course of time her duty exhausted her and she died. At her funeral the sermon was preached from the text :

"Who can find a virtuous woman? For her price is far above rubies."

The old gentleman was much affected; he lamented almost as loudly as he had done when his dapple mare foundered. It was at least a week before he went to the Red Cross Tavern, and almost six months before he was able to find a woman virtuous enough to be worth her price. How very judicious of Providence to make virtue its own reward, for it is the only one it ever gets !

But Miss Gavin had not inherited the character of her admirable ancestor. Had she been in her place she would probably have locked the jolly gentleman out the first time he went to the Red Cross Tavern, and certainly she would have boxed his ears had he attempted to kiss her in his maudlin humor. But Rachel lived when the nineteenth century was on its last legs; she was an embodiment of that transitional period when new customs were casting off the garments of the old and an illusive spirit of discontent manifested itself in the nation. At that time the firmly implanted principles of to-day were but quickening before the travail of birth, and men were dissatisfied with the old without having evolved the new. Theories floated around, like bacteria in an infected atmosphere, waiting to gain a parasitic existence upon an unsettled reason.

A restless, vacillating period it was, and Miss Gavin was an embodiment of the spirit of her times.

Mrs. Algernon Van Dam, a cousin of Miss Gavin on her father's side, and on her own account the well-to-do wife of a well-to-do banker, began a systematic patronage upon

Rachel's arrival in New York. Mrs. Van Dam lived in a very inconvenient house in a very convenient location; somewhere on Fifth Avenue it was, just beyond Fifty-first Street. Mrs. Van Dam had sent Miss Gavin cards to her "at home"; Miss Gavin had not gone. Mrs. Van Dam had called; Miss Gavin had done likewise.

"My dearest child," said Mrs. Van Dam, "you must look upon me quite as a sister, you know. You are *so* impulsive, so unsophisticated. Such naturalness is *so* refreshing." And the next day, from her carriage window, Mrs. Van Dam had seen Miss Gavin coming off the Bowery with a dirty Italian waif by the hand, and she had blushed. An evening or two later she called and found the unsophisticated young person going to dine at a French restaurant, quite alone, and with a crêpe scarf about her head. There were no more cards, no more calls. Mrs. Van Dam bowed upon the street, and that was all.

Alas! poor Rachel! Now Mrs. Van Dam passes her and does not bow, and that is *not* all.

And the Mrs. Van Dams of society continue to flourish as a green bay-tree. Not because they are more virtuous than other people, I beg to submit, but because they appear to be; an imitation, by-the-bye, which has often better results than the original, and is altogether more satisfactory to the person engaged.

For Mrs. Van Dam goes smilingly in to dinner on the arm of Bertie Catchings, who supports Callie French, the ballet-dancer, and beams admiringly upon old General Morehead, who has broken the hearts and the reputations of a dozen women in his day, and whose day will not be over until his life is. But as for Callie French herself, why, she blushes if you call her name, and the dozen victims of General Morehead she passes in the gutter and draws her skirts aside.

And this was the era of the Woman's Crusade!

As for Rachel, she forgot Mrs. Van Dam sooner than that lady forgot her; for she had other things to think of,

and Mrs. Van Dam had not, or if she had she did not think
of them.   Rachel went about her work with steadfast feet.
The world was to her a gigantic machine by which her success was ground out; men and women objects necessary
to the accomplishment of that success.

She was not St. Peter's ideal, nor was she the ideal of
any one else.   She did not believe that meekness and humility were the crown of womanhood, and if you had told
her that "man was made for God, but woman for man,"
very probably she would have laughed.   She was honest
and good-tempered and brave, and perhaps very little else,
except charming, and now and then very nearly if not quite
beautiful.   She had seen a good deal of Michael Akershem
since that evening in her studio.   Several times he had
dropped in about dusk, and she had met him once or twice
at dinner in the restaurant around the corner.   On the
whole, she had thought very little about him.   She was
working upon an oil canvas for the March exhibit, and, as
usual, her work absorbed her lesser interests.   One evening she ran against him on Twenty-third Street, as she
came out of a little Japanese shop.   Her hands were filled
with bundles, and Michael took them from her, but Miss
Gavin demurred.   "You may carry this," she said, "for it
has only a cup towel in it; and you may carry this because
it is marmalade, and, if you break it, you sha'n't have any
with your tea any more ; but you can't take this because
it is a palette, and you'd be sure to hold it awkwardly and
let it drop.   I got it in place of one Madame broke while
she was cleaning it.   She thought she heard her husband
coming up-stairs, and she screamed and let it fall.   She
would be such a very useful little woman if she did not have
that unfortunate habit of feeling presentiments.   Anyway,
I've warned her that if he does come back I shall ring up
the police."

Michael laughed.   Then he looked down into her mirthful face—the dimpling eyes, the sensitive corners of her
mouth that trembled and twitched upward, and the laugh

softened into a smile. "A mouse defying a lion," he said; "a man could crush you with a blow of one finger."

"Perhaps," admitted Miss Gavin, "but I hardly think you will find one foolhardy enough to try it."

Then they both laughed and walked homeward.

"You may come in," said Rachel, when they had reached the flat; "I'll give you some marmalade, since you were kind enough not to drop the jar. Madame Laroque is coming down, and we're going to dine at a little French restaurant around the corner, and be waited on by a charming Irish waiter named Pat. Should you like to dine with us?"

Like! He would have liked fire and brimstone at that moment had she been hospitable enough to offer it. He went in, and Rachel made tea and spread marmalade upon his bread for him, as children do, and talked and laughed and dimpled until he almost forgot that he was an outcast and at war with the whole human race.

Then Madame Laroque came down. She was a demure little woman with pink cheeks, and eyes that looked as though they had gotten very wide open once and had never resumed their natural size. She rarely spoke, and when she did it was to say "yes" or "no," as the case might require.

Presently Rachel went into her bedroom, and came out with a soft Persian scarf thrown over her head and around her shoulders. The drapery suited her well, and Michael had never seen her more bewitching. Her eyes shone like clouded stars; the little dimples beside them were never at rest, but came and went and came again like tiny ripples; the corners of her mouth twitched upward and then lay still; and she laughed, and away they went, regardless of regularity. Every change of thought passed in a fleeting gleam or shade across her sensitive face.

At the restaurant they were waited upon by the amiable Pat. Michael sat opposite Rachel, and between the spoonfuls of her lukewarm soup she beamed upon him, as she beamed upon Madame Laroque, with her deep, gray glance.

There was a feeling of peace and homeliness which Michael, buffeted as he had been about the world, had never known before. He began to doubt if he really hated the entire human race; surely he did not hate one small atom of it—that could not be. He felt secure in her presence; sure of a steadfast hold upon faith and strength; sure, too, of a quick responsive sympathy — a sympathy which rained upon him from beautiful, deep-set eyes.

He was conscious of an illusive sense of exaltation— something indefinable and indefinite, and yet something which seemed to lift him above material phenomena. He did not seek to analyze the sensation; he did not recognize the symptoms, as one accustomed to the malady of love would have done. He only knew that he was glad to be with this one woman, to say nothing of Madame Laroque, and that she possessed an all-pervading charm of personality.

Rachel was in high good-humor; she laughed and sparkled with an effervescent flow of mirth.

"I have dined here twenty-four times within the last month," she said. "It is delightful unless the cook is in a bad humor. If he is, he refuses to give one anything save his own selections. Why, once he was so provoking. I ordered bouillon, and Pat came back and said the cook wouldn't let him have any. Then I ordered birds, and the cook actually sent me word that he wasn't going to broil any birds, but that I might have chops. I detest chops; so I said, 'Pat, show me the kitchen,' and Pat left me at the door, and just as I opened it the old scalawag heaved a soup-tureen at my head. I caught it on the fly, and when he saw me he almost had a fit. I declare I never saw any one grow so purple in the face except my little Italian model when he swallowed a wax plum by mistake. But the cook begged my pardon and gave me some bouillon, and all ended happily."

"Yes!" said Madame Laroque. Madame was a charming person. When one says "yes" when you expect it, and "no" when you expect it, what more can mortal man desire?

"I didn't like his mayonnaise," continued Rachel, "so I gave him my own recipe, and he makes it deliciously, doesn't he?"

"Deliciously!" said Michael, who loathed it.

"Yes," said Madame, who loved it.

Rachel talked, Michael looked at her, and Madame Laroque ate her dinner, which proves her to have been a sensible woman. But Madame had weighed love and her Frenchman in the balance, and had found both wanting. When one finds sentiment worthless, one turns to food, and probably is consoled.

They drank their coffee and left, and Michael walked home with them, saying good-night before Rachel's door.

As he took her cool, frank hand in his an electric current seemed to start from his finger-tips, darting through his veins to his heart. He watched her loosen the Persian scarf and let it fall back upon her shoulders, showing the white curves of her throat. He bent his gaze upon her, looking down into her upturned face. A massive consciousness of unworthiness oppressed him; the knowledge that she was far, immeasurably far, beyond him.

"Good-night," he said; "think well of me." And he dropped her hand and turned away. Rachel went into her studio and talked to Madame Laroque about Frenchmen for an hour. She hadn't any opinion upon the subject, but as it was the only one upon which Madame had any, they were compelled to recourse to it. Then Madame went to bed, and Rachel found the papers Michael had left a week ago and read them very carefully; after which she let down her fine dark hair, and sat before the fire brushing it until it glowed from the friction.

She felt peaceful and happy. As yet no electric thrills had broken the calm serenity of her pulse, no tumult of any kind disturbed her frank good-humor. With each long, firm stroke of the brush she was soothed into drowsiness. "I am so sleepy," she said, presently, speaking softly to herself. Then, before going to bed, she crossed

the room in her bare feet to where the unfinished canvas of
the Magdalen stood, strong and awful behind the heavy curtain.   Very white and slim in her nightgown, Rachel stood
before it, lifting the hangings as she looked at it in the dim
firelight.   The painted woman seemed to quicken and come
to life, to look back at the living woman with a great forewarning in her awful eyes.

But Rachel only saw in it the work of her own strong
hands—her great work.

"Let me finish it, O God!" she prayed.   "Let me make
of it a great, great thing. Give me this, and I will ask
nothing else my whole life long; but, O God! God! give
me this!"

She knelt down upon the floor, clasping her hands like a
child, her face wrapt and white, the dark plait winding like
a serpent along her gown.

"Give me my ambition," she prayed, "and nothing else
—nothing else, O God!"

Then she rose from her knees and went to her bed in
the adjoining room.

Upon New-year's Day Michael took a holiday. It was his first holiday, and he found some difficulty in deciding what to do with it; before it was an hour old it had developed into a white elephant upon his hands.

In the morning he awoke with a definite intention of enjoying himself and an indefinite idea as to what manner of enjoyment it should be. Then, in a nebulous obscurity, his thoughts gathered about a shining centre, and the centre was Rachel Gavin. An indeterminate impulse prompted him at once to seek and to shun her presence. Against his judgment he desired her, but the desire was no less urgent because unauthorized. The tide of his undisciplined nature strained towards her as though impelled by some magnetic attraction. The illusive subtlety of personality fascinated as it enthralled him; the feminine quality had fallen over him as a spell.

He arose early, rendered restless by his mental turmoil. The room stifled him, and he descended to the sidewalk and wandered for hours in a drifting snow. He entered a florist's—cautiously, as a thief might—and emerged bearing a paper box containing violets. With the violets under his arm he returned to his room and set about making his toilet, an operation of some length, consequent upon an unusual decision. For the first time in his life he wilfully resolved to sacrifice comfort to adornment, and it was with a fluctuating sense of self-respect that he discarded his flannel blouse.

Then, hearing Driscoll's step upon the landing, he hid the violets under the bed and began sorting a pile of cravats.

"Happy New-year!" began Driscoll as he entered; after which he gave vent to a prolonged whistle. "Ye gods!" he exclaimed, "behold the mould of fashion."

Michael blushed to the roots of his hair. "It strikes me," he returned, stiffly, "that I have on just about what you have."

"But I am numbered among the Philistines."

The flush passed from Michael's face; he threw back his head impatiently. "I don't see that a boiled shirt affects my principles," he protested.

Driscoll shrugged his shoulders with his habitual loose-jointed movement, which reminded one of an automatic supple jack. "Vanity, thy name is man," he observed, reproachfully. Then, a sudden suspicion seizing him, he wheeled round with a jerk. "Why, bless me, if you aren't using cologne!" he said, with disgust; "or is it powder?"

Frowning heavily, Michael tossed the cravats upon the bed, managing at the same time to administer a vicious kick to the violets.

"Don't be any more of an ass than you're obliged to be," he retorted, angrily.

Driscoll seated himself upon the bed, humming a comic song between half-closed lips. With unabated good-humor he watched Michael tie a four-in-hand cravat.

"Pleasant day," he observed, finally.

"Deuced," responded Michael, without turning his eyes.

With shrill amiability Driscoll finished the song, commenced another, broke off, and walked up and down the room. Then he seated himself and gave way to his forebodings.

"It's—it's not a woman?" he remonstrated.

"No, it is not," returned Akershem, with severity.

"Then, let it be what it may, there's a chance of salvation."

Michael surveyed him for a moment in silence. "I don't see why you object to women," he remarked; "they are good enough in their proper places."

" Which is usually the last place in which you find them. But I don't object to women, my dear Shem; I object to them in connection with yourself. A substance may be all right in a free state and the deuce in combination. Everything is in the mixing, you know."

Michael brushed the sleeve of his coat impatiently. " I suppose it depends upon the woman," he observed at last.

"And the man," added Driscoll. " As for that, everything has its uses; marriage is an institution admirably adapted to fools."

" I wasn't speaking of marriage."

" Oh, you weren't, weren't you? When a man begins talking of women the subject of matrimony isn't far off."

Michael was silent, determination settling upon his face. When next he spoke it was with a metallic ring of decision.

" I can't go with you to-day," he said. " I've other plans on hand."

Driscoll shrugged his shoulders. " You have mysteries," he remarked. " Mysteries are always immoral." Then he sighed. " Shem is no longer innocent."

" So much the better for Shem. Innocence is milk-and-water ignorance."

" Exactly. I've often wondered why the students of the tree of the knowledge of good and evil were always so proficient in the latter branch. It's because if one learns anything it must be vice; virtue is merely the passive state. Oh, the ignorant are the innocent, the simple are the saintly."

" Which argues you a Solomon."

" By no means. With me evil is an intuition, with you an acquirement. I have not lost my innocence because I have none to lose. As for you, alas!—"

" Don't be an infernal drivel of a fool!"

" Strong language, that; but to the point. Oh, my dear Shem, yours is the assurance of youth. In time you'll learn that vice palls upon the taste no less than virtue. One should follow neither the broad road that leads to gout, nor the narrow one that leads to nothing; there are many by-paths connecting the two."

"Philosophic utterances inspired by my descent downward," commented Michael, dryly.

"I weep for your native innocence." Then Driscoll rose, shook himself, and departed. "I'm not wanted," he declared, plaintively, as a parting shot. "The light of my righteous countenance is a reproach. I leave you to your base intentions."

When he had gone Michael threw open the window and stood looking across the rows of blackened chimney-pots. A little heap of snow lay upon the sill, and he bent down and blew it out into space. A breath of intense cold passed across his face, and, looking downward, he saw the frozen streets gleaming like silver in the morning light.

He turned away, took up his hat, stooped to draw the violets from their hiding-place, and passed out, slamming the door after him. Upon the threshold of Rachel's studio he placed the box and stole quietly away. Reaching the ground-floor, he sought out a severe-looking waiter. "Has every one at your table breakfasted, Samuel?" he inquired. Samuel replied that they had—leastways, everybody except the fat gentleman with the puffy face, who didn't count.

"And Miss Gavin? Did she go out afterwards?"

No, Miss Gavin had not gone out afterwards; he thought she had returned to her room.

Michael got into the elevator, rode to the fifth landing, and got out; after which he got in again and rode down. This operation he repeated six times, to the speechless indignation of the elevator boy, a proper-minded youth with principles, and the strongest of whose principles related to the culpability of making unnecessary exertions. Michael felt the indignation and winced beneath it. Then he blushed at the possibility of Driscoll's catching sight of him. This contingency caused him to alight suddenly as he descended the sixth time and retire into a shadow at a little distance.

Here he remained until the tinkle of a bell sounded from above, and away shot the elevator to the fifth landing. Upon its downward course he caught sight of the toe of a rubber boot and the hem of a cloth skirt, and his heart leaped within him. Then, as she alighted, he hastened forward.

"I have been waiting for you," he said.

"Indeed!" Her eyes narrowed. "Oh, dear," she smiled, "we're becoming quite civilized."

"I am not," he retorted, angrily.

"I was merely alluding to external indications."

She wore a trim little coat of brown cloth, with a fur tippet about her throat, and in her hand carried a large muff. He noticed that she wore his violets, but she did not allude to them, nor did he. Her hat cast a slight shadow across her forehead, and the same shadow seemed reflected in her eyes.

"I was waiting for you," he repeated.

"Really?" The dimples beside her eyes ran riot, her mouth twitched. "I thought you had developed a mania for riding in the elevator," she said.

"Did you see me?"

She nodded.

"I feared that I might miss you. I have been lying in wait for an hour."

"In wait! and the prey?"

"You were the prey."

"How exciting!"

She threw back her head, and the shadow passed from her forehead. Her eyes grew dark. An atmosphere of illusiveness hovered about her. He could not comprehend her, and in that lay her charm. Her sweetness, her mirth, her audacity were so evanescent that before he closed upon a mood it escaped him.

"And what do you want?"

The desire for mastery waxed strong within him.

"I want you," he retorted, boldly.

7

"Oh, mortal, thy demand is insatiable !" The ring of
bravado in her tones angered him; his will smarted from
the friction.

"Let me go with you to-day," he said. The words were
pleading, but his manner masterful. "Show me how to
have a holiday."

She rebelled. "I am going to see Dupont, and you can't
go there."

"And then?"

"To the Metropolitan Museum. I spend every New-
year's Day at the Metropolitan."

"Take me. I have never been."

"Heathen !"

"Take me."

She laughed good-naturedly. Unconsciously her hand
wandered to the violets upon her breast. He noticed that
the hand was white and strong, with fingers cut square at
the tips; not a beautiful hand in itself, but beautiful in the
delicacy of its touch. A hand with the power of a man
and the lightness of a woman. "Very well," she said, as
yielding from sheer amiability, "as you please. Meet
me at the Museum at one. I must hurry." Nodding
gayly, she ran down the steps and out into the street.
Here her pace slackened, and she gingerly picked her way
along the slippery sidewalk. The cold brought a swift
color to her cheeks; in her furs she looked like a ruddy
incarnation of warmth.

Some hours later she stood upon the corner of Fourteenth Street and Fifth Avenue awaiting the stage. As it
passed she hailed it and got in so hastily that she was precipitated into the arms of a stout gentleman, who exclaimed "Dear me !" in an irritated aside, after depositing
her upon the seat beside him. Then he glanced at her, and
the irritation vanished as he offered to pass her fare. As
the stage jolted along it seemed to jolt her thoughts into a
confused jumble of unassorted ideas. Since morning her
mind had stubbornly confronted Michael Akershem, her

will as stubbornly kept him at bay. Some dominant, magnetic force attracted even as it repelled her. So powerful it was that it seemed to compel rather than allure; the force of a Wallenstein that beat his followers to his banner. In a woman less self-sufficient than Rachel the strength of the man might have inspired an aversion purely feminine; but to Rachel there was a glorious suggestion of mastery that quickened her to combat. A nature as independent as her own must subdue before a weaker one could gain the power to attract. It was the power that she worshipped, and power there was and to spare in Michael Akershem.

In her abstraction she allowed herself to be carried a block beyond her destination, and her walk across the park was considerably lengthened thereby. Beyond the enclosed streets the temperature seemed to fall twenty degrees. The cold was so penetrating that her blood was quickened to rapid action, and the air, entering her lungs, caused her a sharp physical pain. She passed from a walk into a run, and sped lightly along the avenue.

About her the snow lay in an immaculate carpet, untarnished by the soot of the city. From the trees icicles hung like diamond pendants, and the slender branches cast long, purple-toned shadows upon the untrodden ground.

Into the hall Rachel darted with breathless haste. At the far end Michael was leaning against a pillar. As he saw her the light fell across his face like the falling of a sunbeam. He smiled and held out his hand.

"It is so cold!" wailed Rachel. "My poor nose! It is frozen. I know it is frozen!"

She looked at him wistfully. Upon her lashes a tear trembled, and it sparkled beneath the brightness of her glance like a drop of sunshine.

Michael eyed her critically.

"I don't think it is frozen," he answered, seriously, "because it is pink. When it freezes it turns blue. I know, because our office boy got his frost-bitten last week."

She laughed until the tear-drops melted and rained down.

"Oh, dear!" she cried, "what consolation! Not blue, but pink. There is salvation in the shade." And she buried her face in her muff.

They crossed the hall, and he drew her over a register. Then she seated herself upon a bench with her back to the mummy of an Egyptian lady. He looked at her with a devouring earnestness. From beneath the brim of her hat her hair fell in dark curves, and about her throat the soft fur rose until it rested against her cheek. She asked him if he had waited long, and he answered, "Not long—at least, it didn't seem so."

"You had pleasant thoughts?"

"Very. My stock has risen."

"I could have come sooner," she observed; "but it's just as well that I didn't, you were so charmingly engaged."

The spirit of mischief quickened within her. She smiled upon him, he frowned upon her.

"Why do you treat me so?" he asked. "You seem always laughing at me."

"It's a pity you have no sense of humor. You would find yourself so diverting."

His face grew blacker.

"I don't like it!" he exclaimed. "Stop."

She rose and gave herself a little shake. "Come," she said, "I will take you to my shrine."

They mounted the stairs, and she showed him her favorite paintings, laughing good-naturedly at his ignorance.

"Some day," she said, "you shall give me a sitting. I'll paint you in yellow ochre with a crown of withered leaves. It would make a fine subject for 'Melancholia.'" Then she led him through a doorway, crying, "Shut your eyes!" He obeyed, and she drew him forward a few feet. "Look!" she said; and he looked, and looked into the eyes of the "Joan of Arc." "It is my gospel," she said. "I would like to keep an altar-lamp burning before it, and to say prayers morning and night."

"It—it looks a little eccentric," he remarked, from the depths of his ignorance.

"For shame, blasphemer!" Then she gave a little cry and fell behind him. "Oh, dear! oh, dear! There's a wretch coming to copy. Run! I wouldn't see his canvas for worlds. It's a sacrilege!" She fled precipitately, he following. They sat down, and she gave him her muff to hold. It was so soft and fluffy and warm that he felt as though he were holding a part of herself. He turned his nervous gaze upon her face; the light of his eyes mellowed and grew tender.

"Do you know," he began, and paused and began again—"do you know that you are the only woman I have ever known?"

"Pardon me, but weren't you brought up by the hand of Mrs. Watkins?"

"She was a fiend."

"Shade of Mrs. Watkins, arise!" exclaimed Rachel.

"I hated women," he continued, "until I met you."

"Your limited experience destroys the compliment."

"If I had known thousands," he retorted, angrily, "it would have made no difference. I should have hated them all—except you."

"You are very amiable."

He turned upon her in a blaze of wrath. "How dare you?" he demanded—"how dare you treat me so?"

She paled slightly beneath his passionate gaze and her lashes trembled. Then she raised her eyes to his and the light in them blinded him.

"I will conquer you yet," he said, the desire for mastery surging within him.

"Oh, young Alexander!" she retorted, defiantly, "is not the world enough? Do you sigh for the impossible?"

"The impossible?" he emphasized.

"The impossible," her eyes laughed.

Then she stood up and turned to beam upon him. "There is such a thing as luncheon," she suggested. "And see how we shock that prim lady in spectacles."

He made a gesture of impatience. "What does it matter?" he returned. "But are you hungry?"

"Starving."

They descended to the basement, and ate their omelet beneath an appetizing study of John the Baptist's head reposing upon an unwieldy trencher.

"There is nothing quite so satisfying as food," remarked Rachel, radiantly, as she sipped her tea.

"I don't see how you can get so hungry," retorted Michael. "I forget all about food when I am happy, but you don't seem to."

"Never!"—she applied herself to her omelet with renewed zeal—"constancy is my one virtue."

But Michael had grown serious, and when, a little later, they returned to the gallery, he fell back upon the old subject. "You are a puzzle to me," he said—"a surprise puzzle of which one can never be quite sure. You are tantalizing."

"Am I?" she smiled.

"You are independent—so terribly independent."

"Yes, yes," she assented.

"Is it always so?" he asked. "Do you never feel the need of something else—of love?"

"Why, I have so much of it. I assure you, I adore myself."

"Not that! not that!" he exclaimed; "but—well—but love?"

"There are many varieties. I suppose you mean the matrimonially inclined?"

He nodded.

"Well, I never feel the need of it."

"Never?"

"Never; do you?" She laughed into his eyes. Her audacity exasperated him.

"How provoking you are!" he said.

She rose, fastened her coat, and held out her hand for her muff.

"I have wasted an afternoon upon you," she said, "ungrateful creature."

"I am not ungrateful—I—" he reached out his hand and touched hers as it lay upon the back of the bench. She did not withdraw it, and his eyes grew gentle. A person with a catalogue sauntered by and surveyed them disapprovingly.

"Do you know," he said, "that I have seen a danger-signal and I did not heed it?"

"Indeed!"

His eyes glimmered between his twitching lids like burning coals. She felt his gaze upon her and shifted uneasily.

"And I would not heed it," he continued, hotly, "though I were rushing to hell."

IN her abhorrence of a vacuum, Nature, for the further-ance of her favorite hobby, has often to resort to strange devices. If she could but understand that vacuity is some-times better than superfluity!

In the making of Michael Akershem, she had been lavish of expenditure; there was much in his composition that might have been safely dispensed with, leaving society and himself none the worse.

The mental energy confined within the storehouse of his brain was in a continual state of ebullition, escaping in magnetic currents through the will or the senses, as the case might be.

This fund of nervous power, forever transforming yet never at rest, fed, as it were, upon his physical constitution, demanding always some extraneous force upon which to expend itself.

A cross between a civilized and an uncivilized nature, a strangely complex organism, had been the result; a primi-tive revolt from restraint and disregard of consequences, and yet a half-refined sensitiveness to the force of the con-sequences when they appeared to overwhelm him. Be-neath all his blatant, loud-voiced clamor against custom perhaps there existed a shade of regret (inherited from the father who had sinned in secret and suffered not) that re-spectability, which he appeared to scorn, had scorned him in reality. The scoffing may have been the revenge of the worm that stings the heel which treads it down, but that left at peace in the mire might have entertained quite a reverence for the oppressor of its fellows.

Having been impelled in a given direction, he had on the

rebound gone somewhat beyond the normal standard.   In time, would the reactionary force become exhausted and the organism return to its allotted sphere ? Who could say ?

As yet there was more profundity than latitude in his nature—more intensity than endurance.   The habits of his life had developed an almost abnormal fund of egoism, causing him to consider every detail of existence from a relative standpoint.   But for all that, he was sincere and earnest enough ; narrow, it may be, and strongly intolerant, but the intolerance itself was but the offshoot of an intense vitality.   Swift, eccentric, forever seeking satisfaction and never finding it, in his nature the ethereal element was not wanting ; he was mind, as it were, without spirit, intellect without soul.   Until meeting Rachel Gavin he had enter-tained settled convictions, principles he called them, con-cerning his individual relation to the race.   A twentieth-century moralist could hold no more stoical doctrines re-garding the essence and quintessence of love.   A month ago he would have sworn to them before any jury in the State, and now, all unconsciously to himself, they were melt-ing like the shadows of dawn before the sunrise.

One evening, a windy evening in March, he stood with Rachel in her studio.   He had brought her some books, and she was idly running the leaves through her fingers as she talked.   The gray light came softly in and fell over her, lending to the white outline of her face a sombreness akin to the wind-swept sky without.

" How ignorant I am, after all," said Rachel—" I mean, how ignorant I am about *real* things : science and facts and human life !   I am clever about painting—I can draw in charcoal and I can put in colors with a good hand ; but I must be naturally very dull, because my effort in that line has drained all my intellectuality and left my brain a mere waste of nondescript matter.   It's a pity to tell you, if you haven't observed it, but I'm not clever."

" Your confession is unnecessary," said Michael.

"I used to read," Rachel continued, turning her face with the gray light still over it towards him, "but of late I've given it up. When one works all day, one can't study, can one?"

"Yes, one can," said Michael. "The will finds the way in most things."

She frowned and looked up at him; he smiled and looked down upon her.

"How do you suppose I read?" he asked. "Do you suppose I was brought up to follow my own fancies? Do you know that as a boy I ploughed the only field that was ploughed upon the farm and left my ploughing at night, tired and hungry, to grind away at political economy? Many were the mornings I got up by candle-light, trying to get in an hour of reading before the cattle had to be watered and the horses groomed. You may call it ambition and praise it, if you will, but it was not ambition, and there is nothing praiseworthy about it. It was a selfish desire to know more than those people, that I might *be* more than they, and so turn and spit upon them. Hate was my spur, not ambition. They looked down upon an illegitimate hireling from their plane of respectability; but one day I knew the hireling should look down upon them and their legitimacy. It was for that I worked, for that I toiled, for that I studied. The minister lent me what books he had; those that he didn't have I borrowed from the schoolmaster without his knowledge. If a book could have taught me anything and I couldn't have borrowed it, I should have stolen it. As it was, I read Mill, Jevons, Marshall, Fawcett, and the rest. The first three dollars that I earned went to a year's subscription to the Humboldt Library, though at the time I hadn't a whole coat to my back."

He paused abruptly and Rachel looked up at him again, the firelight flickering where the gray light had been. Her face was flushed, her eyes soft, and there was a half-smile about her mouth.

"And this has made you?" she said.

"This made me toil, unceasingly toil."

And he spoke truly. By roughness he was moulded, by bitterness warped. A creature of impulse, he was without the judgment that a systematic training imparts; the emotional side of his nature was easily aroused, and, unless checkmated by will, prevailed.

"I'm sure," Rachel was saying, "I don't need all these books to convince me of evolution. I've read *The Evolution of the Horse*, and believe in it. I've forgotten who wrote it, but I know that I paid twelve and one-half cents for it, and that I read it every morning for a week in my bath. It was *so* interesting that I sometimes forgot and stayed in the water too long, and, after I had finished it, I had pneumonia. The book used to get so soapy and wet, and the last page was entirely obliterated, but it was delicious, and it convinced me perfectly."

"How like a woman!" exclaimed Michael. The girl had spoken lightly, rippling with merriment. She tossed her head with a little defiant gesture, and the dark coil of hair slipped from its place, falling in a heavy wave upon her shoulders. Then, as she put up her hand to rearrange it, her lips curved and quivered in their sensitive, bewitching way.

"Rachel!" said Michael. He said it warmly, and before the curve had died upon her lips he stooped and kissed her.

Rachel gasped a moment in her surprise; and then, with a fierce movement, she pushed him from her. "How—how dare you?" she cried. "I always did hate to kiss men! How dare you?"

And she darted past him into the adjoining room, slamming the door after her. The next moment Michael could have kicked himself; but being a man, and never venting his wrath upon himself when there was anything else around, he kicked a chair instead, and went down-stairs and out into the street. He was conscious that the strongest conviction he had ever entertained was the present one—that he was a fool.

"Now I've gone and done it," he thought, forcibly, "and there's an end."

Going to his office, he met Driscoll, who was leaving, and who inquired what was up.

"The devil's up," replied Michael.

"In that case there're two of them on the earth," said Driscoll, "and we're that much worse off than we thought. I've had one round my way for the past week; he's been entertaining me with rheumatism, and, by Jove! if he doesn't leave off I'll cut and run. I've been regularly down in the depths. I always thought civilization didn't agree with me, and now I know it. I have had the blues to distraction for a fortnight, and it will soon be Florida or Blackwell's Island."

"Thought your optimism wasn't good for much; but, Driscoll—"

"Optimism! Say, old man, don't slander a fellow. I'm willing to answer for the special sins which I have achieved myself, but I don't like having them thrust upon me. The phases of my life have about run through, and it has been a steady, downward course. First I was an idealist (that was early — fools are born, not made, you know); next I was a realist; now I am a pessimist, and, by Jove! if things get much worse I'll become a humorist."

"Hardly," said Michael. "A man does not laugh at life until he finds it worthless. As long as he places any value upon it he regards it seriously. It's a bore!"

"By-the-bye, Shem, run down to Florida with me."

"No."

"You may have all the oranges you can find."

"No!"

"You may fish for tadpoles."

"No!"

"Ah, you're incorrigible! It's no good. I'm thinking of going down myself, solely for the sake of getting rid of animal food. I've become a vegetarian; a man with indigestion should eat only unbolted flour and vegetables. I've been dieting for a week, and you shall see the result."

"Another fad?"

"No fad about it—honest fact. Follow my example. Make them use unbolted flour wherever you breakfast, and don't let them mix any of their damned nonsense in the vegetables. Take them straight."

"Shall you be at the Iconoclast Society next week?"

"If I am not in Florida. I've an engagement to dine. Good-night."

Michael went on his way heavily despondent. Would she ever forgive him? Did she realize what a confounded fool he was? How would it end? She was so practical; so far from any vapid sentimentality; so far above the miry shallows of love in which he was floundering. All night he dreamed restlessly of her anger and its consequences, and came down, haggard and white, in the morning, to find Rachel starting out to the art school.

She nodded and smiled gayly as she passed out, and he ate a hearty breakfast in the ecstasy of his relief.

"She has forgiven me, bless her," he thought; but with Rachel it was less forgiveness than forgetfulness. Until meeting him at breakfast she had not remembered his existence; the kiss had been merely the cause of a moment's resentment, and then she had forgotten it, as she usually managed to forget sentimental episodes. She considered them merely as melodramatic interludes in the drama of life; after the interest of the moment they fell away and left one as unaffected as the ripples leave a mountain lake. Sentiment is one of the side-lights thrown upon life to give it coloring—nothing more.

For several days Michael did not go to the studio. He was restless and distraught; if he was spoken to he snarled, if not he grumbled. Love for Rachel had entered into his being, consuming him with its intensity. Because she was far off and unattainable, the intensity increased fourfold. Some natures love only that which is beyond them: a star in the highest heaven, a flower beyond the meadow fence. Michael's was one of these. It is well for them if the star sets not within their reach, if the flower blooms and withers beyond the bars ; it is well for them, and it is better for the star and the flower.

We may sigh for our ideals, and sob for them as children for the moon ; but if we grasp them and they fall to pieces, which is the way with ideals, we throw them aside and bind our bleeding hands. And when the wounds have healed we look about for fresh ideals, leaving the broken ones strewn upon the mire.

At the end of three days he went to her again. It was light enough for work, and Rachel was cleaning her palette near the window. She held a small scraper in her hand. He noticed that she looked tired, the purple shadows under her eyes had darkened, and her face was white. She was so small, so childlike, so lovable to him at least, that a sudden tenderness overwhelmed him.

"Rachel," he said, "will you listen to me ?"

Rachel looked slightly bored.

"Not if it is long, please," she answered.   "If it's to be long, I'd rather not. I am just as tired as I can be."

"It is not long," he answered.   "It is very short; it is only that—I love you."

"I wish you wouldn't," she said, pettishly. "I can't bear love-making ; it's silly."

"It is not silly," he answered, "and it is not love-making ; it is love—earnest, absorbing love. You may do what you please afterwards, but you must listen to me now. I tell you I love you! I love you! I love you! I have never said these words before in my life, and I never shall again. They are meant for you, and you alone. I don't want an answer from you. I would ask no woman to share my life ; it would mean pain and humiliation to her. It would mean— But I love you! I love you! No, you can't get away; you shall hear me again—I love you !"

He spoke rapidly, his lips trembling, his face white, his magnetic gaze illuminating her, scorching her, as though the scintillating flame were shafts of fire. He reached forward and took her hands, holding them firmly in his own, and bending still upon her that rapt, impassioned glance.

The girl shivered, trembled, and paled until her face seemed of marble. A sudden fear dawned in her eyes; they grew dark with suppressed tears. Then, with an effort, she broke from him in a tempest of wrath.

"You are cruel! cruel! cruel!" she cried. "Why do you come and make me miserable with your nonsense? Why can't you leave me in peace? I wish I had never seen you! I hate you! I hope I shall never see you again! I hate you! I hate you!"

And she threw herself upon the couch and burst into tears.

MADAME LAROQUE was a lady who had had an experience. Now, experiences affect different women in different
ways. It is principally a question of proportion : either the
experience is too big for the woman and it effaces her, or
the woman is too big for the experience and she effaces it.
Unfortunately, Madame Laroque came under the first head ;
her experience was so large that it had overwhelmed her,
and she had never entirely ceased trembling from the
shock. The more she thought of it, the more it surprised
her ; the more it surprised her, the more she thought of it ;
and the bigger the experience got, the smaller became
Madame Laroque.

One day Madame was sick in her room, and towards
evening she sent for Miss Gavin to come and read to her.
Madame never read any book but the Bible. She said it
was the only book that she was absolutely sure contained
no allusion to Frenchmen.

"And even if the Lord did include them in the faithless
and perverse generation," she said, "it is less than they deserve." Madame had known only one Frenchman, but she
generalized. Where is philosophy without generalization?

Rachel read the Psalms. David was a high-spirited man,
Madame said, and she admired him, he knew so well how
to get away with his enemies. She listened complacently,
lying back among the pillows, her small hands playing nervously with the sheet. Madame was of a religious tempera-
ment ; her wall was covered with a number of rather ques-
tionable Madonnas ; at the head of her bed hung a little
Florentine altar, upon which she kept a lamp continually
burning. I think she had a vague idea that it was an offer-

ing by which Providence was bribed to protect her from an influx of foreigners. Whether the terms were accepted or not is doubtful, but so far Madame dwelt unmolested.

Rachel read the Psalms, and then closed the book and leaned back in her chair. There was something infinitely soothing to her in some of the measured phrases. A swift, luxurious tenderness, which is the sheath of religious sentiment, enveloped her.

"As the hart panteth after the water brooks, so panteth my soul after thee, O God."

She was looking at the red flame flickering before the altar, and suddenly she felt that if Madame were away she would like to go up to it and rest her head upon the altarcloth, and clasp her hands before the red flame, and implore peace and protection.

Then, with an effort, she shook herself free from the desire, and glanced at the Madonnas upon the wall; she wondered why Madonnas always reminded one of sheep. "Why couldn't they paint a reasonable-looking one?" she thought. "I'm sure it's a mistake to think that holiness and imbecility are synonymous. I wish I could do one. I should make it more symbolical of mind, less of matter."

"I was just like you," Madame was saying, "when I was your age."

Rachel started and looked at Madame Laroque. She wondered if her expression could ever become as inane.

"I think that hardly possible," she said.

"I don't mean in appearance," continued Madame, "though I was considered a very pretty girl. I mean in mind and ambition."

Rachel started again.

"I might have been an artist," Madame went dreamily on, "if I hadn't been a fool instead."

Rachel was relieved by the explanation.

"Yes?" she said.

"I am sure no one thought me a fool until I married," said Madame. "I had quite a talent for painting. I did

8

several beautiful pastels. Poor, dear papa was so proud
of them he had them framed and hung in the parlor; one
was a lake with an island and some swans floating around.
But I gave up my ambition for marriage; it's the way with
women. You'll do it some day."

"Never!" said Rachel. She said it so sharply that
Madame was alarmed, thinking she might have missed a
noise on the stairs.

"Yes," she said, "you'll give up your art, as I did. The
more sensible a woman is, the bigger fool she becomes
when she falls in love. I suppose the Lord intended it.
I guess He knew if he made women any smarter the race
would come to a stop. I guess He knows best—at least, He
ought to; but it does seem strange to me that He couldn't
have found a better way to arrange things."

Madame had talked rapidly; she was excited, and her
usual placidity was broken; a little pink flush had risen to
her cheeks.

"If you want to be miserable," said Madame, "marry;
if you want to be more so, marry a Frenchman."

"I shall not marry," said Rachel, curtly, but Madame
paid no heed to her.

"Frenchmen are dirty," she said. "They chew bad
tobacco and beat their wives." The fact that M. Laroque
had acquired both habits upon American soil in no wise
modified Madame's convictions. "They're a bad lot," she
said.

Rachel placed the book upon the table, nodded good-
bye to Madame Laroque, and went down-stairs. She was
thinking; for weeks she had been groping in the dusk of a
terrible uncertainty. Slowly she was awakening to the
knowledge that a change was taking place in her life—in
herself; some indescribable distraction, some mental restlessness hindering the progress of her work. She had
been unhappy and uneasy; the hand with which she held
her brush faltered; for the first time in her life the stroke
of the artist was not firm. It was maddening her; it was

as if she were passing through some period of mental fever. Her pulse was high; its every throb was quickened into unhealthy action. She began to look at things from an abnormal standpoint; she was no longer frank and unfettered. "What is it?" she asked, but she could not answer; she only laid her brushes aside, and, resting her head upon her palette, wept—the bitterest tears of her life.

Something had come between her and her art—a terrible shadow, looming dark and tall, casting its black length across all her brilliant future. For weeks she had felt its presence. She had but to turn her head and she would find the shadow at her elbow, waiting to take the brush from her wavering hand, waiting to obliterate the colors from the canvas, waiting to walk beside her for ever and ever.

She shivered and shrank back; she looked upon her unfinished picture—the great Magdalen; she stretched out her hands with a bewildered, appealing gesture. "O God, anything but that—anything but that, O my God! my God!"

She threw herself upon her knees beside it, her bowed head resting against the outlined hem of the painted woman's garment. It was the hour of supreme self-abnegation, the hour when she saw the toil of her life stretching back amidst a desert waste and stretching onward to nothingness. She had reared the temple of her aspirations upon her own heart, and she saw it shiver and crumble to its foundations, a dart hurled by her own faithless hand.

"Not that," she prayed, "not that. Only let me live for my work. I ask so little—so little; I only ask to work— work — work. Steel my heart, make me cruel, hideous, wicked—anything—but leave me my work."

She prayed as a stranger might have prayed who saw a great thing, unknown to him, lured to destruction. She saw with the eye of the mind; from the watch-tower of the intellect she looked down into the heart, and writhed and was sickened at the sight. It was as if a devil and an angel warred within her, one chaining her to the flesh and to earth, the other drawing her upward to the heaven of the mind.

Said the devil, "You are tired of toil; put it by. Laugh, love, live, as other women live; and then die and be for-gotten, as other women are forgotten. It comes to the same in the end. Life is sweet—love."

Said the angel, in its still, small voice, "There is a heaven to be reached—a heaven of the knowledge of work well done; the way to do it lies through barren ways, up steep mountain-sides, and along desert wastes; alone you must set out to it, alone you will reach it."

Still they warred and wrestled within her, and she crouched like a hunted thing upon the floor. For weeks she had not put in a stroke. Her mind was dazed and confused; the old inspiration had flown before the dark presence. She took up a brush, but her hand faltered and she let it fall. She sat before her easel, and her thoughts fluttered like swallows before they settle to rest. She had grown white and thin; the shadows under her eyes looked like the marks of inky fingers. The old, independent, audacious air had left her; she had grown self-centred and intense.

"What is it?" asked Charles Dupont, the critic. "Ra-chel, it is that your heart is not in it; get it back, my child, get it back, or your work is over. A woman is not like a man—a man may have many interests, a woman but one, or they are all worthless."

"It is not fair!" cried Rachel, passionately, "it is not fair! Why should men have everything in this world?"

"Ask the Creator, my child; He willed it, not I."

Rachel had gone furiously to work. She stood before the glass, shaking her clinched fist at her image. "Rachel Gavin," she said, "you are a fool—an utter, utter fool!"

Then she shut herself in her studio and set to work. For six hours she did not leave her easel; her lips were firmly set, her eyes were strained with determination. She worked without pausing, without looking up, but without inspira-tion. It was an effort, and she knew it. Some hidden undercurrent of feeling was retarding thought; the old absorbed concentration had become impossible to her; a distracting duality of interest was weakening every stroke of her brush. Let her will rebel as it would, it could not dominate emotion. Thought and feeling were at strife; one must triumph before peace was restored. In a man, thought would have risen mighty and victorious, surveying with calm neutrality the ruins of the heart's passion, or, it may be, balancing the opposing forces in the scales of judgment; in a woman—ah, when does love triumph that it has not throttled reason? Great love it is—strong to suffer, fearless to bear pain, mighty to sacrifice, but rearing its fair and holy temple upon the ashes of ambition.

The light grew fainter; a long ray of April sunshine came in at the open window, stretching across the faded carpet, across the Japanese screen in the corner, across the couch before the fire, and across the canvas upon which the girl worked. It illumined the strong, bold figure of the Magdalen, the unrestrained drawing of pose, the repentant droop of the head, the passion and misery and sin. The colors seemed to take fire and glow with a living flame. Over Rachel's bowed head the same sweet sunlight fell, resting about her white brow like an aureole. The graven intensity of her face had the look of Parian marble. She was making her last throw for ambition, her last struggle against nature and her own heart.

The little silver clock upon the mantel, with the little silver bird swinging to and fro, rang out the hour. It was growing late; the sunlight was fading westward. In the streets below men and women were going homeward from their work. At least, they could work; they were not denied that. It was better to roll cigarettes in a factory or stitch cotton shirts than to sink into a drone, losing hour by hour the toil of a lifetime—the ambition of an eternity. She rose and laid her brushes by.

"I will work," she said, and she clasped her hands above her head, drawing back to look upon her picture. The figure loomed boldly upon the canvas, the drawing was the drawing of a master. Rachel smiled softly with happiness —that, at least, would not fail her. She looked at the face upon which she had been working—the mouth, the eyes, the brow. The eyes looked back at her, rapt and pregnant with a great foreshadowing; the mouth seemed to quiver with the memory of a past.

Then the girl gave a little convulsive shudder and moaned aloud, for the face had the look of Michael Akershem.

"O God!" she sobbed, her frame shaken with tearless sobs. Her heart was rent, the ambition of a lifetime undone. To a woman the mental toil of an eternity may sink to nothingness before one heart-throb.

Then, as she clung sobbing to her easel, there was a knock at the door. It opened, and Michael Akershem came in.

He glanced at her with a quick surprise, started backward and then forward again.

"Miss Gavin," he said—"Rachel, what is it?"

The tears started to Rachel's eyes and stung her like melted fire. She flushed and shrank away.

"I don't know," she said. "I can't work; I am wretched —wretched." And then she wrung her hands with a desperate gesture.

He came and stood beside her, taking her cold hands very gently in his. He would have looked at the canvas, but she drew him away with a cry.

"Don't—don't—you must not—you shall not look at it!"

But he did look at it, and to him it seemed only a strong, beautiful figure, the work of a master hand. "It is great," he said.

"Oh, how can you?" cried Rachel. "I have ruined it— ruined it. I would have given my life for it, and I have ruined it!"

"Ruined it? Impossible," he said. "Why, it is magnificent. Are you mad?"

For the girl had thrown the curtain over it with a frantic haste. "I am wretched! wretched!" she cried.

Michael held her from him and looked into her face.

"Rachel," he said, "trust me."

The girl lifted her head and looked at him, the tear-drops trembling upon her lashes, her mouth quivering. For a moment the man was silent; he was struggling as she had struggled between love and reason. As with her, will and emotion were unevenly matched. The stronger prevailed. A sudden tumultuous joy took possession of him, putting all other consciousness to flight. "Rachel!" he said; "dearest!" He drew her towards him; he lifted her head, looking down into her eyes. The eyes were hot with his image, and he saw it.

"Dearest," he said again, "dearest!" and he kissed her upon brow and lips. His kisses scorched her like fire, his gaze burned her like a flame.

And Rachel gave up the struggle. A sudden intense, illusive happiness sent the blood beating to her pulses and a warmer light to her face. She forgot her work—her art—her ambition. She had sold them all for this, and she did not regret her bargain; she would have sold them again, and gladly, assisting with dry eyes at the sacrifice.

"You love me, Rachel?" He spoke imperatively.

"Love you!" With a passionate sob she threw back her head, stamping her foot upon the floor. "Don't you see that I love you?" she cried. "My God! I can't help it; I love you!"

"Oh, my beloved!" His kisses fell hotly upon her quivering lips. But as he caught her to him a latent spark of her old independence took fire and flamed forth. She broke from him.

"It is dreadful—dreadful!" she cried.

"But, Rachel, does it make you wretched? I am yours—yours for life or death. I will give up my work to-morrow and marry you."

The girl started.

"Marry me?" she repeated. "How could you?"

He smiled, and, catching her outstretched hands, kissed them.

"I worship you," he said. "I would throw away every chance of my life—every hope, every principle, for you!"

"They would scorn and laugh at you. You have lived your principles for years, and now, at the first bid of a woman, you cast them away. Oh no; I cannot! I cannot!"

"Let them laugh at me. If I have you, what do I care, darling? Darling, can't you understand? I shall resign from my party. I have made it, and I have the right to unmake it. I'll get a position as coal-heaver, brakeman—anything."

"And in six months you would regret it. Do you think that a man's love can extinguish ambition? Only a woman's love can do that. You would live to regret your work, your freedom; you would brand yourself a traitor in your own eyes, and I—my God! I should go mad, for I love you."

She kissed him as he leaned above her.

"Do you think that I could live and know that I had ruined your life?" she asked. "I had rather kill myself now, before you had time to reproach me. I had rather never lay my eyes on you again. Oh, my love! my love!"

Rachel was young, and ignorant, as most young things are. She had not learned that self-immolation is the surest bond by which one binds one's self to another. It is not those who sacrifice themselves to us whom we love, but those to whom we sacrifice ourselves. Perhaps there is a fundamental principle of egoism which sustains it, but the fact is there; we do not cease to value a possession which has cost us a great expenditure of ourselves. Self-immolation on the part of another we are apt to regard lightly, deeming that of small value which places not a greater price upon itself. Oh, we are only wise in our own conceit!

After Michael Akershem had gone, Rachel remained standing before the fireplace in the gathering dusk. She heard his footsteps passing along the hall, she heard him ring the elevator-bell, and then heard the sound of the ropes as it went downward. She knew that the very sound of his footsteps was music in her ears. Such intensity of emotion she had never felt before; it was as if the fount of feeling within her heart, after being frozen for years, had thawed of a sudden and found a channel. She no longer repelled the thought; she hugged it to her heart, and gloried in it as a mother in the joy of her child. It was new and strange, this swift, pulsating happiness, this illusive sense of life and of possession; it was something, she thought, worth living for, worth dying for, worth resigning heaven for, and worth walking barefooted through hell to gain. It was happiness and it was more than happiness—it was pain.

Behind her the veiled Magdalen loomed like a visible forewarning, before her the ruddy coals glowed like a passionate heart of fire. She smiled and sobbed, and bowed her head upon her hands.

That evening Michael delivered an address before the Twentieth Century Society, and was congratulated afterwards upon having made one of the hits of his life. The society was composed principally of workingmen—men who, spending their lives in physical labor, are willing to save themselves mental by taking their opinions second-hand. A brilliant tongue and a magnetic presence are more forcible than logic, and Michael possessed both. He swept over the universe like a thunder-cloud, lashing his audience into frenzy by the scorching fire of his rhetoric. He kicked society from one end of the platform to the other for the space of several hours. When he had finished society might have gathered itself like the Arabs and as shamefacedly slunk away. A man who is in earnest is a power in the nation. By a chemical affinity he attracts as satellites a host of feebler intellects whose earnestness is seeking to gain a parasitic existence. One man conceives, a thousand re-echo his conceptions. If he is in earnest for good, he may act as the leaven of a people; if for evil, his influence, like a subtle poison, may extend to the uttermost ends of the earth.

And Michael had many followers. His sincerity was contagious, his buoyant vitality overmastering. He had become the recognized leader of a certain enthusiastic element—youthful bodies, gravitating towards the centre of energy nearest their environment. He himself, having been forced beyond his given orbit by circumstances and sin, was now in turn leading where his lines had fallen, men in whose individual lives these circumstances had had no part. For sin is sweeping, and there is none so small but its effects may extend beyond the horizon of the sinner and into an existence of which he had had no ken. And, let us judge others as we may, it behooveth us to ascertain that the limits we set to our own actions are the limits of the world and not those of our own poor field of vision. For there are generations and generations in the dim dusk of futurity over whose pathway our shadows are gathering to a close.

If Michael Akershem had died that night he would have left the germ of bitterness and revolt to quicken and bring forth fruit in a thousand minds, turning their day into night, as his had been turned by a wrong which had died to the wronger in the hour of its birth, for no man hath strangled an action.

"And I am your comrade," said Rachel—"your good comrade, for ever and ever."

"For ever and ever," repeated Michael.

"I shall help you with your work. I shall be your best and only friend. You will never be lonely and wretched again. Call me your comrade."

"My blessed comrade!"

"My hero!"

"My star!"

"Oh, I shall be a great help to you, never fear."

And they caught life in their hands, and sought to mould it into a beautiful image. But it is less easy to mould life than it is to wound one's hands in the attempt.

BOOK III

DOMESTICATION

" Human life is naught but error."—*Schiller.*

CHAPTER I

THE editorial rooms of *The Iconoclast* had been put into unusual order; a char-woman, accompanied by a scouring-brush and a bucket of soapsuds, had gone over the floor, and the office boy had turned on every electric jet.

To-night the Iconoclast Society, composed in part of stockholders and well-wishers—that portion of humanity whose wishes have some financial balance—were sitting in judgment upon the record of the month.

Mr. Kyle had the chair. Mr. Kyle was a man of some twenty odd years, with lank, dark hair hanging in a curtain upon his shoulders, and an habitual air of being the Keeper of the World's Conscience, an office which he found so engrossing that, in his concern for the world's conscience, he was inclined to overlook the condition of his own.

On the whole, Mr. Kyle might have been accounted wise had he held his peace, but, unfortunately, peace was the last thing to be mentioned in connection with Mr. Kyle. Not only was he insecure in the possession of his own, a condition by no means rare, but he exerted his ability to the utmost to prevent his neighbors from retaining theirs.

"There is no state of peace," said Mr. Kyle, and, indeed, there was not if Mr. Kyle was by or in ear-shot. He was assistant editor of *The Iconoclast*. He had done more to promote the cause than any man living, Akershem not excepted. He hesitated at no step to serve the party, a fact which the party applauded unanimously and deplored singly.

Next to Kyle came Captain O'Meara, who was fat and fair and somewhat more than forty. Captain O'Meara was a jolly good fellow; his heart was of such excellent quality that one forgot to wonder what had become of his head. Then came Semple, who had been unanimously elected an honorary member.

Across from Kyle, with their faces to the editor's table, sat three gentlemen in three straight-back chairs. The first gentleman was very tall and very narrow—metaphorically speaking, he might have represented mind without matter; literally, bone without flesh. The second gentleman was very short and very narrow; his eyes had a strangely far-sighted look, as if he were considering the prospect of next year's crops upon Mars. The third gentleman was of a moderate height and an immoderate breadth; he had a habit of smacking his lips at intervals, as if he hankered after the flesh-pots of Egypt.

The three gentlemen occupied seats of honor, and looked like devotees before the altar of an unknown god. They were devotees, but at three distinct and different altars—the first being a worshipper of Mind, the second a worshipper of Man, and the third a worshipper of Mammon. The worshipper of Mind was shrivelled, the worshipper of Man was shrunken, and the worshipper of Mammon was swollen and red of face, as if he had feasted upon the sacrament of his idol. The three devotees were the three principal stockholders, graduating in shares from the worshipper of Mind up to the worshipper of Mammon, who could have bought out the rest of the company at a bid. He was the Great Mogul of the enterprise, and was respected accordingly.

Upon Kyle's right hand sat Michael Akershem, his brow black and frowning, and at a little distance Driscoll, his chair tilted backward and his hands in his pockets. He may not have been bored, but such was his expression.

The rest of the company consisted of the many men that make a party. The aristocratic element was represented by Mr. Douglas Van Houne, who had, by dint of unwearied application, drunk himself out of the Keeley cure and into dypsomania; the labor element by Pat McTibs, who was bricklayer to one Watkins Mark, and father of some dozen children now inhabiting the city poor-house. McTibs was an honest man, and had been content to earn an honest living as long as he had the consolation of the doctrines of original sin and predestination to sustain him. The yoke of dogma had kept him securely in the path of sobriety, if not of righteousness. He was content to toil by the sweat of his brow and wrestle with temptations as long as such conduct warranted him the privilege of a heavenly seat looking hellward. But what is the use of keeping to the narrow path if our neighbors are not damned for going astray? In a moment of missionary zeal Kyle had succeeded in opening McTibs's eyes to the futility of things hoped for, and the enormity of his making an honest living when he might make a dishonest one instead. He represented to him the beauty of Communism, that blessed state, when by forking out your own penny you may pocket your neighbor's shilling. McTibs realized that Communism was the one thing needful; the road to Communism lay in throttling Society. He attempted to throttle Society, which resulted in his being in *The Iconoclast* editorial rooms and his children in the city poor-house.

As for his wife—well, Kyle had converted her also. He had persuaded her that marriage was deceitful, and morality was vain ; and, being persuaded, she had hanged herself.

Who shall say that *The Iconoclast* had not a purpose to serve?

Kyle was speaking excitedly, which was by no means unusual, as he was always excited and generally speaking. Driscoll was listening languidly, contorted between a laugh and a yawn. Semple was drumming upon the table with his finger-tips ; he was slightly startled and somewhat dubious ; once he had interrupted Kyle to say: " Be temperate, my dear sir, be temperate !" He looked as a child might that is watching a toy serpent develop into a boa-constrictor.

" We are standing amidst a rotten rubbish-heap," Kyle

was declaring, enforcing his words by the unrestrained use of his forefinger. "We see around us the decaying remnants of Society, a monster that gorges itself upon the blood of Labor!" ("Hear! hear!" from McTibs.) "We see a foul and polluted system gradually crumbling to dust! It is for us to complete the work of destruction—to hurl, Prometheus-like, a dart at our gigantic foe! To wrestle with the dragon until it is overthrown! We have power to check its bloody course, we may save the millions that perish yearly beneath this social juggernaut!" ("Be temperate, my dear sir, be temperate!" from Semple.) "We see wretchedness and poverty and crime around us, and for this wretchedness, this poverty, this crime, Society is responsible! For all the evils stalking abroad to-day, evils glutted with human lives, preying upon the rights of manhood—for these Society must be held to a strict account! We see nakedness in a land of wealth! We see starvation in a land of plenty! We have shared the misery of the multitude —our hearts are withered, the springs of our life dry and athirst!" ("Hear! hear!" from Mr. Douglas Van Houne, who was aroused from a pleasant doze by the word thirst.)

The worshipper of Mind had risen, and was standing, tall and gaunt, before the table.

"Mr. Kyle is an enthusiast," he said; "he speaks in the language of poetry. He has portrayed our social condition in gorgeous word-painting, not in the cold, bare prose of Science. But—let him exaggerate as he will—our condition is sufficiently serious. From our present state of inequalities and ignorance there is but one broad, upward way for humanity, a road that leads from the depths of sin and superstition to the cool heights of knowledge and demonstrable facts—there is such a road, and that road is Science. Without Science we should never have left the Middle Ages. Without Science we should still be trembling before a god in every breeze, preaching persecution and damnation as essential principles. There is but one salvation for mankind, and that is—"

"Humanity!" shrieked the worshipper of Man, starting to his feet. "What has brought us forth from a howling wilderness of beasts into civilization and liberty? Humanity! What has restrained us from feeding man upon man, and caused us to stretch forth a hand of human fellowship? Humanity! What has promoted sympathy and philanthropy, dotting the world with charitable institutions, protecting the weak against the strong? What, I say, has done this?"

"Nothing!" shouted Kyle, suddenly losing his head and bringing his hand down upon the table with a powerful crash.

"Science," said the worshipper of Mind, in a hollow tone.

"Religion," breathed a still, small voice from the background.

"Wealth," responded the worshipper of Mammon.

"I ask: What has done this?" repeated the worshipper of Man, "and I answer: Humanity! I ask the name of the noblest power in the universe, and I answer: Humanity! I ask what has led us forth from kinship with the lion and the tiger, and made us lords of the earth and master of the elements, and again I answer: Humanity! Of all the attributes of Humanity the greatest is Morality. It is the fundamental principle underlying progress—"

"Morality," said the worshipper of Mammon, "is in the eye of the beholder."

The high-priest of Humanity went smoothly on: "Morality should be the foundation-stone of all government. We will eradicate all suggestions of our origin. We will rise, like gods, to survey the path of our ascent. Behind us in our progress we will leave all save the noblest attributes of mankind. From the world we will sweep all wrong-doing, all manner of sinfulness, and all things evil—"

"You will leave us nothing to live for," said Driscoll, reproachfully. "Impropriety is the spice of life."

"Mr. Driscoll," returned the debater, "such levity is indecent; it is worse than indecent, it is sacrilegious."

9

"But what a bore the world was before the Lord tried his hand on the devil!" ventured Driscoll.

"Sir," said the worshipper of Mind, "worse than indecency is ignorance. Can a man in your position, in this the end of the nineteenth century, speak of a person or a devil being *created?*"

"No more hyperbole!" exclaimed the worshipper of Mammon, smacking his lips, and seeming suddenly to return from the flesh-pots. "What I've got to say is just this: this paper has got to modify principles in proportion to its subscription-list; if the list grows smaller, the views have got to go. I've a pretty little sum in this business, and I ain't going to have it stuck on a little question of *opinion.*"

"Sir," said the worshipper of Man, "there is principle."

"Principle," responded the worshipper of Mammon, waving it to limbo, "is all very well, provided you choose the principle that pays." After which he concluded with a vigorous sweep.

"I guess I've got as much to say as anybody else, and what I say is this: if there is any row of that sort, I'll sell out at a sacrifice and put my capital into the *Sunday-School Missionary.* I've been considering an opportunity for the last month."

There was an awe-struck silence. Mind, personified in its representative, shrank to nothingness; Man withered past resistance; Mammon was supreme.

"That's all I've got to say," he added, moving towards the door, "but I guess it's enough." Then he went out and the meeting adjourned.

Semple laughed, and slapped Akershem upon the shoulder. "Your disciples have outstripped their master, eh, old man?"

"They're a confounded lot," answered Akershem, grimly. "It's no easy task to drive a team that pulls in opposite directions. No two of them want the same thing."

"And not one of them knows what the thing is that he

wants. Every man is chasing a shadow, and the worst of
it is that he doesn't know of what it is the shadow."

Kyle joined them.

"I've been telling Mr. Akershem," said Semple to him,
"that moderation is the leaven we need to balance our
measures. Nothing must be done in haste, Mr. Kyle."

"And nothing will be done by laggards," returned Kyle,
excitedly; then, leaving them, he made a descent upon a
seedy individual moving towards the door, and they passed
out, arm in arm.

"You'll have trouble with that fellow yet," said Semple;
"he's a fanatic, pure and simple."

"We'll keep him down," returned Michael, laughing,
but he went off with the warning ringing in his ears. Long
—long afterwards he remembered the words, and sighed
at the vanity which makes us value such warnings only
when the evil has overwhelmed us and the prophecy is
fulfilled.

As he passed Rachel's door that night, on his way up-
stairs, it opened and she came out.

"I heard your step," she said, making him a low courtesy,
"and—has Sir Pioneer brought his lady a stone in place of
a crown?"

"He has brought his lady a heart," answered Michael,
softly, and he caught her hands and held her from him, his
eyes glowing with the sight of her. The dim light fell
over her with an illusive brightness, shimmering upon her
head and in her eyes. With her she brought an impression
of warmth, as though her gown had caught its hues from the
flames of the fire she had left.

Love had strangely glorified her; she was supremely
beautiful, with the beauty which is a part of love—that
great transforming power which evolves an Esther from a
Jael, a Madonna from a Magdalen.

Michael looked at her in breathless ardor. Love quickened her pulses like wine; it sparkled in her eyes, it quivered upon her lips, it rippled in the dimples of cheek and

brow; it wrapped her about, and possessed her with an exuberant vitality.

So salient it was that it startled him, and, breaking the silence, he drew back. "I am not worthy to touch the hem of your garment," he said.

With a swift gesture the girl clasped her hands upon his breast, looking into his face.

"You are the breath of my life," she said. "My hero! My love! My idol!" For a moment he trembled before the abnegation in her eyes. He looked into them and saw his own image, dominant, supreme. He held her heart in the hollow of his hand, and he knew it. For a moment he hesitated, awed by the sublimity of her passion. Then he flung his arms about her, gathering her to his breast. "My beauty and my beloved!" he said. He kissed her hotly, passionately, with a sudden abandonment of self-restraint; and Rachel, who would have been stung by the delicate touch of another man, flushed into an exquisite ecstasy beneath the storm of his kisses. Insensible to all other love, she was as wax to the fire of his.

"I adore you!" he said—"I adore you!"

And perhaps he did. Who knows?

Mr. Daniel O'Connell Kyle had entered upon life handicapped by limited prospects and an illustrious name. In his own mind there existed an uncertainty as to which had most hampered him—the name, which he was not able to live up to, or the prospects, which he was not able to live beyond. Besides these major disabilities, which might have been ascribed to the inscrutableness of a dispensing Providence, there were minor difficulties which an experienced eye might have traced to the agency of a discerning Satan. The chastenings of the Lord and the aggravations of the devil were so opportune in their concurrence that, to an unholy mind, it suggested a secret understanding between the parties. It was as if Providence and Satan were in league for his undoing.

Kyle the elder, of whom history makes no mention because it discounts possibilities, was a man of great promise and small fulfilment. The only ability which he ever cultivated was an ability to get into trouble, combined with an equal ability to stay there. A friend, who stood bail for him upon a number of appearances in the police court, was heard to remark upon the last occasion that if there was a clear road ahead of him and a row around the corner, Kyle would land in the row, an assertion which that gentleman accepted as a tribute to his daring. He was born in Ireland, and would probably have died there had Fenianism been permitted to flourish upon its native soil. But with the suppression of that movement he followed in the footsteps of Mitchel and landed in America, a dashing young patriot, with melting eyes and a persuasive eloquence of tongue. Having considered right at home, he preferred to consider might abroad, and accordingly offered his services for the invasion of the South. After the war he settled in New York, and, having still the eyes and the tongue, he took unto himself a wife of German parentage—a step which resulted from the contact of his own palate with a dish of cutlets belonging to the lady of his choice. On the whole, the marriage was commonplace. Given two tempers and the time, the ordinary marriage produces anarchy, and Kyle's was by no means an exception. From bad it became worse, and backsliding followed upon bickering. His wife had a way that was painful to others if pleasant to herself, and Kyle was driven to solace himself at the only hospitable spot in the neighborhood, which chanced to be a beer saloon. He grew stout and husky and red of face, and, in time, lost all resemblance to the dashing young Fenian of '58. But the Old Country dwelt in his heart, and he never drank a toast that did not embrace "Ould Ireland" and his fellow-rioters. Then when his son came, his heart leaped in memory of the silver-tongued O'Connell, and he had given the child his name. The little Daniel wrought no change in the slovenly household. He remembered a home whose chief factor was unpleasantness, and the one bright spot was his father's improvident generosity. The young child was fed upon tales of the daring rescue of Kelly and the romantic adventures of John Mitchel, and he waxed fierce upon the strong meat of Fenianism. There were brain pictures of a lighted saloon and glimpses of rough-voiced men hushed into silence while his father stood upon a flour-barrel in their midst. The rich Irish brogue had thrilled the boy as it thrilled the exiles about him, and the sham passion had awakened a real passion in his own breast.

The elder Kyle knew his power, and he made it felt. The flour-barrel became a patch of the Emerald Isle, and he a patriot declaiming his allegiance. There was fire still in the melting glance, and grace in the ranting gestures.

" They are slaves who fear to speak
  For the fallen and the weak;
  They are slaves who would not choose
  Hatred, scoffing, and abuse
  Rather than in silence shrink
  From the truth they needs must think;
  They are slaves who dare not be
  In the right with two or three!"

And beneath the melting eyes the boy had chosen to be
in the right with one, and that one his father.

So much for Irish eloquence and Irish eyes.

As he grew to manhood his father died, leaving him still
in the right, but alone. The next five years were spent in
an unprovoked onslaught upon the world, the flesh, and the
devil. One disadvantage of being in the right is that one
has not the devil for an ally, an individual who, if an implacable foe, is the most influential of friends.

With a singular disinterestedness, Kyle undertook to re-
adjust the eternal order of things to his personal satisfaction. He was burning with the zeal of wholesome reforma-
tion, and prepared to grant no quarter to the iniquities
that were, and that, despite such energetic reorganizers,
forever should be, since iniquity is only less omnipotent
than Providence. After a season of public abuse his zeal
diminished for lack of wherewithal upon which to survive.
Upon a closer inspection he became less ready to sacrifice
himself for the general good. He decided to forego the
cup of martyrdom and to leave men to wrangle over their
petty quarrels among themselves. Poverty, that inexorable
throttler of ambition, checkmated his individual exertions.
With the demand of his stomach the appeal of his brain
was disregarded. For a time he existed, as it were, upon
the Irish question, but even the Irish question becomes exhausted; and when he endeavored to supply the demand
by drawing upon his imagination, it cost him his position.

Then his energies were expended in the effort to keep
his head above the quagmire of a submerged humanity.

He gravitated to a neighborhood upon the east side, literally the centre of the level of decency, and by slow stages ascended from the first to the twelfth landing. He had learned by this time that the public has prepared a sacrificial altar upon its own account, and that the inclinations of the victim are seldom consulted.

From his twelfth-story attic Kyle looked down upon the human comedy, and his heart withered at the sight. When one is compressed into a writhing mass with mankind one is apt to lose a good deal of altruism, drop by drop. Ethical philosophers are found among those who are well off in this world's necessaries, and, consequently, at leisure to arrange for the luxuries of the next. A doctrine of endurance flows easily from our lips when we are enduring jam and our neighbors dry bread, and it is still possible for us to become resigned to the afflictions of our brother.

As an antidote to circumstances Kyle took to opium. Borrowed illusions are better than none, and when one has not food one might as well have fancies.

From his father he had inherited the silver tongue and eyes like melting suns, and upon Saturday afternoon he exerted his eloquence upon the idlers swarming the public squares. He became quite a power in a small way, reducing a mob to silence or inciting it to frenzy by the force of his speech. It was a ranting oratory, but it did damage among the people, and for a time he occupied the post of public divinity.

Then came the great railway strike, and he got mixed with it in some unaccountable manner. His utterances, the result of too little food and too much opium, drew upon him the attention of law and order, personified in the police, and he was commanded to keep silent in public places. They might as well have ordered Niagara to become still water; speech was as necessary to Kyle as rain to a bursting cloud. He continued to speak at the top of his voice, and his speech was loud indeed. One evening in Union Square, as he stood declaiming to a growing audience, a sudden tremor shook the crowd, and some one beside him called out a sharp warning :

"The cops are arter you !"

His defiance grew bolder, and he was opening his mouth to retort when he felt his arm seized of a sudden and himself drawn upon the sidewalk.

"Are you a fool ?" demanded his captor. He looked up, seeing a strong, thick-set man, with an ugly, rough-featured face and a mop of coarse dark hair. Kyle shook him off ; then something in the man's personality overmastered him.

"No, I am not," he answered.

"It's a pity you don't prove it," retorted the other. He lifted his hat, running his hand impatiently through his hair. His eyes narrowed until they flickered between his blinking lids like shafts of yellow light.

"What is your name ?" he asked.

Kyle opened his mouth to say "It's none of your business," but the man smiled, and he changed his mind and said, simply : "Daniel Kyle."

"Ah ! the same who applied for work at the office of *The Iconoclast ?*"

"The same."

"You are out of employment ?"

"Yes."

The man looked at him for a moment with nervous intensity. Then he spoke brusquely. "That's all," he said. "Go home and keep quiet."

Kyle had turned away, but his name was called after him and he paused. The man was holding out his hand.

"My name is Akershem," he said ; and added, "You sha'n't be idle long. I have work for you. I'll look you up. Yes, I have your address." And, with an abrupt nod, he left him.

Kyle climbed up to his attic, and, upon the strength of the contingency, ate the bread and cheese which he had been saving for to-morrow's breakfast.

"I register a vow," he said, solemnly, "that if ever I

have as much as fifty cents to spend on a single meal I won't have a piece of cheese in smelling distance." After which he threw himself upon the bed, and decided upon the number of dishes he would order had he the ordering of a dinner. He had gotten as far as lobster salad when the thought of Akershem caused him to square up suddenly.

"If he keeps his word I'll be delivered from bondage. I'll be free! free!" And he hurrahed in his ecstasy, until a little seamstress living across the hall sent in to inform him that the baby was down with measles.

As for Akershem, he was convinced that in discovering Kyle he had discovered the link uniting *The Iconoclast* with the working world. A man who was at once a power with the people and a disciple of himself he had long looked for, and in Kyle's eloquence he believed that he had found a telling weapon. For himself, his natural reserve and the engrossing nature of his employment put all such personal ambition out of the question.

It was with a certain enthusiasm that he set out some days later to look up his promising subject, and, indeed, had his enthusiasm been less, the search might well have dissipated it. A fastidious aversion to ill-kept surroundings, together with an inherited feeling of kinship to the inhabitants of such surroundings, had served to raise the editor of *The Iconoclast* above the class into which he had been born, and his repugnance to these classes was increased by the very nearness of the relationship. For the men who have least sympathy with ignorance are the men who, by their individual efforts, have raised themselves above it, as the men who are the most unmerciful to evil-doers are those who have lived down evil in themselves.

The dirt, the squalor, the terrible lack of ventilation, oppressed him with the old sense of indecency. It was as though a man, inhaling the stale odor of decaying vegetables and hearkening to the distracting clamor of guttural voices, must become isolated, by mere lack of self-respect, from all respectability.

Reaching the tenement where Kyle lived, Michael ascended to the twelfth landing and knocked at the door upon the right. The door chanced to be the wrong one. It was opened by the little seamstress, who informed him that a gentleman of the name he mentioned lived across the hall. "But if he owes you anything, I guess you'd best call again," she added. "The poor young gentleman has been hard up of late."

Michael crossed the hall and knocked at the door designated. "Come in!" called a voice, and he entered.

At first he was conscious only of lack of space and a curious oppression. Then his eyes cleared of the smoke, and he saw that the room was bare and squalid, with broken window-panes and blackened walls. Upon a small pine table in the centre a newspaper was spread, and upon the newspaper a knife, a loaf of bread, and a bit of cheese. An empty beer-bottle stood upon the chair. A spasmodic seizure of emotion caused Michael to turn quickly in search of Kyle. The sudden leaping of his pulse was almost painful in its intensity, and he cleared his throat before speaking. Kyle had risen from the bed upon which he had been sitting, and was standing, in his shirt-sleeves, before him, a curious mixture of pride and humility upon his face.

"I lost no time in looking you up," said Michael. "I wanted you immediately." A vague wonder as to what he could put him to immediately caused him to repeat, with additional emphasis as he glanced about the room, "Immediately."

"Yes," responded Kyle, with an awkward embarrassment, "yes." His own power of speech had deserted him, and all the time he was telling himself that it was the opportunity of his life. "Yes," he repeated again. Michael laid his hand upon his arm with a gesture that would have astonished Driscoll in its cordiality.

"I like you, Mr. Kyle," he said, "and if you stay in this place it sha'n't be my fault; we'll settle about terms later, but now—" and his mouth relaxed beneath the warmth of his speech. "Come with me," he said; "I'll put you up for a day or two." Even as he spoke he was surprised at his own impetuosity, and because he was surprised he clung to it with his natural doggedness. "I'll find room for you with me," he repeated.

Kyle put up his hand with a bewildered gesture. "I—I don't understand," he stammered; "you may give me work, but—but I am a beggar. I haven't a cent. I—"

Michael broke in brusquely. "I have been there," he said, "and I know all about it. I have eaten a crust that a dog would pass by."

"You—you are very generous," said Kyle, gently. "It —it does not seem like you. I don't know what it means."

Michael laughed with a sudden boyish mirth. "Pshaw!" he exclaimed, "it means that I have been there, my dear fellow." Then he looked at his watch. "We'll dine in half an hour," he said, "and then to business."

Kyle put on his coat, took up his hat, and followed him into the hall. Upon the threshold of the room he paused to look back upon the poverty from which he believed himself passing forever. Standing there in his picturesque attitude, with his beautiful eyes lingering upon the squalid attic, he might have been an artistic spirit breathing an invocation, instead of a material body buoyant with release.

"Good-bye to dirt and cheese!" he exclaimed, hilariously. His wild Irish spirits had returned; it was like returning to life from the grave. With an unrestrained delight he slipped his arm within Michael Akershem's. "I am a man again," he said. And together they descended the narrow stairs and passed out into the street.

CHAPTER III

DRISCOLL met Akershem at the corner of Fifteenth Street and Broadway.

"Shem," he began, "is this thing true?" He looked worried, and his whimsical manner seemed half assumed.

Michael shambled beside him in silence. Then he spoke with a slow indifference.

"What?" he asked. "Has Van Houne drunk himself to death, or has Mr. Mushington sold out?" As Driscoll looked at him he blushed, the nervous blinking of his lids growing faster, and the flame of his glance mellowing like the flame of a shaded lamp. "What do you mean?" he demanded, more seriously.

The other spoke with an awkward hesitancy. "I mean this story about you and Miss Gavin. Is it true? Is she—"

"It is a lie!" broke in Michael, hotly. "Whatever it is, it is a lie. Only lies are worth repeating." Beneath the cool, keen gaze his affected carelessness gave way.

Driscoll spoke next.

"Is it true that she—she loves you?" he asked. Even as he questioned he smiled—a slow, cynical smile—at his own concern.

"Yes."

"Then it is true that she would make a fool of herself for you," he said, angrily. "Good God! a woman in love is as helpless as a babe unborn. If the man is a scoundrel he can make her swear that black is white—and believe it."

Michael winced.

"The more unselfish a woman is," continued Driscoll, ruthlessly, "the easier it is for a man to shoulder his sin upon her. A noble woman has made many a man a black-guard." He paused abruptly, and then, with a sudden change of tone, went on again, laying one muscular hand upon Michael's arm. "Shem, listen to me. Give up this infernal nonsense. Call it what you will, your fight against conventions is nothing more or less than a fight against morality. Men aren't so good that they should be allowed full liberty to do evil; it would be pretty sure to end in their doing it. Give it up. If not for your own sake, for—Rachel Gavin."

"Don't! don't!" pleaded Michael, feebly.

"Marry her if she will marry you, and thank God that you weren't a born fool. It isn't every man that has pearls cast in the mire at his feet."

"Driscoll, there is principle."

"Principle!" His laugh cut like steel. "The only use some people make of their principles is to sacrifice other people to them."

"Driscoll!"

"Oh, call it principle if you choose. It sounds better than selfishness and means about the same. As long as it pleases you to trample upon the woman who loves you in an insane desire to benefit those who spit upon you, go ahead. When the romantic side of being spit upon has palled upon you, you'll turn and go backwards; but"—and he set his teeth firmly—"a man never learns that he's a fool except by experience, and to learn by experience means to learn too late!"

"Stop, Driscoll! There are some things I'll not take even from you. I—"

"You will not take the truth," responded Driscoll. "And if you don't, you'll never get it from anybody else." Then he left him and boarded a passing car.

Michael turned and walked homeward. His head was bent, and as he passed rapidly along a confused tangle of thought seemed to whirl within his brain. Even amidst the hurrying crowd, rendered buoyant by the first smack of

frost, there were some who turned to follow his moving
figure, arrested by the salient individuality of the man.   In
the very ugliness of his roughly hewn profile there was a
terrible suggestion of power.

Remote and far off, across the graded rows of blackened
chimney-pots, across the fevered, restless city, a gray haze
was rising, like dew, upon the gorgeous rose-garden of the
west.   Awhile since its colors had dazzled the vision with
their roseate splendor, paining the senses with the tran-
scendence of human conception.   Now the rose was fading into gray, the flame into ashes ; but one fleeting vestige
remained of its opulent bloom.

Michael raised his head and looked westward.   He was
eager and elated.   The slight shadow cast upon his self-
complacency by the meeting with Driscoll had departed ;
his good-humor reasserted itself, and he smiled slightly as
he hurried through the streets.

All else had faded before him, submerged in the thought
—Rachel loved him ! He had been ill-used and desperate,
but Rachel loved him ! His life had been a battle; he had
lived and hated as other men had lived and loved ; he had
toiled while children played ; he had warred while men had
slept; he had known despair and degradation, but—Rachel
loved him !

Like a star the thought of Rachel seemed moving on before him, shining above his way, shedding its white light
down upon the mire where he trod.   For the first time in
his life he revelled in the ecstasy of loving, which is as far
beyond the ecstasy of being loved as the star is beyond the
moth.

All the weight of years fell from him, all memory of that
stretch of time when his bread had been bitterness and his
heart the temple of wrath.   He forgot the things that had
been, his revolt from the things that were, and his repining
over the things that might have been.   He knew only that
a wonderful change had swept over him, something terrible
and new, which sent the warm blood to his pulses and a

sudden scarlet exaltation to his brain. He was lost in amazement at the state which men call happiness, and for which he had never been in need of a name.

He stopped and gave money to a beggar upon the sidewalk—a wretched creature in a threadbare shawl, who ground "Home, Sweet Home," out of a broken music-box. He spoke to her kindly, and when she whined "God bless you!" he turned and gave to her again. Even the blessing of God—granting there was a God—seemed not unbefitting his mental altitude. For his birthright, for his bitterness, and for his bloody tears he might extend and receive the forgiveness of God. Yes, he would be willing to come to terms with God at last.

He passed on, the discordant tune following him along the block. He bought *The Herald* at the corner. He wanted to take the little newsboy by the hand and tell him that life was beautiful; but he felt that the little newsboy would not understand, so he took his paper and went upon his way. And when the boy ran after him, crying, "Here's *The Iconoclast*, sir," he bought it to recall what he had thought and said yesterday about the eternal unfitness of the universe. Then he went into the florist's, buying violets for Rachel, feeling a thrill as he took the box in his hand, knowing that all her sweet life through he, and he alone, might lavish them upon her.

Rachel met him upon the landing.

As he mounted the stairs he saw her face smiling down upon him, and he thought of the evening-star in the afterglow without.

She wore a closely fitting gown of filmy black that clung about her like a cloud, showing to perfection the ivory white of her throat, the dark of her heavy brows. Her eyes narrowed as she saw him, with a wistful contraction of the pupils implying gravity.

"Why, Rachel," he said, "have you been crying?" There was an inflection of reproach in his voice which she met smilingly, keeping with an effort the nervous corners of her mouth at rest. He took her hand, and together they passed into her studio.

"And now," he said, "we will have the truth and the whole truth." His natural peremptoriness of manner asserted itself, as it always did when his acquired civility was checkmated. There was much truth in Rachel's assertion that at heart he was a despot.

• "It is nothing," protested Rachel.

"The whole truth," repeated Michael.

He spoke authoritatively, but he stooped and kissed her lips as she smiled up at him. With a return of vivacity the girl laughed and yielded.

"It is only a visitor," she said.

"A visitor," repeated Michael, the word suggesting the best parlor in the farmer's cottage, and possibilities of severe-minded ladies in sunbonnets.

"I don't suppose you know Miss Serina Parks?" She tilted her head sideways with a fascinating *abandon*.

Michael disclaimed that honor. "Don't do that," he said, "or you'll make me kiss you."

Higher went her eyebrows and farther aside the little head. "How can I tell you if you behave so badly?" she asked. Perhaps I sha'n't tell you, after all."

"I do not know Miss Parks."

She laughed delightfully. "Lucky fellow!" she exclaimed. "Never say, Mike, that your cup of misery is complete. As long as Providence might have made Miss Serina known to you and did not, it has reserved one misfortune for the future."

"But who is she?"

"A lady who handles the Ten Commandments with care, and collects the fragments that her neighbors have shattered. She is a missionary—that is, she confines her attentions exclusively to the unregenerate. She visits eternally. I'm sure if she ever reaches heaven she will be continually making return trips to hell." Then she seized his arms, turning her eyes full upon him. "She only visits

10

the unregenerate," she said, slowly, "and—she visited—me !"

With a sob she finished, hiding her face against his shoulder. Michael clasped her with a passionate tenderness, the lamps suddenly alight in his eyes.

"What do you mean, Rachel? My darling, *what* do you mean ?"

"I didn't understand until she came," said the girl, still slowly and distinctly. "I didn't know that they said cruel things about me. I thought they just let me alone. But she carries tuberoses to all sorts of wicked women. She never carries them to good women—never—never ; but she brought them to me. She only prays with bad women, but she wanted to pray with me." She threw her head back with a disdainful gesture. "It is weakness," she said, "I oughtn't to care, but I can't help caring—a little."

"Tuberoses !" exclaimed Michael, savagely, as though the enormity of the offence consisted in the choice of blossoms. "She dared to bring *you* tuberoses !" Like a yellow flame the rage in his eyes leaped forth. "It is a dastardly insult !" he cried. Then he looked at Rachel as she stood before him, and a wonderful softening passed over his face. He took her hand and kissed it. "My lady," he said. There was a reverence in his voice that she had never heard before—a new tone which thrilled her strangely. "Are you afraid ?" he asked.

And she answered, "I am afraid of nothing with—" She hesitated.

"With me," he finished. His eyes warmed, and he followed with his touch the line of her as it defined her white forehead.

"I did not say it," she protested.

"But you thought it !"

"Sir Audacity !"

Her glance dazzled him. He threw out his hand in sudden bewilderment.

"How you love me !" he said.

It was that winter that Akershem said he began to live. Until then he had struggled for existence in a desultory, hand-to-mouth fashion. The meeting with Rachel was the genesis of his soul. She weaned him from his melancholia so skilfully that he was unconscious that it had been done. She infused a share of her own light-heartedness into him. She herself was so vitally alert, so buoyant with the essence of youth and life, that optimism was infectious. And with her optimism was a quality, not a conception. It pervaded her whole organism ; through it she looked upon the external world, by its light she read the fulfilment of her own aspirations.

"There is such a change in you, Mike," Rachel had said one day; "you really look like a gentleman."

"I wish only to look like a man," retorted Michael, insistently; but he wore his hair shorter, nevertheless. He was happy, or believed himself to be, which is perhaps as near as any of us come to the presence of a mirage. Happiness is a term which we use as we use heaven—the evidence of a state neither seen nor felt.

But so long as we have faith in our fairy tales we are none the worse. It is the awakening that shows us the fevered eye and quivering pulse, the wages of our ecstatic delirium. In fairy tales the dragon is always slain and the good triumphant, and love, if we wait long enough, will transform the beast. In real life—but which is the real and which is the fairy tale?

They were happy in their life together that winter. Rachel had put her palette and her brushes by. She did not shed tears now. There was a terrible satisfaction in being able to bring her ambition and her art bound and prostrate before her love.

She could see Michael standing in her studio, his shadow falling upon her unfinished picture, and she could smile as a woman smiles who has found the man who has mastered her. A sad smile, think you? Look upon life and see.

"And what do I care for a painting, a mere canvas with

daubs of color, when I have you—you, the pulse of my heart!" She was unwise. Probably. What has love to do with wisdom?

She was ignorant. Certainly. What has passion to do with knowledge?

All during the winter and spring they had learned to know each other. Perhaps some of the first frantic ecstasy suffered. We do not waste time in wishing for that which we have. Not that we value it less; but when one may wish, let it be for something one does not hold in the hollow of one's hand. And idealism, that gaudy coloring matter of passion, fades when it is brought beneath the trenchant white light of knowledge. Ideals, like mountains, are best at a distance.

But the winter passed quickly enough. Many a merry evening they had, dining first at one place, then at another; always finding something to laugh over, some recollection of their early lives to be recalled. A jolly little Bohemian she was, and much of the Bohemian world had she known.

Sometimes they went to the opera. There was Calvé that year, and Maurel, and the De Reszkes, and a host of others. And, best of all, Melba the adorable, with a voice like the rippling of ecstasy over sorrow and a smile like the glancing of the dawn.

He liked to watch her as she listened to music, her little head held back, her eyes growing deep and solemn like the heart of a storm, her quivering beautiful lips apart.

He told her of his hard-worked years, showed her the streets through which he had walked in his feverish youth, and told her of the nights when he had roamed up and down, across the bridge and back again, weak from hunger, mad with pain.

He showed her the square where he had fainted, and told her of the woman who had held his head upon her arm.

"Wherever she is," said Rachel, "may God bless her!"

And perhaps God did.

To Michael now those days seemed far—far off. He

could speak lightly of starvation and despair, as we speak lightly of a past pain, remembering, not the pain itself, but the association of ideas which it suggests. All the reckless ambition of his boyhood, all the weighty heritage of shame and ignorance, no longer, represented life to him. He was able to look back impersonally upon them, and to separate in distinct consciousness the boy of eight years back and the man of to-day. He looked upon his youth, not as a romancer "reverencing its dreams," but as a moralist condoning its passion.

His philosophy had undergone modifications. He read to Rachel, but he did not read his old masters. Instinctively he felt that she had naught in common with them. Schopenhauer and Von Hartmann were put back upon the shelf; the dust gathered and thickened upon Rousseau and Proudhon; Voltaire went the way of all philosophers. And Rachel was supreme. He had discovered by this time that she was not an angel, but he had found to his satisfaction that she was something far more interesting—a witch.

She bewitched him in the audacity of her brilliant mirth, when her eyes were like laughing stars and the dimples beside them played at hide-and-seek, and her mouth quivered with the merriment that would not be shut in. She bewitched him in her gravity, when her beauty, which was all radiance and expression, had died away, leaving a strained and pallid abstraction. Perhaps at such times he loved her best, for her fascination was distinctive and apart from beauty of form or color. Upon her plainest days it was sometimes most vivid, and consisted more in the mobility of her personality than in any definite quality.

In the spring came Michael's breaking down and Rachel's nursing—lavish, enthusiastic.

He remembered lying for hours upon the sofa in her studio, watching her small flitting figure, as uncertain as a gleam of sunshine. The making of the beef-tea was gone through so absorbingly that he loved to watch the play of her long, white fingers, the earnestness with which she peered into the jar as it sizzled and boiled in the kettle of water. He watched her as she knelt before the fire, the long fork held out before the ruddy coals, the light falling over her bowed head, her eyes looking up at him from the rug, laughing, wistful.

And then she would spread the napkin upon the waiter, strain the beef-tea, and bring it to him, sitting beside him until he drained the last drop. In Michael's last severe illness, when he was shrieking in the madness of fever, his voice grew suddenly low and appealing, and he cried : " Is this your broth, Rachel ? I want only Rachel's broth !" And when one of the hospital nurses said, " This is Rachel's broth," he took it from her and drank it down like a child. And turning upon his cot he stared out into vacancy with his delirious eyes, seeing her standing beside him, her hand outstretched, smiling—smiling—

But by-gones are by-gones. Time jogs on and we with it. Whither? Whither?

JOHN DRISCOLL stood upon the steps of his club. In one hand he held a cigar, in the other a match, with the blue flame slowly flickering out. He had forgotten that his original intention was to apply the match to the cigar.

A military-looking gentleman, running down the steps behind him, paused to slap him on the shoulder.

"Hello!" he exclaimed. "Is it a matter of public interest?"

"I was merely wondering," returned Driscoll, "if I was a particular fool, or if it is an attribute of man in general?"

"For purely personal reasons, I incline to believe the former," remarked the military gentleman as he passed on.

Driscoll drew a long breath, and shrugged his shoulders with his habitual loose-jointed movement. Then he uttered a half-suppressed exclamation as he put the match between his lips and threw the cigar into the gutter; after which he uttered a more forcible exclamation and threw the match in its wake.

"Damn it!" he said. And a little later, "Still more damn!"

Then he drew out his cigar-case and fell to smoking savagely.

"It's no business of mine," he continued, "but I'm such an infernal meddler. Why can't I let other people's affairs alone? I'll be holding myself accountable for the devil next, and apologizing for him to the Almighty."

He descended the steps, passing languidly along the sidewalk.

"Why did I introduce them?" he said, half aloud. "I might have known something would come of it—something always does come of it. Half the trouble in life comes

of introducing two fools. Look at that missionary I introduced to the girl I loved. Look at that typewriter I introduced to my father; she married the property and the old
man before my back was turned—"

"Stop a bit!" called some one from behind. He turned,
and Kyle joined him.

"You look used up," remarked Kyle, pleasantly.

"Decidedly so," responded Driscoll.

"Sorry, but I want that paper you promised me. Begun
on it yet?"

"No."

"Oh, well, I suppose you'll take your time; you usually
do, but I wish you'd go ahead. Going in for luncheon?
So am I."

They entered the restaurant together and made for a distant table.

Kyle beckoned to a waiter, and gave the order with the
sharp, peremptory manner which so ill accorded with his
principles. Then he shook back the hair from his eyes and
began upon the crackers beside his plate.

"I have it!" exclaimed Driscoll, in an audible aside,
awakening from an abstracted silence.

Kyle looked slightly amused. "What's the row?" he
inquired, persuasively.

"Oh, I was merely alluding to an ancestor of mine," returned the other, in a whimsical drawl. "I like to trace
cause and effect, you know. I like ascertaining the exact
source of a misfortune. I have an intemperate conscience,
my dear Kyle, and for the past six hours I have sought its
fountain-head. Now I have it. I only wish I had him,"
he added, savagely.

"A weak conscience is only second to a weak digestion,"
remarked Kyle, sympathetically.

"Second!" Driscoll bent his heavy brows upon him.
"I assure you, an indiscretion sits heavier upon my conscience than a—a plum-pudding upon my digestion. If
that's not a malady, I don't know one!"

Kyle laughed with the quick twitching of the nostrils which accompanied it. "A case of your grandfather having the fun and you the gout, I suppose," he suggested.

Driscoll crumbled his bread between his fingers in a moment's abstraction; then he smiled. "I had a grandfather who was a Puritan," he said, "which means that he was a sinner with a conscience. The only recorded fact concerning him states that he stole a feather-bed; it also states that upon his death he made restitution of the feather-bed to its rightful owners. Don't start, my dear Kyle; it is not his method of acquiring the feather-bed that I object to— I waive that in respect for the end in view. Personally I consider feather-beds highly desirable possessions, and had his conscience been in a healthy condition he would have bequeathed it to his lineal descendants. But the feather-bed is a mere instance. It is the conscience I object to, and the conscience I have inherited."

"Conscience," said Kyle, dogmatically, "represents a fetich to which good people sacrifice their own happiness, bad people their neighbors'."

"Quite right; but unfortunately so few of us are able to grasp that convincing truth. If there is a law in this universe more durable than the Persistence of Force, it is the law of the Persistence of Error. Witness the number of us that are unable to throw off the effects of early training. Why, if there is one document that is firmly embedded in my mind it is the Shorter Catechism. It is a moral alphabet, and its maxims come to my finger-tips as easily as A B C. I acquired it with twelve painful years; and philosophers may come and philosophers may go, but the Shorter Catechism abides forever. Somehow I can't get over the conviction that when I follow the Catechism I am right, when I go contrary to it I am wrong."

He smiled upon Kyle, and Kyle cast upon him, from beneath his lowered lids, a quick, scrutinizing glance, as if in doubt of the sincerity of his words. One was forced to take Driscoll's earnestness, if he was ever in earnest, upon trust. "It is a lack of independence, I know," continued Driscoll. "Nine-tenths of the virtuous people are good from sheer inability to be bad. A fool may follow in the straight and narrow path, but it takes a clever man to leave new tracks in the broad one."

Kyle tapped his coffee-cup with the forefinger of his right hand.

"Ah!" he said, softly, with a sudden relish of his luncheon. Then he rose, and they passed out into the street.

At the corner they separated, Kyle going to his work, Driscoll to his idleness.

He had gone but a short way when his gait lost suddenly its languid listlessness, and a quick interest awoke in his face. Along the block before him moved swiftly a straight, slim figure. For a moment Driscoll started in pursuit. Then his pace slackened and he fell back, his eyes following the figure with a pained wistfulness until it disappeared around a distant corner.

Then he shook himself and laughed.

"A woman," he remarked, irrelevantly, "is a fool until she falls in love, and then she's a damn fool." With which philosophic utterance he went upon his way.

After the opera that night Driscoll went with Mrs. Van Dam and several of Mrs. Van Dam's acquaintances to the Waldorf for supper. Mrs. Van Dam might be described as the logical product of an exact equilibrium. Her earthly possessions were so nicely adjusted upon the scales of fate that the weight of a feather upon either side would have disturbed the balance and she would have been found wanting. Her virtue, as an instance, was less the result of a positive tendency in that direction than a negative capacity for the opposite course. Being beautiful, she might have been a Lais; being plain, she became a Lucretia. She possessed worldly wisdom to a degree that enabled her to appreciate the fact that to shine in infamy requires certain extraneous qualities which may be dispensed with in a less ambitious career. To be successfully vicious necessitates charm of manner; but a severe exterior is not unbefitting a virtuous soul. Having grasped this essential verity, Mrs. Van Dam relapsed into an inflexible respectability; and, attaining that state, meted out impartial judgment upon the offenders whose less nicely adjusted balances have decided them upon an adverse direction.

Such is the power of accident in our choice of attitudes.

Physically she was a small woman, with a figure suggesting that the Lord, in his search for material, had overlooked the possibilities of the backbone in favor of the rib. Her features were considered saintly by those who had only seen saints upon canvas and associated the term with immobility. Mr. Van Dam sat across from her. He was fat and well fed, possessing, indeed, all the attributes of a happy mortal. The fact that he was not so was due to circumstances, not to composition.

A gentleman upon Mrs. Van Dam's right was looking down upon his Newburg with sentimental fondness. "If I eat lobster, and if I don't eat lobster, I shall regret it," he remarked, plaintively.

"A sin of commission or omission," suggested Mr. Van Dam, with a sudden interest in the decision.

"If it lies between doing a thing and refraining from doing it, I always do it," announced a gentleman with a large mouth and an enormous nose. "To act means to live."

"Except when it means to die," amended the sentimental gentleman, resignedly, as he took up his fork.

Suddenly the gentleman with the enormous nose was heard from. "There's Akershem with a lady," he said. "I didn't know he affected the advancing sex."

"Ah, he has retrograded, you see," commented a young lady beside him. Then she looked at Mrs. Van Dam. "Why, it is your young cousin," she said; "where has she been hiding such an age?"

Mrs. Van Dam looked at her with eyes that saw not. So stony was her stare that it seemed to penetrate the walls and to traverse Fifth Avenue. Her voice was ominously distinct. "I have no young cousin," she said. Rachel Gavin, sitting within reach of her, heard the words, and a sudden wave of color mounted to her white forehead. Instinctively she shrank away, drawing nearer to Michael Akershem. In her eyes there was the look of a fawn that a huntsman has driven to bay.

From beneath his lowered lids Driscoll looked at her, seeing the hunted glance, seeing the wave of scarlet sweep across her brow, seeing also that the look Michael bent upon her was a look of adoration but not of comprehension. His sensibilities, blunted as they had been, failed to recognize the dart that wounded her sensitive nature. This Driscoll understood, and, like one who suddenly awakes to his surroundings, he spoke, fixing his keen glance upon his hostess. "Why, there is Miss Gavin," he said. "If you will pardon me, I'll ask her about her picture." He crossed over and took Rachel's hand, meeting her proud glance of gratitude with an amused indifference. Akershem's manner of conscious possession irritated him, and his nonchalance was heavier than usual, as he stood beside them waiting for the tremor to leave Rachel's lips.

"So you have been to the opera," he said, lightly. "That's good; there is only one thing better than the sound of music, and that is no sound at all."

"Oh, dear," sighed Rachel. "It was beautiful—so beautiful!" The light leaped to her eyes—that rich, luminous light that shed its kindly beams in an indiscriminate cordiality. Michael watched her silently, his face warming with delight in her, until his irregular features grew soft and harmonious.

"Well, yes," conceded Driscoll, coolly, "Mrs. Van Dam really said some witty things."

Rachel frowned spitefully. "She might have said them as well at home," she said.

"By no means: the singers invoke a spirit of emulation. I assure you, whenever I go to the opera I take my note-book along prepared to jot down clever speeches. There must be something inspiring in the music of *Faust*, for the garden scene never fails to sharpen the wits of my friends." Then he grew serious. "We missed you at the oil exhibit," he said. "No work of yours was hung."

The girl looked at him wistfully, her eyes narrowing, the smile leaving her lips. "Oh, I was never much of a painter, you know," she said, and her voice was almost appealing. "It was a case of mistaken vocation."

His eyes were merciless in their keenness. "So you have joined our grand army of the unsuccessful," he added.

The bitterness of tone caused her to cast a startled look upon him. "You—you regret it?" she faltered. "You regret my work?"

"I regret a wasted talent," he answered, harshly.

She did not reply, and he left them and went back to Mrs. Van Dam, who received him disapprovingly, and to Mr. Van Dam, who asked, in a drowsy tone, "who his charming friend was?" And Rachel finished her supper, and went home with the flush still lingering upon her face.

"Are you sure you are happy?" she asked—"quite, quite happy, dearest?"

And he answered by a glance.

Then she lifted her resolute eyes to his, and said in her heart: "It is worth it—worth it ten thousand times!" But she did not forget Driscoll and the bitterness of his lament over her buried talent. Despite her indomitable pride she acknowledged a vague gratitude; and when, some evenings later, Michael brought him up to dinner, she received him with an affectionate cordiality. "I told him we were to dine in your studio," Michael explained, "and I wanted him to get a glimpse of you at home."

"It was just right," assented Rachel, and she smiled brightly upon him. At the moment she was stirring mayonnaise in a tiny china bowl, and she gave him the hand that held the spoon. The black sleeve was rolled back from her elbow, and there was an appealing innocence

about the curves of her slim white arm. To Driscoll she
seemed a naughty child that had strayed beyond the camp
of the Philistines. He wondered if it wasn't all play, her
art and her ambition and her love and the whole sunny
stretch of her short life. Was the tie that bound her to
Michael Akershem more durable than the passing fancy of
a young human thing for companionship? Was it not the
mistake of a soul in the old, old search for happiness? She
was but a child as yet, and children must have playthings;
but when the child puts aside childish things, would she
put aside her love along with them?

But she was healthy and warm with her red young blood,
and the call of a warm young thing for happiness is not to
be hushed by the chill of the philosopher's stone. It is
only when we have called and called until our throats are
dry and happiness has not come that we take up philosophy. We leave the sermons of life to the dust upon the
shelves until the sweet mad poetry has drained our passions dry; then we turn back for the sermons, which are as
dry as ourselves. But youth, tragic youth, has first to be
cheated.

Driscoll glanced about him with a careful scrutiny. He
took in the details of the room, the charming feminine
touches that lent it its originality. It was a room which reflected Rachel at every turn. The table had been spread
by the girl herself, and when she had finished the mayonnaise, turned down her sleeves, and seated herself behind
the bowl of flame-colored nasturtiums, Driscoll acknowledged to himself that it was good. Good! Far, far too
good—too good for Michael Akershem and for himself.

Across the flame-colored nasturtiums her deep eyes shone
upon him, her scarlet lips broke into sensitive curves as she
talked, her whole radiant personality fell over him as the
falling of a spell. Was she in earnest, or was it all play?

"Who is going to smoke?" asked Michael, when the dinner things had been removed, and they still lingered about
the table.

Rachel paused, with the sugar-tongs held in her hands, a lump of sugar in the sugar-tongs.

"*You* aren't," she responded. "You've had your share of cigars to-day." Then she turned her eyes upon Driscoll. "You may, Mr. Driscoll," she said.

"Am I one of the blessed?" he asked. "But what about Shem?"

"Shem knows he can't have any," she answered, sweetly.

"Just one," pleaded Michael.

"Not one," and she passed him his coffee.

He demurred, but yielded. "You are severe," he protested.

"That has nothing whatever to do with it," returned she. And she smiled so delightfully that Michael swore he didn't want a single one, and Driscoll threw his into the grate. Then they drew their chairs about the fire and talked until the hours went on, and Driscoll left, taking Michael along with him.

In the street he turned and looked at Akershem with a sudden inscrutable earnestness.

"Upon my soul, Shem," he said, "I never envied a living man until to-night." And then he added, under his breath, "No, I don't envy you, because you will never understand."

THE next year left an indelible impression upon Michael Akershem. It showed the immense factor which happiness or unhappiness may be in the making of man. It was as if the check arresting his development had been suddenly withdrawn, and his nature as suddenly veered into a discovered channel. Not that Michael was satisfied—far from it; but his dissatisfaction had taken a new and startling direction. The bitter lines about his mouth faded into a general expression of uncertainty; his speech was less cynical, more honest. He was fast acquiring the air of a man who sees in the world the oyster ready for his opening.

Perhaps, of all men, John Driscoll was the first to notice the change. The desperate, revolutionary spirit from which he had feared so much he now watched with growing complacency, seeing in it a flame which, sooner or later, must burn itself out. One may play with opinions as long as there is no danger of one's cutting one's self.

Michael was beginning to realize that life might turn out to be a pretty good thing—too good to be squandered in altruism, so called. And as long as life seems good to us we are content to leave in the hands of Providence the slaying of public dragons. It is not of happy men that martyrs are made, and Akershem was beginning to play the reformer after Driscoll's heart, the wise one who leaves his schemes as well as his stones to be tested by others. But despite the awakened regard for personal attainment, there was a feature of Michael's evolution from revolutionist to reformer which Driscoll puzzled over. It was the heightened variability of his moods, as if, by cheating himself into a conviction, he were trying to escape the resultant twinges of conscience.

Egoism had been the cardinal element of Michael's nature—this Driscoll knew—an egoism which was all but unconscious of itself, and which was concentrated into an abnormal desire for self-satisfaction. That self-satisfaction to be complete must contain self-esteem, Driscoll also knew, and the varying gloom and shade of Akershem's demeanor made him wonder if the reformer held the mere agitator as worthy of respect as he had held the revolutionist.

And that Michael now wrote beyond his convictions was evident. But little force had gone from *The Iconoclast*. The leaders were as brilliantly invective as of old, but in the man himself fanaticism seemed exhausting itself in wavering outbursts. It was the stock in trade doled out from the editor's chair, and once out of office he seemed to have left the mantle of his Iconoclasm behind him. Upon Kyle, his idolater and disciple, perhaps his mantle was destined to fall. But Kyle hardly seemed to favor the possible transference. He had a slavish, almost superstitious reverence for Akershem, the man whose mental force had dominated his own weaker intellect until it seemed that he had received the other's passion untempered by the other's judgment.

Of the two men, Kyle was, unquestionably, the more unselfish, the more fanatical, the readier to offer soul and brain to the party juggernaut. Akershem was the saner.

And now Michael was slackening all but imperceptibly in his zeal. His mind was divided, and a mind divided against itself is without foundations. His abstraction was the result of an unsuccessful attempt to cheat himself into overlooking his own insufficiency, and with a mind whose reason and desire were concomitant this was no difficult matter. "I will be what I will be" might have been paraphrased for him into "I am what I will to be." It was not that he refused to confront his soul, but that in confronting it he cast over it the glamour of personality, looking

11

down upon himself through himself. Life had taught him that reason may be bound and fettered by desire, and yet hold itself supreme in right of a beggary of names.

"There's a change in you," said Semple to Michael one day, "and I like it; you're better company." Michael laughed. His laugh had always seemed singularly lacking in a humorous quality, and there was no change in that.

"I have taken your advice," he answered, "and I feel that we must move slowly. Desperate attempts end in desperate failures."

"Quite right! quite right! There is nothing like moderation."

"Nothing—when one upsets the world for a pastime."

There was a twinkle in Semple's short-sighted eyes. "You needn't sneer," he said; "when a man gets to middle age he wants a warrant against boredom. Every man tries to find one—science, philosophy, dissipation, what you will. Now, to a man who wants action and has no especial taste for impropriety, reform is the thing."

"Glad you're suited. It seems to me a useless sort of thing, though a frenzy may be vastly diverting, one can't work one's self into it over nothing. A man wants to see the fruits of his endeavor."

"That's a weakness of youth, my dear Akershem. When a man has passed into his fifties he'd much rather not see the fruits of his endeavor. He wants to be always looking ahead to them. No man wants to reach the top of the hill; when he does he may as well sit down and wait to die. Pessimism is the affectation of youth, the reality of age."

"And your immense influence has for its support—"

"Diversion! A sure one, I warrant you. This is between ourselves, of course. I don't placard my motives, but—" Then he changed his tone. "You'll dine with us on Thursday, won't you? Quite informally. My wife wishes to know you, and if you don't wish to know her now you will after Thursday. You'll come? All right." And they parted.

Michael went home, changed his clothes, and went in to see Rachel.

"Semple got hold of me," he said, "and made me promise to dine there."

"Oh, well," said Rachel, "but I don't like Semple."

"Why?"

"I don't know. I think it's because he's—he's insincere."

"Insincere! How?"

"Oh, how can I tell? But I know he is; I feel it. He rubs his hands so, and he's—he's fishy."

Which was somewhat unjust; but justice was hardly one of Rachel's strong points.

Concerning Semple, Michael found that his own tolerance had strengthened. He even began to entertain a reverence for so well balanced a judgment, and his contempt for what he had called "Semple's artifice" was rapidly waning in admiration for his sagacity. On the whole, he was glad he had accepted Semple's invitation, and when Thursday came it was with no small interest that he went to keep his engagement.

A cheery blaze of light greeted him in the hall—a ruddy light of open fires and shaded lamps. At his entrance there was a scampering of children's feet and a voice heard, saying:

"No, no, Johnny, positively you can't look at him; he isn't a show. Go to bed."

Then in a moment Mrs. Semple descended with outstretched hand and cordial voice, several children clinging to her skirts, and a general air of motherliness about her. Michael felt a delightful ease at the first sound of her voice; she seemed the embodiment of home and comfort. "I couldn't get the children to bed," she said, cheerily, "until they had had a peep at you—just one peep, and then they go to nurse." There was something beautiful in the way her large white hands passed over the tiny heads and the patience with which she submitted to the ruthless clutching at her light skirts. "Say good-night," she said, "and run away." And after Michael had shaken hands with a boy or so, and kissed several of whose sex he was uncertain, they were borne off by a nurse in a voluminous apron.

Mrs. Semple was a large woman with a somewhat shape-less figure and a pleasant face. Her face was so pleasant that one forgot to notice that her features were irregular and her chin too full. One might have called her a noble-looking woman without stopping to explain what the term signified. The geniality of her expression, the tactful charm of her manner, caused her size and the awkwardness of her movements to dwindle into veriest insignificance.

She talked to him of his work, of the success of his jour-nalism, of a lecture she had heard him deliver, and of her husband's enthusiastic interest in his future, until, by-and-by, Semple himself came in and Michael saw the agitator at home. The deference and honor with which he treated his wife were at once evident. There was no turn in the conversation that he did not appeal to her judgment; when she spoke he listened gravely, if he differed he entered into a full argument. Never by the slightest sign did he ignore the value of her opinion or bring the question of her sex before them. She spoke as coolly and independently as if she were a man and he her associate in business affairs. It was a strange and surprising experience to Michael, who knew the vacillating restlessness of Semple's nature, and who had seen wives of a year or two ignored or treated as dolls in dolls' houses. Here was a woman, neither young nor beautiful, who had been married twenty years, who was the mother of a large family, and who held the undeviating esteem of a man as changeable as Hedley Semple. How was it?

"You should hear my wife on the platform," said Semple, suddenly. "You're a new woman, aren't you, Carolina?"

"A pretty old one," she answered, cheerily. "My oldest boy will be seventeen in March."

"She's abreast with me," he explained, "in my work, and

sometimes she gets ahead. She works for the emancipation of women, and it is as much as your sanity is worth to
get into a controversy with her on the subject. She can
show you more logic in an hour than you ever imagined the
woman's suffragists possessed. I—"

But the other guests arrived, and Michael found that the
dinner was hardly so informal as he had been led to expect. There were several ladies ; all wore rustling silks,
and one of them was very beautiful. She was introduced
as Miss Rankin, and he heard Mrs. Semple call her "Ger-
trude." She was tall and of superb physique, with a brilliant color, and coal-black hair worn smoothly braided upon
the crown of her head. He learned that she had just left
Vassar, that she was a Theosophist, and was upon her way
to Madame Somebody of somewhere, who was to instruct
her in the art of spiritualism. She carried herself languidly and spoke as from an elevation, seeming to have an eye
for things spiritual and looking like a magnificent specimen
of things temporal.

Then there was Miss Patskey, who was of uncertain
years, tall and thin, with a gray front that had not always
been in her possession. She was a woman of extraordinary
attainments, having an aptitude for scientific pursuits, and
was just completing a work upon "The Habits of Centipedes," which she alluded to frequently, remarking that our
ignorance of the habits of those domestic insects was depressing. At every allusion Miss Rankin was seen to put
her spoon aside, shift her spiritual vision, and shudder.

Next came Miss Allard, who taught mathematics in a
public school. She was fresh and plain looking when over-
shadowed by Miss Rankin's superb proportions, but Michael
liked the strength of her honest face crowned by the halo
of rich red hair. Her skin was of the transparent order
that is rarely seen unaccompanied by red hair, but her eyes,
instead of being blue, were hazel. Once he met her full,
level glance, and found her eyes limpid with an emotion-
less tranquillity.

Miss Rankin was taken in to dinner by an English Member of Parliament, who displayed a lively interest in the habits of the centipedes as well as the habits of Americans, but who dressed with a meritorious disregard of the latter. He was making a tour of the United States in the interest of a theory he hoped to formulate concerning republican governments—whether for or against, Michael did not discover. The M.P. had been in America exactly three weeks, during which space he had received enough impressions to supply the demands of the most prominent periodicals, to which he was contributing lengthy articles upon "America and Americans," "Characteristics of American Women," and "American Types." About the last paper he seemed somewhat confused, and Michael heard him apply to Semple for data.

"My dear sir," interrupted Kyle, who was of the party, leaning across the table, and speaking in a high-pitched, dictatorial voice, "there's no such thing as an American type or a typical American. It's all nonsense. But, of course, if you ram it down our throats we will believe you. It's a weakness of Americans to read the folderol foreigners are always writing about them."

The M.P. put up his eye-glass and eyed the speaker curiously. But for his inherent good-breeding he should have liked to have taken this specimen down in a series of notes.

"Give us time," began a mild-voiced young man from the other end of the table. His name was Self, and he was a Methodist clergyman, having strayed into satanic meshes through his admiration for Miss Allard. "We are making a nation," he declared—"a great nation."

Mr. Self was a gentleman of a great many ideals and a very few ideas. His ideals were his own, stamped with the pattern of their creator; his ideas were borrowed—notably from Thomas à Kempis and Mr. Jeremy Taylor. His ideals he used as whips, whereby he lashed his congregation into the narrow path; his ideas he reserved as a conscience - balm, when he was inclined on his own part to traverse the broad one.

"We are making a great nation," he repeated, with amiable emphasis.

Miss Patskey fixed her eyes upon him, whereupon he was suppressed.

"Take a composite photograph of the nations of the earth," asserted she, "and you have a typical American."

But the Englishman was speaking to Michael. "I hear that you are from Virginia, Mr. Akershem," he said, "and I feel a peculiar interest in Virginia. I intend spending some weeks there upon my return from the West, in order to have an opportunity of studying the negro character. Can you suggest the part of the country most suitable to my intention?"

Michael felt that he was verging upon unsafe ground, but he entered into a discussion respecting the relative advantages of the various sections. He was somewhat relieved when Mrs. Semple called the Englishman's attention to the general conversation.

"We are discussing," she said, in her pleasant voice, "the greatest need of the American people. Mr. Kyle thinks independence spiced with action; Miss Patskey the emancipation of women; and Mr. Self is divided between prohibition and religion."

"Spiritualism," announced Miss Rankin, bringing her glorious eyes to bear upon the M.P., and speaking as if she were issuing oracles from Mount Olympus—"spiritualism is the need of our people. We are singularly lacking in ethereal qualities. The presence of a Madame Blavatsky among us would work miracles. We need to look upward to higher things; we are exhausting ourselves in the debasing pursuit of wealth."

"I agree with you, Miss Rankin," cried Mr. Self, in mild excitement. Miss Rankin bowed her priestess-like head in acknowledgment of his intelligence.

"We need patriotism," said Michael; "our patriotism

was exhausted in the Revolution. Our constitution to-day is no better than a stagnant organism, supporting a parasitic growth of politicians."

"But this—this praiseworthy, shall I call it?—desire to know what is thought of your institutions by travellers, is this not patriotism?" The Englishman leaned forward, intent upon sifting the matter to an explanation.

"Oh, I think our patriotism is all right," said Semple, reassuringly. "Let a foreign power assail our dignity, and see what will come of it. But as long as we can't have war, why not let us have wealth?"

"Oh, it is the love of wealth that is wrecking our national character," argued Mr. Self. "I agree with Miss Rankin: we have too much sordid realism. We need idealism. We need to turn to the frugal existence of our Puritan ancestors, putting aside all the vicious results of these decadent days. We need to do away with the liquor traffic and woman's suffrage."

Miss Rankin started, a slow flush mantling her beautiful face. "I did not mean that," she retorted, haughtily.

"In woman's suffrage," said Miss Patskey, repeating a lesson by rote, "behold the salvation of our people."

"And in the liquor traffic the consolation of man," added Semple. "So you're overruled, Mr. Self."

"But, after all," concluded Mrs. Semple, "it remains for me to solve the riddle, and to suggest that our greatest need is the need of manners."

The M.P. was struck with the discrimination shown in the remark. "Now, I'd really thought of that myself, you know." He emphasized and proceeded to make a mental memorandum of the coincidence.

Michael, looking up, met Miss Allard's eyes across the table, and again he noticed how clear they were. Then he looked at Miss Rankin and back again, and thought how plain and commonplace Miss Allard was.

When the gentlemen came into the drawing-room the Englishman pleaded an engagement and left, impressed with the fact that well-served dinners are a pleasant feature of American customs. Miss Rankin gathered her diaphanous drapery around her, bowed her stately head, and was driven away, chaperoned by Miss Patskey, who had tied her head up in a gray woollen muffler.

Then several small figures in white nightgowns came bounding into the drawing-room.

"I heard Anna," piped a chorus of trebles. "And I smelled cake, an' I want both."

And Anna, who was Miss Allard, marshalled them off to bed.

"The children adore Anna," said Mrs. Semple, "and so do I. She is so wholesome."

Michael, walking home through the night, found himself haunted by Mrs. Semple's serene graciousness. A charming woman she was, he told himself, and he seemed to see her large, bounteous figure, enhanced by the cheerful setting-off of her fireside—a rare womanly presence, in whom the restless heart of her husband had trusted for twenty years. What was it that to a man so impatient of restraint as Hedley Semple had made his marriage bonds not irksome, but a veritable assistance? Michael questioned, and, so questioning, gave it up.

ONE evening during the following week, Michael, passing Semple's after dusk, saw Miss Allard descend the steps and pass along the sidewalk before him.

With a mechanical inertness his eyes followed the swift onward tendency of her movements, lingering upon every flexible line of her figure as it flitted through the pellucid light effect. The electric light seemed invested with a curious fluidity. It was as if it shimmered in visible waves upon the sustaining atmosphere.

There was a buoyant energy about the girl's figure, a lightness as if she had walked upon springy turf with a pristine disregard of the weight of gravity.

Michael contracted his gaze to more intent observation. He understood what Mrs. Semple had meant when she said "Anna is so wholesome." There was not a possibility of the morbid depression of the times in any line of the girl's form. She was all health and action, a reincarnation of a woodland Diana, passing at nightfall through the New York streets. It was not that she was beautiful, for she was not; it was only that she was healthy, untainted by the degeneration of the day, as untainted as if she had lived upon sylvan meads and fed upon the milk and butter of a mountain dairy. An appropriate milkmaid she might have made for all the clear-cut purity of her profile, carrying her bucket with the firm, swinging movement of her unfettered arms, carolling in the rarefied atmosphere of the pastures. Suddenly she turned the corner, and Michael overtook her with several long strides. "You are late," he said. "May I not see you safely home?"

Miss Allard turned upon him with her fresh, wholesome

smile. He could but notice the serenity of her quiet face, brightened by the glory of her hair.

"I hardly think my safety depends upon it," she observed, with her cheery laugh that seemed sylvan in its heartiness; "but as you choose." She had drawn herself to her full height with an unconscious dignity of carriage. He thought, with a touch of offended vanity, that she seemed not wholly pleased with the meeting—but perhaps it was his fancy, after all.

"I am late," she admitted, after considering the suggestion. "Nannie will worry."

"Nannie?"

"My niece," she explained. "I have had her since she was a tiny child. We lived in the country until her parents died."

"Oh!" The chastened rusticity of her personality was explained. Perhaps she *had* been fed upon milk and eggs, and that trick of walking—evidently the meadows had been springy.

"You lived out-of-doors," he said, unconsciously speaking his impression aloud.

"Out-of-doors?" Her eyes questioned his sanity.

"I—I beg your pardon, but I was seeking to explain your difference from the women of to-day. Mrs. Semple says that you are wholesome—the result of country air, I suppose.

"Perhaps." There was a rising breeze in her laugh, suggesting buttercups and pastures green. "All wild things are wholesome, are they not? I grew wild."

He bent his ruthless gaze upon her. "You are like a tonic," he said, simply. Then he added, "And what a pity it is! you will not escape the contagion — you will catch one of the 'isms' floating around and go mad, like the rest of us."

"Are you mad?"

"It is deadly. The degeneration has attacked us. It is the *fin de siècle* disease."

"It is transient. From the fever we shall but gain stamina for fresh exertions."

"Ah, it hasn't attacked you yet."

"I am not sufficiently civilized. The disease is not strong enough to contend with rusticity." With all the soft outlines of her lips there was no lack of decision, for all at once the lines of determination were written upon her face. She looked up at him thoughtfully. "I did not know," she said, "until a moment ago that you were the Mr. Akershem—of *The Iconoclast*."

"Yes." Michael's vanity responded to the appeal, but he started slightly at her next remark.

"I am so sorry," she said.

"Sorry! Why?"

The words seemed to have slipped from her almost unconsciously; for as he repeated them the color in her cheeks deepened. But, having committed herself, she did not flinch.

"Sorry that you have thrown yourself away."

Rudeness was hardly compatible with the simple earnestness of her voice, rising perceptibly in its flute-like notes; if not rudeness, then ignorance. But he turned to look at her, and the supposition fled. He fixed his magnetic regard upon her. For the first time in his life he was brought face to face with the inflexible convictions of an incorruptible character. An almost primitive adherence to principle was the dominant element of Miss Allard's nature.

"Thrown myself away?" repeated Michael. "Why, I have accomplished more than any man of my age that I know."

He said it honestly, with a desire to right himself in her eyes.

"You see one side," proceeded Miss Allard, in her even tones. "Perhaps I cannot see that side, but I see the other and—is it worth it?" Then she broke off. "I beg your pardon," she said, with the same cordial smile. "I should not have spoken. Won't you come in? Good-evening!"

But as he turned to go he looked back at her as she stood in the doorway. "Some day," he said, "will you explain?"

And she answered: "Some day—perhaps."

A child had come to the door—a slight, crippled girl, who leaned upon a crutch. Anna Allard stooped and lifted her in her arms, and he saw her head resting upon the child's upturned face. Then the door closed upon them, and he went out into the night.

Miss Allard's personality was an enigma to him. There was a depth that he could not fathom, for all its limpid serenity — some indefinable attribute which he failed to grasp. It was not the fact of her evident disapprobation— thousands showed that: he had been harried by the news-papers and assailed from all the pulpits in the land. Nor was it that she was reasonable in her disapproval; liberal-ity, though uncommon, was not impossible, and he had en-countered it occasionally.

But his impressions were fleeting; he concluded that Miss Allard was a good young woman with a fine carriage and a healthy interest in life, and so forgot her and her grave arraignment.

Fate deals largely in small circumstances. Like life, if she ignored the infinitesimal she would go a-begging for the infinite. Her puppets are impelled onward in a given line; following the rhythm of motion, they circle through time, and but for the attraction of existing forces might cir-cle indefinitely. But the curl of an eyelash, the turn of an ankle, a moment's vanity, and lo! the circle is broken and a collision has come. Then the combination of gases goes to pieces, and from the chaos another combination rises, phœnix-like, and passes into space. And the littleness and the greatness are in no wise diminished.

Michael dropped in at Semple's one afternoon, and as he was leaving Mrs. Semple handed him a note.

"Will you leave this at Anna's?" she said. "The servants that aren't sick are busy, and I can't get a messenger. I hate to trouble you." Michael took the note and left. He had no intention of asking for Miss Allard, but the crippled child came to the door, and, without taking the note, called "This way" as she limped along the passage.

Reaching the first landing, she threw open a door, revealing Miss Allard in the meritorious employment of darning stockings.

She looked up quickly with an unruffled welcome, but with a swift flush rising to her clear cheek. As she laid the work-basket aside he noticed how neatly the small packages were folded, and what an air of orderliness pervaded the room. He gave her the note, and she thanked him, but in a precise, business-like manner, as if there was no possible reason for his lingering. As none suggested itself, he turned to go, lifting, at the same time, an open volume which had slipped to the floor. It was Weismann's "Heredity," and a sudden interest awoke in his face.

"You read Weismann?" he asked. "Do you agree with him?"

"He is interesting," responded Miss Allard, with a noncommittal expression. The answer provoked Michael, it was so distinctly an evasion of his question; and to remark that Weismann was interesting seemed to him as superfluous as remarking that pain was unpleasant. There was a displeased flash in his eyes, but her indifference disarmed him. How can one be angry with a woman if the woman doesn't care? And apparently she did not care. The flash died from his eyes, but they still rested upon her; there was a trimness about her figure that showed itself in the narrow white bands at her throat and wrists, in the set of her black gown, in the shimmering braids of her red hair. She was a woman that a sick man might roll his delirious eyes upon and feel refreshed, or a Don Juan turn to from his voluptuousness as he would turn to pure water from Eastern wines. Michael was glad that he had seen her, as we are glad that we have tasted the fresh air of the country-side.

His hand was upon the door, and he was passing out when suddenly the memory of their last conversation occurred to him, and he veered round. His movement was so sudden that Anna, who had risen, started back, and he surprised the relief in her eyes.

"Will you tell me," he asked, "what you meant by 'the other side'?"

"'The other side'?" repeated she, inquiringly.

"The side of my work that you had seen," he explained.

For a moment she was silent, her steadfast gaze upon his face. Her head rested against a Persian scarf, and the dull tones accentuated the lights in her glorious hair.

"Shall I tell you?" she asked. The direction of her glance shifted, and wandered through the window to the budding branches of a tree without. "Perhaps I should not have spoken. Meddling does no good, and I'm not a missionary, but—but your paper has a wide circulation. It enters thousands of homes; people read it for your language and your style who otherwise would shrink from an expression of your opinions. Its influence is sweeping, and its influence is *your* influence." The flute-like quality of her voice was at its highest. Its penetration was almost painful, its decision merciless. "I work among the poor—the very poor. I see the harm done by useless agitators—by men who write and speak things they dare not act upon, but which ignorant men and women accept as a gospel. No, I do not mean Mr. Semple; he does not half the harm that you do."

Her accusing voice, pitilessly clear, rang upon him like a clarion; before her level glance his nervous lids quivered and fell. Then he raised his head in protest, shaking back the heavy waves of his hair.

"Harm!" he emphasized; "your words are badly chosen."

"It is not your motive that I call harmful," she said, more gently—so gently that he almost forgave her. "It is not your cause—I do not judge that—I but see the effects."

"And they?"

"There was a family upon Hester Street, an old woman, several grandchildren, and a boy—a bright, enthusiastic fellow, the main support of the family. He had been the support for five years, and was not more than twenty—the apple of the old woman's eye—"

"Well?" for she had paused.

"The first time I heard your name—I remember it well, for the old woman was sick and I had gone to see her—*The Iconoclast* lay upon the table, a newspaper print of yourself was pinned upon the wall, the boy stood in the centre of the room. The old woman was speaking; she said, 'Them Akershemites will be the ruin of you.' And the boy rushed from the room in a rage. I asked her what she meant, and as she pointed to the print of yourself she said, 'My boy is possessed with his notions, and they will be the ruin of him.' The boy banded together a small party, calling themselves Akershemites; they were inspired by a hatred of their employers, of every form of restraint. They made depredations upon the small storekeepers in the neighborhood, which ended in a row in which one of them was shot. We tried to get the boy a situation, but he would not sacrifice his liberty. The old woman and the children went to the almshouse, and a month later the boy cut his throat." She had spoken coldly and distinctly, but when Michael looked at her he saw that her eyes were suffused with tears.

"But," he said, with an angry intonation, "you are unjust. The boy did not follow my teaching. Clearly you are ignorant of my doctrines, else why should you make me responsible for a lawless riot?"

"I hold you indirectly responsible," she replied. "Can a cause be good of which the effects are so disastrous? Shall I go on?"

"Yes."

"There are many from which to choose. I have seen much misery. Some"—with a laugh—"I grant you, had never heard your name, others had. There was a man with a wife and five small children. As long as duty bound him to his post he supported them; then he became your disciple, and you—well, he deserted them for a younger woman, that was all. You may say it was the natural evil of the man's nature. So it was. But until your latitudinarianism released him from his conventional scruples, that nature was kept down by training and inherited belief. Yours is an ideal theory, Mr. Akershem, intended for an ideal humanity, with an innate desire to do right and a superhuman recognition of good and evil. The world as it is to-day cannot stand your views. You have done harm. But I have said enough."

"Yes," retorted Michael, bitterly, "you have said enough." His face was pallid, and his breath came quickly. "You have sought to fling all the misery of the world upon my shoulders. This is the result of my honest endeavor to help mankind—this—" His emotion touched her almost against herself.

"Is it worth it?" she asked, gently. "You, who can do so much good, is it worth it?" She reached out and touched his arm with a soothing, unconscious gesture, such as she would have used to a child in pain, but he shook her hand away.

"Since you have made me a devil you are pleased to pity me! Am I to answer for every boy that has killed himself, or every man that has deserted his wife?"

"I am sorry that you are hurt," said Anna, "but I cannot unsay what I have said."

"Why should you unsay?" he retorted. "It is little to me what people say of my—" Then he broke off abruptly. "I beg your pardon," he said. "Good-afternoon."

And he went down-stairs, while she returned to her darning.

Michael had gone out raging. He was furious with Miss Allard, with the world, with himself. The imperturbability of the girl's manner irritated him unbearably. She seemed so secure in her position—so assured that right and com-

12

mon-sense were on her side. If he might have accused
her of impetuosity, of intolerance, of exaggeration, he would
have felt less wroth with her. But she was so wholesome-
ly practical, so free from any morbidity of judgment.

"How dare she?" he cried, passionately—"how dare
she hold me accountable for the imbecility of those beg-
gars?"

Had Driscoll, had Semple, had Rachel herself accused
him of wielding a heinous influence he might have passed
it over with superficial concern. But a stranger, and that
stranger a woman who, like Miss Allard, was serenely convinced of the justice of her charge, and asserted as one who
knew whereof she spoke—it was maddening!

And, then, was it *true?*

He held his breath for a moment, shuddering at the possibility. A curious revulsion of feeling swept over him,
and in an instant—an instant such as we have all endured
—he realized the utter littleness of it all, the pettiness of
his revolt, and the impotence, for good or evil, of his mental cyclone.

Walking rapidly, he passed his office and turned into the
Bowery. He read the signs, "Corned - beef & Onions, 10
cents," as he had read them for the last seven years, with a
shrinking disgust—a loathing for poverty and filth. With
all his socialistic tendencies, he shrank from the unwashed
half of society with a delicacy that was pitiable. As nearly united as he stood to the lower walks of life, the only
feeling that personal contact with the representatives of
those walks aroused in him was a feeling of profound disgust. The aristocratic side of his nature was strong enough
to overpower the radical in a question of direct intercourse
with that portion of humanity to whom he believed his existence to be dedicated. He might declare the equality of
man in a glowing paraphrase while sitting next a patrician
in a clean shirt-front, but before a soggy inhabitant of Bax-
ter Street his enthusiasm for human fellowship was lost in
the practical dissent of eyes and nostrils.

His sympathies were radical, his tastes aristocratic, and as yet he had managed to equalize the two.

When he had walked some distance he stopped before the door of a third-class bar-room. After a moment's hesitation he entered, nodding to the proprietor across the counter. It was a squalid room, reeking with the fumes of bad whiskey, dense with the smoke of bad cigars. Several straggling foreigners lounged upon the tables.

"Give me a drink," said Michael. And as the proprietor filled his glass he spoke to him with attempted familiarity. "You do a good business?" he inquired, pushing a second glass towards him.

The man, a heavy German with a bloated face and an all-over greasiness, nodded gruffly. "It might be vorse," he admitted.

Upon the counter lay a pile of papers. Michael motioned to them. "Do they sell well?" he asked.

The man nodded, leering with his bloodshot eyes.

"Which is ahead?"

"*Ze Vorld.*"

"And *The Iconoclast?*"

Michael picked it up, pointing with his forefinger to the leader. He remembered that he had thought it particularly impressive.

"Now, say, my friend, what do you think of this?" he asked.

The man drained his glass and wiped his mouth upon the back of his hand.

"Zat," he observed, smacking his heavy lips, "ees—vat does you say?—r-rot."

Michael's laugh rang out so suddenly that a group of men at the back of the store lounged over, glasses in hand.

"Zat," repeated the proprietor, "ees r-rot; but it pays."

"Exactly. And the man who writes that rot. You know him?"

"I haf knowed him. He haf drunk much of my viskey." He leered again.

"What do you think of him?" He would have liked to have chucked the lying old codger into the beer-vat.

"Ze man—ze man he knows as much of life as he knows of—sauerkraut."

"Exactly," observed the man who had written it; "just about as much about life, my old philosopher, as he does about sauerkraut."

"*The Iconoclast!*" called a young fellow in a blue smock, tossing a nickel across the counter. He took the paper and departed.

"Zat boy," observed the philosopher, "ees mad — daft mad wid ze rot."

Michael left the shop, walking rapidly in the direction of his office.

"Kyle," he said, suddenly bursting into the editor's office, "write the leader for to-morrow, will you?"

Kyle looked up concernedly. "Not used up?" he asked. "We can't do without you. The work would fall through."

"Damn the work!" said Michael Akershem. And he passed into the next room, slamming the door after him. Going to the desk, he took from it a couple of printed sheets, and, folding them once, he tore them deliberately in half, letting the pieces fall into the waste-basket. "It *is* rot," he said.

As he went out again Kyle rose and followed him. "Take care of yourself," he said; "the people need you."

"Damn the people!" responded Michael Akershem.

Miss Allard stood before her mirror. It was morning. Through the open window came the cheerful far-off sound of church-bells, ringing across all the wealth of May and sunshine.

She had just fastened her hat by means of a silver hatpin, and beneath the flapping brim of black all the warmth of her hair shimmered with aureolic lustre. The figure reflected by the mirror was a thing to gladden the eyes and refresh the heart, rich-hued, supple, and straight-limbed—a a woman strong to endure.

She put up her hand, arranging with a few careful touches the muslin band at the neck of her black gown. In garb she might have been the sister of some holy order; in person, a pure-eyed young rustic, fresh from her vernal showers.

She turned away, lifting the prayer-book from the bureau. In the next room the child called to her, and she stood looking down at it with a suppressed anxiety.

"Shall I stay with my pet?" she asked.

But the child shook her head. Marie was coming to play. Marie was clever.

Then Anna stooped to kiss her and passed out. Down the stairs she went, singing softly to herself. In the hall below a young married woman stood with her husband. As Anna passed the woman turned and smiled upon him with a quick, resistless tenderness. The girl caught the look and imprisoned it in her own heart.

Then she opened the door and stepped into the spring sunshine, and into the presence of Michael Akershem.

Like a vision she broke upon him in the doorway, a supple, straight-limbed figure with a crown of ruddy hair and a fresh, grave smile—a vision of honest, wholesome woman-hood. The smile faded, he could but notice, as she held out her hand.

"I wish to talk to you," he said, "about—about my work, but I am too late."

"I go to my mission chapel," she said. And added, "Perhaps you would like to come."

"Are you also engaged in cramming religion down inde-fensible throats," he asked—"in offering a creed in place of bread?"

But he walked beside her through all the supernal radi-ance of the springtime.

"It is more digestible, at least, than the bread that you offer," she said. "Stolen food sits heavily. You from your office chair offer them, through the medium of a news-paper, the belongings of other people; we go among them, working to impart a love of cleanliness and order, to fight the effect of your influence. Our maxim is that the object of religion is to add to the general happiness—a utilitarian dogma, you see, but it has served us well. And you—what do you know of the poor?"

"Nothing; I know as much of New York tenement life as I know of the tenement life upon Mars." He looked into her fresh, plain-featured face, and met her amused glance.

"O Apostle of Modernism!" she said, "whose conviction is in proportion to his ignorance. If this hysterical century could taste of the tree of knowledge, how many 'isms' would go to air! Do you know, you remind me of the small boy who said in his composition, 'Human beings don't eat to-matoes,' and when asked for his authority, replied: 'I don't'!"

But Michael did not laugh. He never laughed except when he was amused, and Anna did not amuse him. He felt that she must be taken seriously, and that in her mirth she belied herself.

As Michael entered the little chapel he seemed awkwardly at a disadvantage. Since his childhood he had not been inside of a church, and there surged upon his memory, overborne by later experiences, the phantom recollections of his youth—gloomy phantoms, thronging ghoul-like above the graves of his childhood years.

He sat through the short service rapt and abstracted, hearing not the voice of the preacher, seeing not the whitewashed walls nor the work-worn faces of the congregation.

Beside him sat Anna Allard, her pure face uplifted, the glory of her hair "making a sunshine in the shady place," but he knew her not.

Manhood, the errors of ignorance, the sins of knowledge, had passed from him with the heated world without. The whitewashed walls were the walls of the little chapel upon the hillside; the slow voice of the preacher, the voice of his childhood's friend; the gaudy stained-glass window above the altar, the window he had stared at upon a Sunday until he had known the colors in Charity's robe and the features upon the beggar's face, tint for tint.

He was back again, and he was young and eager, with his passions surging fresh and strong, and the power for loving good and hating evil swelling unsubdued within his breast. Upon his right hand sat the farmer, his heavy head nodding from side to side, and beyond him the farmer's wife, her black straw bonnet tied by purple strings, the pin in her carpet-shawl standing in dagger-like erectness; and in the long pew at their side the ten children, in ten blue-checked pinafores, with ten flaxen braids, from Betty, who lent the gospel hymns the ardor of a war-cry, to little Luly, whose drowsy head nodded like a flower upon its stalk.

And the voice, falling sad and stern: "For all that is of the world, the lust of the flesh, and the lust of the eyes, and the pride of life is not of the Father, but of the world. . . . And the world passeth away, and the lust thereof; but he that doeth the will of God abideth forever—"

Abideth forever!

And beneath the minister's eye, in the foremost pew, sits pretty Emily in her blue-lined bonnet, her eyes cast heavenward like a saint—eyes not more blue than saint-like, not more saint-like than sunny.

Ah, pretty, pretty Emily, the desire of his youth! And from the height of Emily he descends to the peaks of the far-off, smoke-wreathed mountains, terrible in their eternal calm. Those mountains were to him the limits of the world, godlike barriers, beyond which yawned the colorless gulf of infinity. Now he had crossed those barriers, and had found that the finite was only a little less removed, the infinite unthinkable.

Again the voice: " For this is the promise that He hath promised us, even life eternal. . . ."

Life eternal!

Why, he has but to turn his head, he knows, and life and the tumult of living will be over and done with; but one step from the passionate noise of time to the passionless silence of eternity.

Beyond the vine-wrapped walls of the church, beyond the moss-grown ledge of the open window, the long, pale grasses, a visible dirge, bend above the storm-stained marble slabs. From his corner of the pew upon the Sundays of nineteen years he has watched three of these marble slabs, standing like sentinels above three sunken graves.

" Sacred to the memory of Mary Elizabeth !"

" Sacred to the memory of Hannah Maria !"

" Sacred to the memory of Susan Virginia !"

How alike they must have been, those sisters, and what small sisters, whose memories were protected by three tiny slabs and three fallen graves! Why, one pale, long grass was not more like unto another than was one sunken grave to the sunken graves beside it.

And again he heard a voice that was not the voice of the preacher, but the voice of a royal philosopher, sounding along the ages, and speaking, in living tones, across nigh two thousand years; and the voice spoke, saying:

"Consider that soon thou wilt be ashes, and either a name, or not even a name; *and a name is but sound and echo.* . . . And the things which are valued in life are empty and rotten and trifling, and justice and truth are fled. . . . Throwing away, then, all things, hold to those only which are few. . . ."

A name is but sound and echo!

And for the sake of a sound and an echo he had striven long and suffered and been sore bespent. He had put aside reason and the quiet which reason begets, and had toiled in a world amidst the little things thereof, which were many, forsaking the great, which were few.

"For the soul is a whirl, and fortune hard to divine, and fame a thing devoid of judgment. . . . And everything which belongs to the body is a stream, and what belongs to the soul is a dream and a vapor, and life is a warfare and a stranger's sojourn, and after-fame is oblivion. . . ."

Fame is but sound and echo!

And his greed of glory, his lust of power, the pride of his eyes, were less in the immutable void of eternity than the waving of the long, pale grasses in the wind.

"I shall give you a chance to extend your knowledge of human nature, Mr. Akershem."

He turned almost instantly, to meet Anna Allard's eyes. Apparently the service had had no depressing effect on her; she was as cheerful as usual.

"I am not sure that it is desirable," he answered, shortly.

"I am sure that it is desirable for other people," returned she. "Perhaps if you knew them a little better you'd let them alone."

Her frankness irritated him again; for all his concessions she had not yielded a letter of her convictions; and he knew that she entertained not the remotest intention of so doing. The unswerving constancy of purpose at once perplexed and attracted him; it was the subtle force that exercised its ascendency over his nature in its new-born uncertainty. Weakening in his own, stability of convictions in another he recognized wonderingly.

They had turned into Mulberry Street, and the density of the atmosphere oppressed him. The old loathing, the old intolerable disgust for poverty seized upon him, and he longed to flee to cleanliness and space.

Through swarms of Italian women, deep-bosomed and heavy of tread, they passed rapidly. The broken, guttural tones, robbed of their native melody, grated upon Michael's ears ; the stale odors of decaying vegetables stored in reeking cellars offended his nostrils. He hated it all, hated the squalor, the filth, the inevitable degradation. It was an everlasting reminder of the destiny that he had missed by a slip of the cup.

Anna Allard passed along with healthy indifference, her skirts held slightly aside, her brows unbent. Again her personality impressed him in its forcible uprightness. She possessed, in a great measure, that illusive quality called goodness, which so few good people possess, and which may be defined as a mean between spiritual unsophistication and worldly wisdom. It was said of Miss Allard that she was good, implying that a persuasive sanctity was one of her attributes—a sixth sense, as it were, conveying religious impressions. Whether the impression conveyed was as potent as the manner of conveying it or not is a subject for dispute, and one upon which my profane pen need offer no suggestion.

But Michael felt, without defining, the attraction. It was not Miss Allard's indomitable rectitude that caused him to become conscious of a state of moral inanition ; it was the charm with which she managed to endow that rectitude. A Mulberry Street missionary, possessing a withered profile and a shrinking manner, might have been doubly virtuous with but slight success. And, after all, there are few of us capable of dissociating the attraction of virtue from the attraction of the earthly habiliments which it chooses to adopt. They left Mulberry Street, and she took him into

several tenements, bringing him face to face with the powers
of poverty and dirt. A terrible pity took possession of him,
a pity prompting him to sit in his office chair and hurl editorial thunderbolts at the oppressors of the poor. There
was no desire to speak to them or to touch them; there
was a sensitive shrinking from the crippled man upon his
pallet bed, and from the little red-eyed seamstress in her
curl-papers and her soiled gown. He started when Anna
Allard lifted an unwashed baby in her arms. And yet the
memory of her as she stood there clung to him and followed
him far into the night. A young Madonna, the straight and
supple figure, the outstretched arms, the wonderful tenderness upon her fresh-hued face, the wonderful, wonderful
halo of her hair; and, above and beyond it all, the rays of
sunshine falling, white and holy, into the squalid room, falling like a benediction upon woman and child, wrapping in
a luminous stillness child and woman—an eternal symbol
of an eternal motherhood.

At that moment he realized the emptiness of ambition,
the futility of reward. Was he who loathed pain the one
to close the gaping wound? He who shrank from filth the
one to purge from uncleanliness?

And ambition? What a petty thing it is in the midst of
a world of men, living, begetting, and passing into dust!

"For fame is a thing devoid of judgment, and after-
fame oblivion, and a name is but sound and echo."

He walked the streets that night pursued by his self-dis-
trust. He despised himself that he had fought for the sake
of fighting, not for the sake of the cause; for what men
might say of him he had wrestled for the things that were,
baptizing his battle-field with bloody sweat. For a name
he had given his salvation.

"And a name is but sound and echo."

Onward before him in the night, against the blackness
of drawn clouds, moved the memory of Anna Allard, the
holy of holies in her eyes, her eyes upon the young child.
What was it that brought that look into a woman's face?

What might a man not sustain, smiling, for the sake of such a look?

Then, like a flash, one word broke upon his thoughts, and he paused and stood still as if he hearkened to a spoken name—"Rachel!"

Could it be that he had forgotten Rachel? Rachel who, he had told himself, was the breath of his life! Rachel whom he had loved with the passion of his youth and the strength of his manhood!

He went to her studio, and found her light still burning. As he entered she gave a little cry, and ran towards him with outstretched hands.

"Why, Mike, you bad, bad boy, where have you been?"

Her gladness, her trust, her utter lack of suspicion, touched him, and he stooped to kiss her with a poignant sense of remorse.

As she looked up at him a sudden fear, vague and illusive, flamed in her face, and she spoke quickly:

"Mike, is there anything wrong?"

"Wrong! No, dear."

And then a sudden cowardly shame took possession of him, for he had noticed the details of her toilet, and contrasted the careless drapery, the wind-blown hair, with Anna Allard's dainty trimness. Rachel was beautiful just then, but, to do him justice, he was not a man to be overborne by physical beauty; it was only an attribute to him, not a thing desirable for its own sake.

It was cowardly to criticise Rachel; he had never done so before; and yet at that moment the fall of her gown seemed careless, the loosened coil of her hair a trifle unkempt. He hated himself for the thought, but the thought would not be shut out.

Then he started, for the girl, who had been watching him, suddenly threw herself upon him with a breathless sob.

"Love me! love me! *love* me!" she cried. "I care for nothing but you—nothing but you! Let the world despise me, but you—you love me!"

Her eyes, deep and solemn, like the heart of a storm, bound him by a spell; the slim white hands clung to him and would not let him go.

With a swift repentance he caught her to him. "My star!" he said.

Still her eyes cast over him their wonderful spell. "Swear that you love me—swear it!"

"I swear it!"

She threw back her head with one of her impetuous movements, her face gleaming whiter in the dim light, a rapturous worship thrilling in her voice.

"I adore you!" she said.

Again the cursed thought: Would a good woman have loved him as Rachel loved him? Was not the worship she offered up to him a proof of her own unworthiness? Nay, a good woman sees ever between herself and the man she loves the inviolable shield of her own honor!

Ah, the thrice-accursed thought! Would it never let him rest?

It was the old, old expiation that Nature has demanded and woman paid since the day upon which woman and desire met and knew each other.

Ah, the old, old expiation!

CHAPTER VIII

" HELLO, Shem !"

Akershem looked up.

"Your entrance is rough on nerves," he remarked, irritably.

Driscoll leaned in the doorway, surveying the world in general and the editor in particular with his accustomed complacency.

"I say, Shem, what is the matter with *The Iconoclast?*"

Akershem shifted uneasily, running his hand impatiently through his hair. He looked worn and harassed, and the lines upon his forehead had deepened.

"Matter?" he echoed. "Why, nothing."

Driscoll shook out a folded paper and held it towards him.

"For the past fortnight who has served us with editorials?" he asked. "Not yourself, my good fellow; and don't tell me that this is Kyle's work, for I know better. Why, here are two whole columns, and not an abusive epithet to speak of. Who's your man?"

Michael kicked the paper viciously under the desk.

"To tell the truth, I got Springer to do it. He's one of our reporters, you know—a sensible fellow—"

"That fool! Why don't you do the work yourself?"

"Confound your catechizing! I'll not have it!"

Driscoll gave a long, low whistle. "Well, of all the dashed impudence!" he said; then added, amiably, "I'm off to Java, you know."

"To Java?"

"Oh, the reports of Dr. Dubois and his Pleistocene discovery made me feverish. I am convinced that only criminal negligence has prevented our verifying Darwinism by producing the bones of our ancestors. I'll satisfy myself in regard to the Java find, and then I'll get up an anthropological expedition for the purpose of making explorations in tropical Asia. I am inclined to believe that man originated thereabouts, and I intend to search for the exact spot." His eyes were glowing with enthusiasm, his face flushed. The old restless spirit was in possession. He pursued the dangerous, sweet divinity—change.

Akershem was devoid of sympathy. "What a pity you weren't born a beggar!" he said; "you might have accomplished something."

Perhaps of the affections of Michael's life the affection for John Driscoll was the strongest; certainly it was the steadiest. And yet when Driscoll had gone he felt vaguely relieved; he half wished that the Java scheme would materialize. For the past two weeks he had been undergoing a curious revulsion from his old nature, and the presence of Driscoll seemed a living reproach. And with his new-born sensitiveness he dreaded reproach; he craved not only self-esteem, but the esteem of his fellow-men.

Impatiently he rose, and paced up and down the uncarpeted floor. He felt feverish, alert—eager to sweep the past aside, and to start, unfettered, in pursuit of the future.

With the past he knew that Rachel was associated; Rachel, who had given him life when he was famished, sympathy when he was sore beset; Rachel, who had been passionately content to cast her art and ambition as a stepping-stone before his feet, and who, when upon that stepping-stone he could not reach the goal, had raised it by the throw of her own heart.

The morning sunlight flitted across the floor, bringing to his memory the flitting figure of Rachel—Rachel, with luminous eyes, with tender, quivering lips, the Love who had been offered up upon the altar of his own divinity.

Upon the scales of his judgment his life and his life's ambition were found wanting when weighed in the balance

with Rachel's.   And yet, though Rachel was fair, Rachel be-
longed to the past—to the past, with his old bitterness that
needed a balm, his old ambition that craved a ballast.

In his future Rachel had no place.   Now he wanted
more—far more—than Rachel could give.   He wanted the
one thing that she had not.   He wanted the honor of good
men and good women.   He wanted a clean future, unbe-
smirched by any blot upon the closed pages of his past.

Then, dimly, as one who sees through a glass darkly, he
felt that the respect he wanted was the respect of Anna
Allard, the homage of her fearless rectitude, her implacable
honor.   To him, in his limited experience, the esteem of
Anna Allard meant the esteem of the other half of the
world—the better half, with its trust and purity and faith.

He knew then, and he had always known; that the desire
for Anna Allard was not the desire for love.   Love in his
nature must hold ever a secondary place—must serve ever
as the handmaid of ambition.   And with love he had been
surfeited—but honor lay still unattained.

And he felt no remorse before the memory of Rachel.
It seemed to him but natural that she should fill the part
which she had chosen in his life.   If she was to be buried,
a victim to his discarded theories, it was because she had
accepted those theories, discarding upon her side the laws
of her conscience.   And the thought again : A pure woman
would have spurned passion for the sake of principle !

Ah, the old, old expiation !

A man is never so merciless as to a dead desire, never
so implacable as to the woman whom he has once loved
and loves no longer.   In the whole course of his life Michael had never been so severe as he was to Rachel Gavin,
never so unmerciful as when he held himself most just.
And he judged her as he had never judged himself, because with himself the wrong had not been of his own begetting, but had descended to him in place of a name.   But
Rachel—with Rachel it had been love, not mistaken principle, and it was for that love that he judged her.

" Please, sir, will you speak to me?"

With a start he turned to meet her brimming glance. She stood before him, dressed as he had first seen her—in the artist's blouse and cap, with a drawing-block in her hand and her hand outstretched. At the apparition he fell back, surprised into a quick remorse; then he looked at her, and his heart hardened. Had he found her overburdened with a sense of her own unworthiness it might have been different. At a word of serious realization, he told himself, his anger would have melted. But, alas! poor Rachel; responsibility sat restlessly upon her—all eyes are not dimmed by tears.

What was life to her, he asked himself, if she met it so lightly? Had she not played with ambition as with a toy, and might not love be as frivolously dealt with? Why should he fan the waning embers of his remorse for the sake of a pain that would be over and done with in the curl of an eyelash? And his heart hardened, and he drew back.

"I forced an entrance," said Rachel; "a guard in the guise of a reporter tried to stop me, but I told him that I had important news about the murder trial, so he let me in. Aren't you glad he did?"

She laughed, and by that laugh she lost her kingdom. A well of merriment overflowed and rippled upon the air; laughter was in her deep, gray eyes, where the tears were hardly dry, laughter was upon her lips, laughter dimpled across cheek and brow; she was all laughter. The little cap upon her head slipped jauntily aside, and the dark line of hair was sharply defined upon her white, blue-veined forehead. She was the old, audacious Rachel, whom he had met and pondered over some two years ago—a charming Rachel, but a Rachel whose day was done.

"Aren't you glad?" she repeated, and she rested her hands upon his shoulders and looked into his face. "Don't you want those items dreadfully?"

"I am busy," he answered.

13

"Aren't you glad to see me?" she questioned, lightly, as if forcing a foregone conclusion. As she spoke she gave him a little shake.

"I am busy."

"Busy! Nonsense! Why, you were walking up and down this blessed floor as idle as—as that reporter. What were you thinking of?"

"Many things."

"What? Was I among them?"

"Yes."

"Really? Then if you have time to think of me, why haven't you time to talk to me?"

"I was thinking seriously."

"Well, I never! And can't you talk seriously, too?"

"To you?" he asked, and smiled. "Why, you look like an escaped sunbeam."

"What a pretty speech! But shall I look like a cloud?" And she bent her heavy brows upon him, closing her eyes until only the smutty purple shadows under them were visible. "Do you like me now?"

"It does not suit you."

"What is the matter? Are you angry?" Something tender and childish about her smote him suddenly with a sharp pain. How young she looked!

"Oh no!" he answered; "not that, dear."

"Am I good?"

"Yes."

"Am I pretty?"

"Yes."

"Then what is the matter? Why can't you become nice and good-humored?"

Then like a flash all the gayety vanished; a wondering look settled upon her face, and the sweet, fresh merriment fled.

"There is something wrong, dearest; what is it?"

He shook his head; but, with a sudden, passionate intensity, she spoke:

"How *dare* you say nothing is wrong when you look like that? Something *is* wrong, and I will know! I will know!"

"What will you know?"

"Why you look like this—why you wish me to go—what it all means. Tell me!"

He took her hands very gently. What slender hands they were!

"There is nothing wrong that I can tell you, Rachel; nothing is wrong. Shall I go out with you for a walk?"

"No."

All the slumbering force of her nature had awakened, and thrilled in her voice. For a moment she was silent; then, drawing her hands from his grasp, she stood white and straight before him. The words came slowly:

"For some time, Mike, I have felt—I mean I have thought—that—that something had come between us. I tried not to see it; but one cannot shut one's eyes, and—and I fear that it is so."

"Rachel!"

"What it is I do not know. I have thought and thought until my head ached, and I could think of nothing that I had done or said that could have made the difference." Her voice was clear and steady now. "It may be that I am mistaken. If I have been unjust, forgive me. I know you have many things to do in life besides to love; and yet"—then she looked at him, her solemn eyes summoning him to judgment—"is it true?" she said.

"Rachel!" A note of pity softened his voice, and, like a flash, it told upon her. He almost held his breath at the change. A warm light leaped to her face; the flame in her eyes blinded him as they swept over him, hot with pain. She drew back, straightening herself to her full height as to withstand a charge, and throwing back her head with a gesture of resistless pride.

"Because I have loved you," she said, "do not think that I cannot forget you."

He moved forward, but the coldness of her voice checked him, and he stood still.

" If we have played with love," she said, "we have played with it together, and neither of us has been wounded in the farce. I need no pity. I chose to love you, and, when I choose, I can forget you."

Then her voice broke, and she fell to trembling as he reached forward and caught her in his arms. "My dear! my love!" he cried, "forgive me! I am only a poor blundering fool; forgive me!"

But her vehemence had died away, leaving her weak and sobbing upon his breast. "I—I lied," she said. "I love you—and I did not choose to love you—and—and I *can't* forget you."

He loved her still, he told himself. He did not tell himself, but perhaps he dimly felt, that it was a love from which reverence was slipping away. What he could not tell himself was that this mental revolution, which shadowed Rachel, was the result of an illumination cast for him by Rachel herself upon human life—and human fulfilments. His love for her had been born of a desire for the unattainable, and had fed upon sympathy; and that sympathy failing to extend to changed conditions, he found that mere love was of all things frail the frailest.

He kissed her and cursed himself; and, with sobs still echoing in her voice, she left him and went into the street.

At first she walked heavily, feeling wretched and undone. But the air was so fresh, the sky so blue, the world so pulsating with energy, that one must put aside borrowed cares and be glad with nature. And, after all, it had been a mistake—he loved her, she was sure he loved her, and what mattered all else? So she quickened her steps and walked briskly along the crowded streets, shooting soft, luminous glances from beneath her drooping lids, putting away doubt and distrust.

Then as she reached her door she caught sight of an organ-grinder with a monkey upon his back, and she called to the man, taking the grinning little animal from him and caressing it in her arms. It was so cunning and so tiny; and when it climbed upon her shoulders and laid violent hands upon her cap she forgot her depression and bubbled with delight.

"He's such a little dear," she said to the man—"such a darling little dear." And she gave him the change in her purse.

Then the man, who was an Italian and skilled in beggary, doffed his battered hat. "The Lord bless your sunshiny face," he said; and he made the monkey practise his ridiculous little tricks, while the sunshiny face shone upon him and the sweet laugh rang out.

A passer-by, one who was once young but was now old, and whose youth and age had been spent in the ways that lead to the getting of wealth, heard the laugh and turned to see from whence it came. He saw, and his withered heart grew green again at the sight, and he forgot, for the moment, that joy was vain and gold the only good. "A happy woman," he said, and smiled enviously.

And yet where the laughter sparkled in the deep, gray eyes the tears were hardly dried; in the rippling laugh, if one listened, one heard the echo of a sob, and beneath the mirth, in her heart, a heaviness was weighing her down.

Alas, poor Rachel! all eyes are not dimmed by tears.

CHAPTER IX

Summer had come—throbbing, passionate summer, when Nature had ripened into the fulness of maternity. The earth had quickened joyously into fertility; not a meadow but teemed with emerald verdure, not a barren space but grew pregnant with life.

In the city the fog of soot and smoke hung heavily; the sweet, glad sunshine, reaching the tenement roofs, shifted in leaden rays as if robbed of the essence of its gladness.

Summer in the country, with its free, wide stretches of purpling moors and its ecstatic insight into the sacred heart of things, is as unlike the city summer, with its palpitating humanity and its tainted atmosphere, as life is unlike death. The one is the world as God planned it; the other as man has made it.

Rachel Gavin fretted and pined in her fifth-story front. She kept close during the long, hot days, and only stole out, wan and white, in the twilight for a breath of evening. In imagination she saw herself roaming over tangled fields and in shadowy woodland ways, her sketch-book and camping-stool strapped upon her arm. But the city fenced her in, and her straitened means, the result of her idleness, had to be lengthened by stringent economy. She had not allowed Michael Akershem to give her so much as a paint-brush, and the stratagems to which she resorted in her financial straits were many and varied. Once he had brought her a diamond ring, and she had turned upon him like a flame. "How dare you?" she had cried, passionately. "Do you wish to insult me? And I despise diamonds!" He had been a little vexed and a great deal startled. "I shall be beholden to no man," she had said.

"I will take nothing from you, do you hear? Nothing! nothing!"

"Forgive me," he had answered; "it is as you will."

But he had grown dimly conscious of a lack of comprehension. The delicacy of Rachel's decision had been beyond his power of perception. As some visions are unable to grasp, in a certain color, minute variations of shade, so in a wide survey of a fact, subtle distinctions were lost upon Michael Akershem. That Rachel's determination was the one salvation to which her pride adhered he did not suspect, and he would have failed as utterly in an attempt to distinguish between the position as she now saw it and as she should have seen it had she arrayed herself in his diamonds. To his mother, toiling in the harvest-fields, a nicety in point of morals could not have been more incomprehensible.

But Rachel said, "I have accepted your convictions for your sake; you may also abide by mine." And he was silenced.

So it was not only her watch that was pawned this summer; a pink coral necklace of her great-grandmother's lay unreclaimed for several months in the glass case of one Israel Meyerbeer, and her guitar passed under those gold balls never to return—at least, into her possession. She suffered silently, however, for her pride set a seal upon her paling lips. She packed Madame Laroque and her belongings off to the seaside, watching her depart with smiling eyes; and when the old flower-woman at the corner clapped her withered hands, where the chilblains were barely healed, and declared that she felt the summer in her bones, Rachel answered with her ringing laugh. She had lost her watch and her great-grandmother's necklace and her peace of mind, but, outwardly, she had not lost her frank good-humor.

Rachel was not the only one who sighed in spirit, torturing her imagination with visions of the country-side. The heat had penetrated into the office of *The Iconoclast*, and the printer's devils groaned themselves blue, while in the composing-room the foreman mopped his streaming brow and thundered maledictions after the recreant editor.

Michael was out of town. For the first time in his nine years of journalistic work he had taken a vacation. It was Hedley Semple who had borne him off for a fortnight's shooting in the White Mountains. Mrs. Semple was ensconced with the children and several friends in a dilapidated farm-house which she had purchased near North Conway, and Akershem had been drawn into the party. Like a bit of untried life to him was this happy-go-lucky holiday, spent in the midst of the mountains, with Hedley Semple's enthusiastic sportsmanship and the frank cordiality of Mrs. Semple's large and pervasive presence. It was a pleasant fortnight, and Michael entered into the high-spirited informality with a boyish zest, grasping at the youth which he had missed. For the first time he was thrown with a crowd of wholesome, unaffected young people —girls who had no theories and no missions but the general theory that life is pleasant enough in its way, and the mission to endeavor to make it more so. It was refreshing to him ; it robbed him of half his cynicism, and knocked the life out of his fundamental maxim of social depravity.

When he returned to the city he was in excellent health and spirits, and it was with a masterful determination that he took up his work again—the work that he was beginning to hate.

One day in September, as he worked in the composing-room, a sudden disgust for his employment swept over him, and, rising, he walked rapidly up and down the room.

"Mr. Akershem," said the foreman, "can you let me have those three sticks of copy ?"

Michael sat down again, taking up his pen with an air of supreme self-mastery.

There came a peal from the telephone bell, and he looked up impatiently. "That is the twentieth time in the last half-minute," he said.

The telephone boy turned, the trumpet still at his ear. "Cockril & Holmeson," he said, "say that in your account of the strike at their works you put the wages the strikers were receiving at half a cent too low."

He looked at the foreman as he spoke, but Michael uttered an exclamation and returned to his work.

The bell rang again. The boy looked up. "Mr. Coggins says we made him say that Anarchism was not an unnatural outcome of—"

"Pshaw! I don't care what he said."

Michael sighed. "That infernal telephone again!" he exclaimed.

"Please, sir"—the telephone boy addressed vacancy and looked dejected—"Miss Caroline Houston, of Thirty-first Street, says if we don't retract that libel concerning her in to-day's issue she'll—she'll—she didn't say what she'd do, but she's coming up in a few minutes."

"And the last form going to press," muttered the foreman, helplessly, while Michael cried : "Tell the next person to go to the devil!"

For a moment there was silence. Michael tossed a covered sheet aside and took up a blank. A reporter looked in at the door, and, seeing the state of affairs, cautiously looked out again.

The telephone rang sharply, imperatively, with a finishing snap at the end.

"Please, sir."

No answer.

"Mr. Akershem!"

"Well?"

"A gentleman to speak to you."

"Tell him he can't."

The words were shouted through the telephone.

"He says he must speak to you, sir."

"Tell him to go to thunder."

"Please, sir, he says he won't, and he won't budge till he speaks to you."

In a rage Michael rose and strode to the trumpet. "Who, in the devil's name, are you?" he shouted.

"Hello, there!" came Driscoll's voice. "I've something to say to you."

"Can't say it. I wish you'd find some other amusement. We're going to press."

He gave an angry jerk and left the telephone, picking up his papers from the table. He cast a sympathetic look at the foreman, who held his head in one hand as he took down notes with the other. His tone softened wonderfully. The better side of his nature came out to his fellow-workman. "Come into my room, if you like, Jenkins," he said; "I'll give you this in twenty minutes."

And he passed into his office.

It was not until some hours later that he recalled Driscoll and his urgent desire for an interview, and shortly after dinner he went to hunt him up.

He found Driscoll in his sitting-room, waiting patiently for the last of the dinner things to be removed from the small table.

"Hello!" he said. "Draw up and have some coffee and a cigar. "You'll find that box of Havanas to your right first-rate." Michael sat down and glanced about him. There was an air of solid comfort about Driscoll's rooms which never failed to impress him, and which he had striven long and unavailingly to copy.

"How comfortable you look!" remarked Michael. "I wish I could reach your degree of perfection in that line."

"My greatest talent," returned Driscoll, with complacent assurance. "I tell you, there is more real science in making life pleasant than in tracing its origin."

"Was it Tertullian who said that to be happy is to flaunt one's self in the face of the Creator? And there is some truth in it. I am never particularly cheerful that I don't wonder what particular misfortune Providence has prepared next in order. But you had something to say to me."

"And I have. I met Splicer, managing editor of *The*

Journal of Economics, you know. Well, his health has failed, and he has to quit work. He thought he might get me into his place. It's a pretty responsible position, you see, but I told him political economy was too stagnant for my taste, and took the liberty of suggesting yourself. He was wild in your praise, said in controversy you hadn't your match. Indeed, he magnified your ability considerably. You know you scored him once on the sanitary advantages of ash barrels, which accounts for it. He said he would have been glad to use his influence for you had you been less unsound, and I ventured to hint at the moderation of your views."

"It is not so. My views have not altered. I shall not leave *The Iconoclast.*"

"Oh, well, suit yourself. It's a pretty good chance, however, if they offer it to you, which isn't likely. I thought I might as well prepare you—"

"I shouldn't accept it," returned Michael, insistently. But as he walked home, after leaving Driscoll, he knew that his determination had been but momentary, and that he was already beginning to waver in his allegiance to *The Iconoclast.* In view of the foreseen contingency, his present work became more distasteful. It was uncongenial; not enough so, perhaps, to cause him to throw it aside with no immediate opening in view, but uncongenial enough to warrant his exchanging it for an equally successful and more respectable position. And even if he was not sufficiently quixotic to sacrifice his future to his principles, still he was sufficiently ambitious to attempt, were it possible, to gratify principle and ambition at a single stroke. Yes; after all, if the position were offered he would consider an acceptance. In his primitive disregard of consequences he overlooked the difficulties of his reversion. By an open and barefaced desertion to pass from his own party to the front ranks of his opponents seemed, in its way, feasible enough. That his party might resent his desertion did not occur to him.

Cheerfully sanguine with regard to the opportunity he desired, he went home and smoked a peaceful pipe in the satisfaction of his decision. With the thought of his changed position had awakened the thought of Anna Allard. For a moment he allowed himself to indulge in a soothing reverie. He saw her beside him, bending above his chair—the keeper of his home and his heart—her serene judgment sustaining him through life. He saw her grave smile illumined by the glory of her hair; saw her bend above him with his image in her eyes; saw them threading together, through youth and through age, into eternity, the pathway of their lives. He thought of her calmly, with not one quiver of his pulse. He desired her mentally. She personified the proprieties of life—nothing more. From his wine husks he was preparing to return to virtue, and virtue wore the hair and eyes of Anna Allard.

Then he put the thought from him angrily, and fell to thinking of Rachel.

The next day, going to his office, he found Kyle awaiting him. The young fanatic had grown more fanatical of late; his appearance had become generally unkempt, and there was a strangely lurid light in his eyes.

"We needed copy," he began; "and as you left none I ventured to look into your desk. I found an article upon "Tyrannicide" which I made use of. It suited us exactly."

A flame kindled in Michael's eyes.

"I consider it officious," he said. "The thing was written two years ago and not intended for publication. I shall have it recalled."

"It is too late," returned Kyle, doggedly; "I have given it to Jenkins. I had no idea you'd cut up so. I shouldn't, in your place."

One of his rare smiles flashed across Michael's face, giving him a brilliantly youthful look.

"I don't believe you would," he said, frankly. "I beg your pardon, Kyle; I was hasty."

"And there is something else," continued the other. "Paul Stretnorf was here. He wishes you to deliver your lecture upon Russian Nihilism before his society. I told him I was sure he might count upon you. It is important, you know."

Michael started. The smile passed from his face, leaving a harassed expression.

"You are getting me into a peck of trouble, Kyle. I can't do it."

"You must," persisted Kyle, passionately. "I as good as gave my word for you. The demand is imperative. Why, one would think that you were—" He checked himself.

"That I were what?" demanded Michael.

"Nothing, old man; but we must have the lecture."

"That I were what?"

Kyle threw back his head and fixed his lurid gaze upon him. "That you were playing trimmer!" he said, in a passionate undertone.

For a moment Michael looked at him, growing white to the lips. He realized in a flash that his part was less easy than he had believed it, that what he called principle other men would call perfidy, and that because of that principle or perfidy he should have to reckon with Kyle.

"Do this for me, Akershem," said Kyle.

Michael hesitated, his gaze abstracted, the vein upon his forehead growing livid from contraction, his eyelids twitching nervously. Then he reached forward and laid his hand upon Kyle's shoulder.

"You believe in me, Kyle?" he said, and there was a certain wistfulness in his voice.

"Unto death," responded the other.

The old brilliant smile illumined Akershem's face as he spoke. "I will deliver the lecture," he said.

BOOK IV

REVERSION

" It is not only what we have inherited from our fathers and mothers that walks in us. It is all sorts of dead ideals and lifeless old beliefs. They have no vitality, but they cling to us all the same, and we can't get rid of them. . . . And then we are, one and all, so pitifully afraid of the light."—*Ibsen*.

CHAPTER I

To Rachel Gavin the days seemed crowding past like gray gnomes glutted with presage of evil. With passionate incredulity she blinded her eyes, feeling in the darkness their leering presences around her. Then she looked and understood. She understood that the way upon which she had walked was the way of a quicksand; that the things upon which she had looked were but phantasmagoric nothings; that the rock upon which she had anchored had crumbled, as rocks will. There remained only the end.

"But I will be happy!" cried Rachel, in all the passion of her vehement youth—"I will be happy!" And she had grown beautiful from the assumption of omnipotence, as if an infusion of fresh blood stained the white of her skin with its scarlet flame. Against the tenacity of her will what power could prevail? In her eyes happiness had clothed itself in the image of Michael Akershem. As he was the one thing needful to her existence, so the vigor of the desire with which she desired him redeemed the shrinking value of her self-esteem. The buoyancy of her belief in him had exalted her above conventions; but despised conventions avenge themselves as inevitably as despised truths. It may be that we have never clearly defined wherein lies the difference between them.

But if Rachel suffered now, she made no sign. If she missed the intensity of Michael's first affection, she missed it silently. If the carefully acquired courtesy with which he treated her showed pale beside the flaming memory of that turbulent devotion, who was the wiser?

Before her always, sometimes shrouded by unnatural lethargy, sometimes veiled by a natural sanguineness, loomed,

in a terrible obscurity, the dread of entering upon that valley of humiliation which is found at the end of the way of
false ideals.   She resented the gentleness with which Michael treated her ; she resented the superlative considerate-
ness of Michael's friends , and, most bitterly, she resented
the ill-concealed compassion of her former companions.
She who had renounced art scoffed at them that they re-
gretted the renunciation.

When Driscoll came one day and lounged about her
studio, and talked to her in that deferential manner which
she had observed closely of late, it stung her like the sting-
ing of a lash.   She writhed in the nervous tension of her
exasperation.

"I wish you wouldn't treat me as if I were insane or in a
fever," she remarked, irritably.

Driscoll's mouth dropped in astonishment.   He walked
to the window and stood gnawing his mustache abstracted-
ly.   His back expressed an amicable forbearance, his face
a prophetic gloom. The silence was oppressive. There was
a lack of sprightliness about the passers-by that savored
of dejection.   He shook himself resignedly and glanced at
Rachel from the corner of his eye, after which he beat an
almost inaudible tattoo upon the window-pane with the fingers of one hand.   He quoted, gravely :

> "'I never saw a purple cow,
>   I never hope to see one ;
>   But this I'll tell you, anyhow,
>   I'd rather see than be one.'"

With an energy born of boredom he descended to over-
tures.   "Well, he remarked, placidly — "well, as we were
saying, the wind sits in the east."

"If you have anything to say," continued Rachel, with
asperity, "please say it, and have it over.   I hate skirmish-
ing !"

Driscoll's mouth dropped a degree lower, and his eyes
grew wider.

"But I haven't anything to say," he protested, "so how can I say it?" Then he grew hopeful. "I can quote you a line or two if it will answer," he added.

Rachel was not to be mollified. "I don't know the reason," she said, "but I wish you didn't always look as if you were thinking things."

"I assure you," retorted Driscoll, with solemnity, "my mind is a perfect blank."

Rachel laughed nervously, her glance flashing brilliantly through the dark shadows encircling her eyes. She interlaced her fingers restlessly. "Perhaps I am insane," she said; "perhaps that is why you are so civil." And she added, with the recklessness of desperation, "I see no other reason."

He regarded her contemplatively. "If you will know," he returned, with a whimsical disregard of her earnestness, 'I was thinking that the abolition of slavery has more to answer for than is written in history." Then he became suddenly serious. "And I was also thinking," he added, slowly, "that not one of us is worth your putting out your hand to; but it is like you to do it, and it is more like us to want you to."

Rachel started, and the scarlet fled from her face, leaving it like marble. Her lips trembled; the stars were lost behind the rain-clouds in her eyes. She tore at the embroidered edge of her handkerchief nervously. "I—I am so childish!" she said, and burst into tears.

He watched her quietly, pale to the lips. "Don't!" he said, at last, stammering awkwardly. "Don't!" Then he spoke quickly.

"Rachel," he said, "if it had only been—" He checked himself; the word was never spoken. It was the restraint of a man in whom passion had long since been throttled. He regarded Rachel as he regarded the world, with honest cynicism, and a quizzical acknowledgment of what she, as well as the world, might have been to him and was not.

When she looked at him he was conscious only of her eyes—tragic eyes, haunted by tears.

"I am happy," she said, "I am perfectly happy." There was a pitiful refutation in her voice. "It is only my work that troubles me," she added, and looked into his face and saw that the lie was as naught. "It *is* my work," she repeated.

"Of course!" assented Driscoll, heartily — "of course! What else could it be? As a friend of mine used to remark, 'What with your confounded advantages and your cursed attractiveness, you lack only common-sense!' Not that I intentionally cast any aspersions upon your intellect," he added, hastily, "for you will take it up again and I shall yet see the great picture."

"I don't know." Rachel wavered in her answer. Then she stood up, and her glance met his as he leaned above her. A wave of color flooded her face. At the thought of Akershem she reddened before Akershem's friend. A flash of her old iridescence illumined her.

"I have chosen to *live !*" she said.

"As we have all chosen," he answered, simply. "I as well as you, and the world as well as ourselves." And he took the hand that lay in her lap with a gesture that was half consolatory. "And like most choices, we regret it," he said, and left her.

"Do you ever think," asked Rachel of Akershem that night, "how different life would have been for us both had we never loved?"

"Yes," he answered, truthfully, "I have thought."

She flashed a brilliant glance upon his face. The lightness of her voice drowned the pain beneath. "How bare it would have been, and how cold!" she said.

"How brilliant for you!"

"But how cold!"

"Cold! With Fame?"

"It does not warm."

He grew tender.

"Does this?" He put his arm about her, and, as she lifted her head, kissed her lips.

She warmed, a glow overspread her face, and that vivid, illusive flame, at which he had so often marvelled, wrapped her from head to foot.

She laughed softly with happiness. "So you aren't sorry?" she asked.

"Sorry?"

"Not sorry that I failed?"

"You did not try."

The old haunting jealousy of her work was gone, and it pained her.

"I might have been an honor to you," she said, with rash audacity, "to leaven the lump of your reputation."

His brow wrinkled and grew harassed; the twitching of his lids increased. The superficiality of her manner perplexed him; he knew not of the unguessed depths that lay below. He knew only that the recklessness of speech which had at first attracted now repelled him.

"My reputation is not so black as you are pleased to suppose," he retorted.

She laughed provokingly.

"You contrast it with mine," she said, "which, I doubt not, outrivals the raven's wing."

"Don't, Rachel!" he pleaded. "One must consider such things."

"As ebon reputations?" she inquired. "Mine is at your service." Then she made him a mocking courtesy. "Sir Respectability, may your shadow never be less!"

She stood in the falling firelight, a vivid, elastic figure, all the supple curves emphasized by the strenuous motion. From her straight, white brow to her agile feet she was all energy and action. A scintillant charm, born of her spirit and the genial firelight, sent for an instant the swift blood to his brain. But half smiling he turned from her to the ruddy coals, which seemed inert and lifeless. There was nothing vital save herself.

"What a pity that one becomes stupid as soon as one becomes respectable!" she continued. "When we cease to be interesting we become virtuous, it is so much easier. That is why very plump and pudgy people are always so good." She was grave suddenly. A shaft of light falling over her revealed the wistful lines of her lips. "Would you have loved me better had I been a saint?" she asked.

But Michael was thinking of something else suggested by her words, and he did not hear. "Ah! What was that?" he asked, absently.

She stared at him a moment, a sharp terror whitening her face. With a passionate gesture she put out her hand, blindly warding off the black shadow that loomed before her. "It—it is nothing," she faltered. "I was only jesting—as usual."

Her knees trembled, and, yielding to a passing weakness, she knelt beside him, resting her head upon his hand. He was kind, but kindness was mere lack of passion; he was gentle, but gentleness was foreign to his nature. In the old time he had been neither gentle nor kind, but he had loved her. Then he had wounded her by his intensity; now he lacerated her by his tenderness. Then the wounds had been the wounds of love and the pain pleasant; now that love was dead, tenderness was but the empty shroud and little worth. The hand beneath her cheek did not quiver; she missed the old answering throb to her touch.

With a sigh she rose to her feet, looking down upon his abstracted brow. He glanced up and smiled; then, seeing that she was pale, he drew the scarf she wore more closely about her. As he did so his hand brushed her throat, and, as it passed, it left a crimson flush. Abandoning reserve, she stooped quickly and kissed the hand that lay upon her shoulder.

"Good-night!" she said.

"Good-night!" he echoed.

She reached her door and came back. She was trembling with a vague foreboding.

Quietly he drew her into his arms as one draws a child, but she clung to him with a passionate cry.

"Oh, my heart! if there was only love in the world! Only love in all the wide, wide world!"

"There is something else?" he asked, wonderingly.

She shook her head as she turned away. "Everything else," she answered. Then a yearning seized her to have him lie to her, and she lingered, standing with upraised eyes and hanging hands. A forlorn hope burned in her heart that it might all be a dream, and that he would awaken her with a touch. But the hope was forlorn, and it ended forlornly. He looked down upon her passively.

"Rachel," he said. She thrilled and warmed suddenly. "Do you wish anything?"

She grew cold. "No," she answered, and passed out.

At that moment she was waging a revolt against Fate as impotent as Michael Akershem's. A nauseating disgust for mankind seized upon her—a disgust for petty passions that mouldered to dust, and for pettier aspirations that but tainted the heaven to which they aspired. As yet her portion of gall and wormwood was bitter to her lips. She had not learned that when one has drunk deeply one becomes indifferent to the gall and oblivious to the wormwood. It is merely a matter of taste.

The next morning as Michael stooped to kiss her before going to his office she drew back.

"I detest forms and ceremonies," she said.

He regarded her with surprised eyes, his brow contracting.

"Is it only a form?" he asked.

And she answered, "What else?" But in her heart she was longing to have him contradict her as vehemently as he would once have done, forcing back her words with a storm of protestations. The fact that he submitted to her proved, as naught else proved, the dearth of emotion. He smiled at her as he went out; and because he smiled she knew that the words caused him no pain, and because they caused him no pain she hated him and herself.

But that afternoon, when her natural optimism had vanquished the forebodings of the morning, and she had lost
the memory of his smile, repentance took hold of her, and
she looked eagerly forward to reconciliation.

Lightly she determined to meet him as he left the office
and walk homeward, and from a fleeting sentiment she
dressed herself as he had first seen her, wearing the cap
and blouse with a fresh dignity of carriage. The reaction
from the unusual depression sent a swift light to her face,
and the dimples beside the eyes rippled mirthfully. In one
instant she had warmed from the passionate pallor of the
morning to an iridescent vivacity. As she looked at herself in the glass she caught the eyes of her reflection, and
laughed breathlessly from sheer sympathy. Long afterwards she remembered the freshness of the face that had
looked back at her, and the memory was as keen as pain.

She opened the window and leaned out, testing the
warmth of her clothing. A smack of frost was in the air,
and as it brushed her she shivered slightly and drew back.
A light coat lay upon the divan, and she slipped it on,
pausing to give a brisk touch to the wide sleeves. Then
she nodded gayly to herself and went out. In the elevator
she drew on her gloves, carefully fastening the six buttons.
She was humming a silly little French song, and the words,
dancing in her head, made her wrinkle her brow in a quick
grimace:

> "Voyez ce beau garçon?
> C'est l'amant d'Amande."

Buoyant and alert she was, feeling the nervous capability
of action which stirs us in early autumn, and which usually
ends in nothing.

In the street, as she passed with that resolute step which
characterized her, people turned to look after her with
brightened eyes. A lady in a white fur cape caught sight
of her approaching figure, reddened, and turned aside; a
shop-girl carrying a heavy bundle stood still as she passed,

and was torn by the green fangs of envy; a dapper young foreigner put up his glasses, eyed her critically, and heaved a relieved sigh that the eternal American girl might be numbered among the things that abide not.

Rachel paused a moment before a florist's window, the odor of violets floating idly about her thoughts. Looking up, she smiled in answer to a passing nod. It was one of her fellow-students, a woman who had started with her at the Art League. She remembered the rivalry that had existed between them and the victory she had won.

"What was it worth?" she asked. "She has outstripped me now, and who cares?" And she felt a contemptuous pity for that other woman, and for the art students, and for their teachers, and for all who painted with cold brushes upon cold canvas.

"How are they better than stones?" she asked. "They have not lived." And upon the woman who had outstripped her in the race, and all such, she smiled unenvyingly—as unenvyingly as that other woman smiled back upon her.

Optimism, which was as the sunlight of her energetic nature, gilded with its shifting rays the clay upon which she trod. She was uplifted by the surging vitality within her.

Kyle, meeting her upon the corner, raised his hat with an enraptured smile. "Summer lingers yet," he remarked, with a touch of Irish blarney.

Rachel blushed. She had long disliked Kyle and his compliments; they gave her an unpleasant sense of being considered unfettered, and admiration, from all save Akershem, was mere milk and water. "A lingering summer is invariably a very sickly, frost-bitten one," she replied, tartly, "and a very foolish one."

He smiled affably. "You will meet Akershem on the next block," he said; "I passed him." And he hurried on.

Rachel quickened her steps. A sharp wind blew down the street, wrapping her skirts around her and blowing a loose lock of hair across her face. She put up her hand, impatiently brushing the hair aside, and, looking up, she saw Michael Akershem.

With an impulsive movement she went towards him, when she saw that he was looking above and beyond her, and stopped. A tall woman passed her quickly—a fresh, strong woman, with a coil of red hair showing beneath the brim of her hat. Across Michael's face fell a light that was as a reflection of the tall woman's hair. He took her hand and stood looking into her eyes, a passionate admiration in his gaze.

Rachel drew back into the shadow of the crowd; then she passed them and went on her way.

The sun had gone down. It had grown suddenly cold, and with a shiver she fastened the collar of her coat. She was stunned and bruised, and her limbs were heavy. It was not pain that she felt, but weariness. Thinking she had walked too far, she glanced up at a lamp-post—Fourteenth Street. She wondered what had brought her to Fourteenth Street, and, remembering that she needed some embroidery silks, she entered a shop, taking a seat beside the counter. There was some difficulty about the shades, and she selected them very carefully, recalling the shop-girl, as the package was being tied up, to add an intermediate skein. At the moment she thought how absurd it was to bother about silks, and how absurd it was for people to work colored flowers upon white linen. It all seemed so useless. And when she was forced to wait for her change she wondered if the time would never come when such a tedious medium of exchange would be abolished. All the little accessories of civilization seemed so irksome.

A man lost his hat in the street, and it was caught by the wind and carried along the sidewalk. Rachel laughed uncontrollably. What ridiculous things hats were, after all! and why did every one upon the block make a catch at it as it went by? What useless expenditure of energy upon a hat! How happy that man must be to care whether he lost it or not! And she felt that humanity, with its hats and its loves and its hates, was but disgusting. What came of it in the end? Or did it go on forever, with its ambitions that came to nothing; its lies, that deceived not even men themselves?

She shivered as from a chill wind. "What does it matter," she asked, wearily, "whether I saw him or not? One must always be seeing things, and it was not much to see. He looked at her. Yes, to be sure he looked at her. What of that? People usually look at each other when they meet. Coward!" She despised herself for the attempt at self-deception. "He looked at her as he no longer looks at you. He loves her, but he once loved you. His love is adjustable. How convenient!" she laughed, with a sudden recognition of the humorous side.

Reaching her room, she took off her coat, laying it carefully away. After drawing off her gloves she smoothed the fingers before placing them in the drawer. "What useless things gloves are!" she thought. "I shall stop wearing them. Why do people make themselves uncomfortable?" She brushed her hair and sat down near the fire. A heaviness, resembling the effect of an anodyne, stole over her. She looked upon life and all suffering with vague, unsympathetic eyes. She watched the little silver bird upon the clock as it swung to and fro, knowing that when the hour had reached seven, Michael, missing her at dinner, would come to seek her. With a shrinking dread she listened for his footsteps. A crisis had come, she knew, but she knew not whither it would lead her, and just now she was hardly interested in the result. She was conscious only of extreme physical fatigue. The door opened and Akershem came in.

"Rachel!" His buoyant tones cut her like steel. She quivered from head to foot. Her head rested upon the back of a chair, and she put up one hand to shield her eyes from the firelight, and from him. "Rachel, are you asleep?"

She moved slightly. "Only tired," she answered.

"Shall I send you your dinner?" She lowered her hand,

observing him intently as he stood before her. She noticed his hair, the irregularity of his features, the lines about his mouth, and the bewildering blinking of his lids. A little nervous laugh broke from her. Strange that she had never viewed him so dispassionately before.

He came and leaned over her, resting one hand lightly upon her hair. As if stung by his touch she drew back. "Dinner?" she repeated. "I wish none, thank you."

She rose and stood before him, avoiding the contact of his arm. Her hair had fallen in a heavy wave upon her forehead, and she put it back feverishly.

Michael watched her with anxious intentness, the firelight falling over him, revealing his figure, flashing into his brilliant eyes.

"Is it that you regret your work, Rachel?" he asked, suddenly.

Rachel drew back and looked at him, measuring his height with her glance. She was white to the scarlet line of her lips, and her hands trembled. In her eyes a resolution flickered and took flame. She moved a step forward; her fingers stiffened as they interlaced.

"Yes," she said. Then as she turned from him the tears started to her eyes. "Oh, leave me alone!" she cried. "Leave me alone!"

Without a word he left her; and passing into the adjoining room, she threw herself heavily upon the bed.

In the night she awoke in sudden terror. Across the city a clock struck the hour, its solemn tones tolling knell-like upon her excited mood—one! two! Something tangible about the darkness seemed to bear down upon her with stifling force. She remembered her old childish idea that it was a great black monster with fiery eyes, and the impression was so vivid that she half reached out, hoping to find that she was in the little trundle-bed at home, and that from out the darkness her mother's hand would be stretched to soothe her fear. For a moment she lay breathless and still, her thoughts taking no definite shape. Then she strained her ears, hoping to hear the crowing of the genial rooster in the barn-yard, and to learn that day was breaking in the east—only the distant rumble of the elevated road, and faint, uneasy sounds that seemed but the echoes of the noise of departed day. She sat up and reached for the candle, striking a match with nervous fingers. For an instant the pale-blue flame shot up, illumining all the familiar objects that seemed in the half-light invested with grim irony, and dying as quickly down. She struck a fresh one, holding her palm beside the candle to intercept the draught. It ignited, and, placing it on a chair, she crouched shivering upon the bed and looked around her. The dim outlines of her figure, reflected in the gray length of the mirror, impressed her with the shock of a visible presence. In her white nightgown, with the pallor of her face and the dark of her heavy hair, there was a certain solemnity about her. She looked tall and strange and sharply indistinct, as a shadow that is thrown upon a sheet of white. In the silence and dim light she sat silently.

She regarded the room and all the commonplace objects
of every day with curious eyes, as if seeing them clearly for
the first time.   The long shadows cast by the uncertain
candle lent a weirdness to the apartment, the furniture, and
even to the dusk beyond the window.   She looked at the
wardrobe, and wondered why it seemed to move and topple
towards her.   She put up her hand, instinctively warding it
off, and, realizing her hysteria, laughed nervously.   Upon a
chair lay her clothes, thrown carelessly where she had slipped
out of them, and she wondered if they were really insensible
to pain—if there were any objects in this vast universe too
inanimate to suffer.   She followed with her eyes the length
of a stocking and the space of a slender shoe.   How lightly those shoes had trodden the street below only yesterday,
and how heavily had they returned!   Then she looked at
the pictures on the wall — at Murillo's " Magdalen," so
plump and passionless; at a worn engraving of Bellini's
" Gethsemane"; at the " Martyrdom of St. Sebastian."
She smiled, thinking that those hands had striven to render
agony and had failed.   What a mere outline was the passion in the garden ! how languishing the pose of Murillo's
holy sinner !

Upon the bureau stood a photograph of Michael Akershem, and from behind it her own face looked back at her
from the gloomy mirror, as the ghost of the past looks over
the brow of the present.

In one outcry her agony broke forth : " O God !"

She ran her hands through her hair, pressing them into
her temples with almost brutal violence.   After that one
outcry she was silent, but the passion seething within her
seemed to rend her chest asunder.   The expression of her
face but for its quiet would have been despair.

" Let me think," she said, suddenly, her voice sounding
so distinct in the obscurity that she stopped half startled.
" I can't think.   How annoying it is ! I know he loved
me. Yes. And he loves me no longer. I know it. But
what does it mean to know a thing ? And how do I know

it? And what is it, anyway, that I should know? It has been, and it is over. All things are over sooner or later, and what matter is a month, a year, or ten years? In the end he would have gone from me. It is only that it has happened this year instead of the next or the year after."

And then she saw Michael Akershem as he had first appeared to her—impassioned, energetic. She saw his eyes burning with her image. She felt the touch of his hand, the pressure of his arm. With the gesture of a wounded animal she cowered downward, beating the bedclothes with impotent hands. Her dry eyes stared out into the flickering gloom.

"I hate myself! Oh, how I could curse and spit upon myself! What am I — I, a target for the stones of the world—what am I that I should chain him to me?"

A shadow upon the wall, cast by a piece of bric-à-brac, took the shape of the devil's face, mocking her with its grotesqueness. She stared at it with a dull fascination, watching it as it danced upon the papering, leering now this way, now that, but always seeming to draw a little nearer. A nervous fear shook her like an ague. She started up with a desire for human companionship. With the candle in her hand she went to the door, her white gown trailing behind her like an altar-cloth. But with her hand upon the knob she paused, and, turning, walked to the window, leaning out into the chill night, and straining her ears to catch some familiar sound. A policeman strolled by upon his beat, and his resonant tramp acted soothingly upon her overwrought nerves. She laid her head upon the sill, watching his figure as it passed, like a gigantic shadow, beneath a distant light. The cold air blew over her, piercing her thin gown. It was as ice upon the brow of one in fever. Again the clock struck — one! two! one! two! She lay there until the darkness broke and a thin line of gray showed in the east. With the shimmer of dawn she blew out the candle, and, drawing on her dressing-gown, passed into her studio. The chill light penetrated the chinks of the shutters, revealing as through a crystal lens the familiar rooms and all the bare angularities that are softened by the chastened glow of the day. Upon the floor lay the small objects that she had thrown aside the day before—a broken scraper, a glass bottle labelled " Pure Turpentine," and an emptied and distorted tube with a trace of rose madder still adhering to the mouth. In the corner stood her great picture, the dust settling upon the curtain which hung before it.

She looked about her with that sickening tightening of the heart with which we view in the gray dawn the scene where the day before we caught at happiness and missed.

In the grate a heap of ashes lay cold and lifeless. Upon the hearth the tongs had fallen. She remembered that he had dropped them as he stirred the coals the evening before. A white smile at the needless ironies of life crossed her lips. How like that burned-out grate to her own burned-out heart! The chair in which she had sat, the coat she had laid aside, the rug upon which he had stood—these tortured her with a terrible sense of familiarity. Upon the table lay the stump of a cigar and a tiny pile of ashes in a silver holder. She pushed them from her with a hasty gesture. She hated them all—these trivial objects so redolent of associations.

Then she looked at the silver clock, and the little bird upon it seemed to wink at her with its jewelled eyes. She laughed nervously. What an odd little bird it was! and why did the feathers in its tail all point in different ways? Her laugh frightened her, and she glanced fearfully around at the mirror. Above the gray dressing-gown her face showed white and haggard. Beneath her eyes heavy shadows lay.

"Soon there will be nothing left of me," she said— "nothing but a laugh."

Some hours later, when Michael came up from breakfast to inquire for her, she did not see him.

"I have a headache," she said, from behind the locked door. "Come up early. There is a matter for us to discuss." And as his footsteps descended the passage she lay idly listening to them and counting the dragon's eyes upon the ceiling. Her breakfast was on a tray beside her, and she rose presently and drank her tea and ate her roll with a stolid determination.

All the little monotonies of her toilet, she felt, were irksome. The bath was fatiguing, and she was forced to nerve herself to the effort of fastening her clothes and arranging her tangled hair. It seemed to her absurd that she should dress herself and go about her ordinary tasks with unchanged demeanor. She spoke to the maid who came to dust her room as pleasantly as was her wont; she sorted the paints and brushes systematically; and when, later in the day, she went for a walk she was surprised to feel invigorated by the bracing air.

It was not until the afternoon that a nervous reaction sent a flush of excitement to her cheeks. Her brilliancy returned to her, and when Michael Akershem came in he found her awaiting him with shining eyes and scarlet lips. He did not see the quiver of her muscles or know that she was divided between a desire to rush into his arms and a hatred of his presence.

She stood beside the fender, the light from the grate rising behind her and throwing her white-gowned figure into high-relief. Her hands were clasped before her, and her nails were pressed deeply into her sensitive palms. Beside her stood a tea-table, the lingering daylight sparkling prettily over its embroidered cover and over the dainty, gilt-edged cups. A bowl of nasturtiums curled towards her on their slender stems like tongues of flame.

Coming from the cold without, Michael was exhilarated by the genial glow, and in harmony with the radiant interior was the radiant figure of Rachel as she neared him with burning lips and eyes. He would have kissed her, but she drew gently away.

15

"How cold you are!" she said, speaking rapidly from a feverish dread of silence—"how very cold! Sit down. No, not there. You never liked that chair, you know. This one suits you. So you came early, as I said. Yes, there is something to be discussed. Why is it that the word discussion always reminds me of a dissecting-room? I feel that when a person is discussed he is morally dissected and pulled to pieces. But we sha'n't dissect any one but ourselves, shall we?"

She sat down near him, keeping upon the edge of her chair and turning her profile towards him.

"Why dissect ourselves?" he asked. "Unpleasant complications are likely to ensue."

"Oh, but it is necessary," she answered, quickly. "You see, we have been living, as it were, under false pretences. We have pretended to be happy when we were not happy at all. You pretended to me, and I pretended to you. It has been just like a game we used to play when we were children, which we called 'making believe,' and in which we made believe we were something that we were not. Now we must stop making believe. I don't feel like playing any longer; I want to return to my real self. So here I am."

He regarded her fixedly, his eyes narrowing until his gaze seemed as a stream of light thrown from a lantern upon her excited face.

"So here you are," he repeated.

"So here I am." She moved restlessly on the edge of her chair. "And this means that it is all over—all over, do you hear? You go back to your work and I go back to mine; and we will both look upon this as a little game of 'make-believe.'"

"But it was earnest," he said.

She started at his unconscious use of the past tense, and walked hastily to the window; then she came back, and played with the cups upon the tea-table. She raised a lump of sugar in the tongs, but it dropped before it reached the cup. She smiled as he looked at her.

"Is there any superstition about sugar?" she asked. "Only that foolish one about 'Many a slip,' I suppose."

She poured the tea very carefully, and handed the cup to him. As he took it from her he noticed that her hands were trembling.

"Rachel," he protested—"Rachel, I can't understand."

She filled a cup for herself. Her throat was parched, and she swallowed a little before replying.

"Not understand!" she exclaimed, with that lightness of manner which had once been natural. "Well, be quiet, and let me explain. I was always good at explaining things, you know. It means just this: you and I have been very good friends, but friendship isn't the only thing in the world, and we have found it out; and it means—well, you understand." In a moment she went on again: "Perhaps, after a long time, when we are very, very old people, and have gotten as much fame as our hands can hold, we will sit down again and talk it quietly over. By that time it will all seem very amusing," she added. She lifted the cup to her lips again.

He surveyed her in baffled silence; then, rising, he stood before her.

"Is it possible," he asked, slowly, "that you have ceased to love me?"

With a soothing gesture she put her hand to her throat, it felt so strained and drawn.

"So many things are possible," she replied, "that one can't be sure of anything."

He felt vaguely aggrieved. Then he looked into his own heart and his faith in impossibilities weakened. If his love could burn out, why not Rachel's. And yet—

"I do not believe it!" he cried, hotly.

She flushed angrily. "You were always sceptical," she rejoined. She looked at him firmly. The struggle had come, and she knew it; and with the knowledge a nervous excitement quickened her to combat. The thought that he would yield easily maddened her; but she was not a coward, and she faced that as she had faced the rest.

With vivid intensity his figure, as he stood before her, was photographed upon her brain. In all the years that came it was Michael Akershem as he looked that moment that she remembered. The maze of hair, the cut of his coat, the ink-stains upon his finger-tips, the very pattern of his cravat—these dwelt in her mind then and forever after. He himself was half angry, half humbled.

As Rachel stood there, wrapped, as in a mantle, in her indomitable pride, he realized, as he had never realized before, the wealth of her nature, the immensity of the love with which she had loved him. And then a tide of relief swelled within him that the crisis was to be faced and the suspense at an end.

Stung by a quick suspicion, he spoke harshly. "Rachel," he said, "is there some one else?"

A wave of resentment swept over her, staining her cheek; a wrathful light leaped to her eyes. She grew icy. "Why not?" she demanded, insolently. And he, remembering Anna Allard, was silent.

He stretched out his hand without replying. "At least we are friends," he said.

Her hand closed upon his with nervous tension. "Not yet," she answered; "after a time—perhaps."

She swayed and leaned lightly against him, her head resting against his arm. Then by an effort she held herself erect, and, lifting her head, kissed him once. "It was a very nice game," she said.

In a sudden forgetfulness of all save her and what she had been to him, he held her from him, trying to read denial in her eyes.

"Little comrade," he said, "can't we throw up the game? Can't we settle down into commonplaces and matrimony at last?"

The laugh that broke from her was a reaction from her passionate self-control, but he did not know it.

"What a prosaic ending to our theories!" she said. "No; it is better so."

He turned from her towards the door. On his way out he upset her work-table, scattering a pile of colored silks upon the carpet.

"I beg your pardon," he said, bluntly, stooping to gather them up.

"Don't trouble yourself," she answered, looking up. "It is no matter."

And he went out.

Rachel stood beside the table as he had left her. She leaned over the bowl of nasturtiums, crushing a flaming blossom between her fingers; its blood stained her hand. "It would all be so ridiculous," she said, "if one could only see the humorous side."

Her glance fell upon the shrouded canvas, and she went over to it, drawing the curtain hurriedly aside. Taking down her palette, she emptied a tube of yellow ochre upon it, squeezing it out with lavish haste, after which she stirred it absently with a camel's-hair brush.

"There is always something left," she said, and, looking up, found that the twilight had crept in upon her. She laid her palette aside.

"It is too dark to work," she said, "so it won't matter if I cry a little." And she laid her head upon her arm and wept.

CHAPTER III

Michael walked along the corridor, and pressed the electric button summoning the elevator. As he stood waiting he straightened himself with the gesture of one relieved of a grievous weight. " So that is over," he said.

The conviction of its finality was impressed so forcibly upon his brain that, when he reached the ground-floor, he was surprised to find himself wondering what course he should pursue in view of a possible reconciliation. The climax having been precipitated by Rachel, she, he told himself, was alone responsible. But with the sudden removal of suspense, and the passing of the jubilant revulsion succeeding it, a gnawing doubt of his own sincerity assailed him.

He left the house, walking along Eighteenth Street, and turning into Broadway at the corner.

" So that is over," he repeated, in a vehement endeavor to reassure himself.

Then he threw back his head with the impatience of a horse that resents the curb.

" Hang it all!" he exclaimed. " What is the matter with me ?"

A moment before he would have sworn that freedom was the one thing needful; and perhaps it was, but he felt no freer to-day than he had felt yesterday or the day before. The fact that Rachel had annulled the unspoken contract was insufficient. A slow consciousness that he, not Rachel, was responsible for the annulment oppressed him with stubborn insistence. Vainly he sought to intimidate the consciousness by undue influence; he might obscure it by sanguine assurances, but when the assurances were hushed he

knew that it would rise and confront him. He admitted
dimly that six months ago such words from Rachel would
have had no power to release herself or him from their vol-
untary obligations. He was aware, although he refused to
acknowledge it, that for him to retrace his steps and to accuse Rachel of the treachery of which he was unwilling to
accuse himself would be to virtually reseal their broken
faith. And yet—

"It is her choice." And the rising conviction that he
lied irritated him unbearably.

In his uncertainty he walked the streets until midnight,
when he returned to his rooms. As he opened his door he
spoke. "It is over," he said. As he struck a light he
spoke again. "I will see her to-morrow," he said.

That a personal interview indicated a truce to hostilities
he admitted, and with a sinking confidence in his own good
faith he shrank from clinching matters so irrevocably—
upon the side of Rachel. With the cowardliness which
he would have derided in another, he compromised. Standing beside the mantel, he drew out his note-book, and, tearing a leaf from it, scribbled a line:

"You cannot mean it; I refuse to consider this final. If
you loved me, you would not let me go."

This he kept by him until morning, when, before going
to his breakfast, he sent it to Rachel's room. In a moment the messenger returned. There was no answer, he
said.

Vehemently Michael demanded whom he had seen, and,
when he had learned that it had been Rachel herself, was
divided between anger and astonishment.

In a fit of anger, which was increased by a sleepless
night, he went to his office without breakfasting. The disorder upon his desk annoyed him, and he spoke sharply to
a reviewer who inquired for a missing volume. He found
himself unable to concentrate his attention, and the task of
pruning one of Kyle's leaders was so irksome that he gave
it up in disgust. The editing of a paper he felt to be a

species of refined damnation. Suddenly he rose, pushing
all the papers upon his desk into a confused jumble.

"Kyle," he called, "I've given out! Take charge of this
confounded stuff, will you?"

Kyle looked up sympathetically. "Overwork, Akershem," he said. "I should advise your seeking medical
advice."

"Advice is the kind of rot that comes unsought," returned Akershem, crossly. "I want quiet. I'll go off
somewhere."

Kyle laughed softly. "The city editor's lot is not an
easy one," he remarked. But Michael had left the office.

The possibility of encountering Rachel if he returned to
his apartments occurred to him, and he went to a restaurant
for dinner. Then, with a feeling that New York and the
tumult of New York maddened him, he took the ferry, buying a ticket in Jersey City and boarding the first train he
came upon. Action of any kind was better than inertia,
and to be rushing to hell preferable to standing still.

He settled himself, throwing his overcoat upon the seat
facing him, and surveying with an angry glance his fellow-
passengers. Before the train pulled out from the station he
was thrown in a nervous rage by the sounds without—by
the hurry in the station-yard, by the equanimity of the por-
ters, and by the steam from an engine upon the track beside him. A frail lady carrying a milliner's box took the
section in front of him, and he felt an instantaneous dislike
for her, for the bundles beside her, and for the crimps of
her hair. A stout gentleman, entering from the rear, paused
beside him to remove a silk hat and don a travelling-cap,
and he disliked the stout gentleman even more than he had
disliked the frail lady. At the end of the car a baby cried,
and he felt that he disliked the baby most of all.

Then with a jerk that irritated him the train started.
The relief of motion was so great that for a moment the
strain seemed lifted.

An agent passed with an armful of books. He took the

first that was handed him, running the leaves idly through his fingers. It was Mr. Chambers's *King in Yellow*, and the head-lines caught his eye, conveying an impression without an idea: "The Repairer of Reputations." Why should not reputations be repaired? "The Yellow Sign." Why yellow? And then "The Studio" staggered him with the suddenness of a blow. From the page before him, suggested by the words, the familiar room dawned gradually: the glow of the fire in the grate, the faded carpet upon the floor, the Eastern pottery in one corner, the pictures on the wall, the plaster casts above the door, the marble statue of "Hope" upon a little table, the bust of Michael Angelo upon her desk, the hangings at the windows, the paints, the brushes, the canvases — all the objects upon which she had impressed her vivid personality. The recollection was not pleasant; it was by a mechanical predominance of memory over will that it prevailed.

Striving to banish the real by the ideal, he followed the page upon which his eye had fallen:

"He said: 'For whom do you wait?'"

"And I answered: 'When she comes I shall know her.'"

He threw the book aside. For whom did he wait? Then—

"I am a man," he said, "and I will face it."

What it was that he thus determined to confront he did not know. To himself he admitted no possible reason for Rachel's decision. He accepted it mentally, as he had accepted it the evening before, viewing the facts of his life through a discolored veil.

The flickering lights of the train reflected upon the window-pane dazzled him, the swaying motion seemed the result of intoxication. He stared into the obscurity with unseeing eyes. The landscape stretched in a sombre weirdness that was as a triumph of the supernatural. A dim line of pearl-colored clouds in the distance suggested a possible horizon to the blackness—blackness broken only by shrouded outlines of leafless trees and barbed-wire fences, speeding rapidly past, their places being as rapidly refilled.

He brushed the frown from his brow with a single gesture of his hand.   Desire had so long guided him in the guise of reason that it was no great difficulty to follow where it led, deeming himself secure.   It was as if his whole being sprang forward, drawn by some magnetic force, seeking, however dimly, a loadstar in the distance.   What that load-star signified he dared not question.   He even put its existence angrily aside; and yet, ignore it as he would, a calm presence shone as through a nebulous vista, far beyond the tumult of the present, and—ignore it still more doggedly— that presence was Anna Allard.

The severe recoil from the sinking reefs of his fanaticism served as an impetus which impelled him towards conventions.   His nature strained towards that decent ambition of decent people—respectability.   Love and notoriety were his for the asking, but not honor and—Anna Allard.

Beyond the difficulties investing the path that led to the accomplishment of his desire rose the objects desired, the more alluring to his combative nature because unattainable. And yet—   Why unattainable?   Only yesterday he had noticed the altered looks bent upon him.   Only yesterday his hand had been grasped by a man whom he had long held as an opponent—an apostle of respectability.   It had been a new experience and a pleasurable one.   Now that his mind was purged from passion, he could look upon men as they were, not as his diseased imagination had distorted them.   He saw that in his old enmity against the world he had pursued a course devoid of policy.

To get the best that the world can give and hold it grudgingly is a surer revenge than squandering one's birth-right of ability in the waging of a fruitless war.   It was not that he had grown fonder of the world or of those men who called themselves his brothers, but that he realized that the revolt of the one against the many is an ineffectual revolt; that to take all life can offer is wiser than offering one's self a victim upon the sacrificial altar of conventions.

Yes ; he wanted the opportunities that men open only to

men who are like themselves. He wanted his reputation repaired. What an excellent thing it was that one had the power to repair one's reputation! In a flash he remembered the appointment of which Driscoll had spoken. He knew that a word from Driscoll would procure it, and he also knew how gladly Driscoll would speak that word. Driscoll! Why was it that the name of the man whose esteem he most coveted was linked in his mind to the name of the woman who he now knew had hindered his career? Why was it that in facing Driscoll he must face Rachel also? Were they in league against him? Was Driscoll that some one whose existence she had not denied? Then even to his prejudiced eyes the subterfuge showed too weak to stand. Absurdity was bald upon the face of it.

He ground his teeth as one in torture. What was it that haunted him? Without was the blackness of night, within the glare of swinging lamps.

What was it? Passionately he strove to collect himself, but that something—that intangible something, for which he had no name and no acknowledgment—rose from the chaos of thought and confronted him. All the accumulated experience of years, the lingering effects of which acted as his conscience, grouped themselves one by one about him. His sense of gratitude, which served him for a sense of duty, awoke. All the little kindnesses that men had done unto him and forgotten were resurrected from the dust in which they had lain, grouping about a light and gracious vision that glimmered in the night without.

His nature still strained onward through that pale vista leading ahead, but something which fettered him like a chain held him back; and that chain was formed by links of the little kindnesses of men.

In the chain came the farmer in his rusty suit of jeans, turning to look at him with his watery eyes, and passing him the supper which he had saved from his own. Why did that link him to Rachel?

The minister, with his great nose and short chin; the

books which he had loaned him; the seventeen cents jingling in his pocket, as he, a little outcast, darted along the dusty road that evening; his very enjoyment of that circus— why did that link him to Rachel?

The woman who had held his head that night in the public park, the softened look in her eyes as she chafed his forehead, the dime that she had slipped into his hand—why did that link him to Rachel?

And Driscoll? Driscoll, as he sat in his office chair looking with cynical eyes upon life; Driscoll, who had stood as a pillar of fire to his mental night — why, above all, did Driscoll link him to Rachel?

Goaded to frenzy, he raised the window, leaning out into the night, watching the train as it rounded a curve, speeding with fiery eyes into blackness. A hot air laden with cinders blew into his face.

"Will you kindly lower that window? I am subject to neuralgia."

The frail lady was speaking. He looked at her blankly, and she was forced to repeat her request before he complied. The lady retired into her berth, and soon the curtains were put up along the aisle.

A man took the seat beside him, turning to follow drowsily the movements of the porter. It was the stout gentleman with the gray travelling-cap. He folded a single sheet of *The Herald* into a narrow strip, tapping his nose reflectively. "Unusually chilly for this season," he remarked.

Michael stared at him absently. "It is hot," he replied; "or is it cold?"

The stout gentleman bestowed upon him that pleasant smile with which we favor those less gifted than ourselves in the matter of intellect. "Well, cold, rather," he responded, amiably. Then he continued: "We are having trouble out West again, I see."

"Yes," said Michael, turning his dazed eyes to the window. "A blizzard, was it not?"

Another pleasant smile crossed the gentleman's face. "I

was alluding to the strike," he answered. "The blizzard happened yesterday. We don't take account of yesterday's news in Chicago. We take to-day's, and grumble because we can't get to-morrow's."

The gentleman departed to his berth, and Michael put up his hand to screen his eyes from the glaring lamps. The porter touched him upon the arm. "I shall sit up," he said, surlily.

And in the morning, when, upon reaching Richmond, he found himself in time for the returning train, he took it. The trip had saved him from insanity, and decided nothing.

That night he spent at a hotel, and the next morning, drawn by very indecision, he returned to his rooms. On the way he passed Rachel's studio, and from a sudden impulse knocked at the door. There was no answer. Opening it, he was startled by blank walls; the firelight, the hangings, the canvases, the casts, the pictures — all were gone, and Rachel with them. In the haste with which she had deserted her accustomed spot he read a feverish shrinking from himself; in the bare wall and the sacrilegious sacking of this her temple he saw the overthrow of those passionate divinities of the past. It was as one who enters a cathedral that has been suffused with the purple mysticism of mediæval ages to find it naked to the cold, raw light of modern thought. The last shred of romanticism, draping the altar before which he had knelt, was swept aside. Rachel's spirit, that light, elusive essence of modernism, the outcome of an effete civilization, crumbling to dust upon the soil from which she, an untranslatable mixture of the past and the future, had sprung, had escaped as a vapor from the place thereof.

In an agonizing perplexity he left, going to his office. There he found disorder and excitement. Mr. Mushington, the man of money, awaited him. He had a complaint to lodge, and he lodged it with emphasis.

"The paper is going down," he said. "There is a mad-

ness about the editorials which amounts to insanity. Can
you explain it, sir ?"

Akershem looked into his red and bloated face with in-
solent eyes.

"I cannot," he answered. It was his first revolt from
the service of Mammon.

"Then, sir, you know precious little about your business !"

In sudden fury the Gordian knot was severed.

"And will know still less about it in future. Expect my
resignation."

He would let this infernal nonsense go. He was sick of
fanaticism and women. By one stroke he had cut himself
adrift from his old life, ridding himself forever of the past
and of the present. Only the future remained.

He remembered Driscoll and the appointment. That
was his chance, and he would make it good.

As he rushed from the office a group of reporters, assembled about the door, drew back.

"What's up with Akershem?" asked one. "He's as
mad as a March hare."

The sleeplessness, the perplexity, had fed upon him, producing an agony that was almost insanity. He felt his
blood coursing like fire through his veins, and a dull pain
started at the base of his brain. Lights flickered and
danced before his eyes.

The primitive lawlessness of his nature, aggravated by
the swaddling-bands of the hot-bed of civilization, rose in
a tempestuous desire to assert itself. Conventions which,
acting like a moral strait-jacket, curb the normal man, in-
flame the abnormal. But conventions are created and
stamped with the Divine signature, not for the one, but for
the many.

He entered a bar-room, drinking a glass of brandy, but
it failed to drive the lights away. It was as if his eyeballs
were on fire.

With an impetuous haste he rushed to Driscoll's room,

and found that gentleman sitting before the fire, a bottle of brandy at his hand and misery upon his face.

Seeing Akershem, he exclaimed: "The very man! Behold me in the clutches of the devil. He is sawing every bone in my right side to bits. I leave for Florida to-day."

Akershem took no notice. "Look here, Driscoll," he said, excitedly, "I have resigned from *The Iconoclast*. I want that credential for Splicer."

Driscoll looked at him inquiringly. Then, without speaking, he rose and limped to his desk. As he put his right foot to the floor his brow contracted with pain. "It is a temptation never to rise," he remarked, "and having risen, it is an equal temptation never to sit." With pen in hand he paused. "It's all right about the place, Shem," he said. "But"—he hesitated a moment—"Shem, this is a serious affair—more serious for you than for most men. You see, you must square up all your accounts. You can hardly re-adjust your political views until you have made reparation for your discarded social ones."

Michael flinched. "Those have readjusted themselves," he replied, stolidly.

Over Driscoll's face a warm light broke; a flash of relief brightened his eyes. "That's right!" he exclaimed, heartily. "I expected it of you, old fellow. So that explains why I found Miss Gavin's studio deserted when I called there yesterday. Where are you staying?"

A ramifying humiliation shot through Michael's frame. It was like the application of an electric wire to raw flesh. The sensation was so strange that it half startled him. Never in his life had he felt this slow sense of rising shame that he felt before Driscoll—the man who believed in him. A red flush mounted to his brow. Then, with desperate resolve, he raised his eyes. "I cannot tell where Miss Gavin is," he answered, "because I do not know."

The keenness of Driscoll's glance made him wince sharply. "Why, what does it mean?"

Michael laughed; it was a harsh laugh, which grated

from lack of humor. Instinctively he realized the suspicion in Driscoll's mind, and it angered him. "It means," he retorted, fiercely, "that she, like the world, has weighed me in the balance and found me wanting."

A flash of perplexity shot from Driscoll's eyes. "That she might have done so to her advantage, I admit," he said; "that she has done so, I refuse to believe."

Akershem flushed hotly. He was exhausted, and the lights flickered before his eyes. "Then get her to explain," he broke in, passionately, "for I am sick of the whole confounded thing."

"But explain you shall. If there is a grain of manliness left in you you will make good the debt you owe her. Good God, man I do you know that she has sacrificed more for you than your salvation is worth?"

The blinking of Michael's lids grew faster and a yellow flame shot from his eyes. His face was gray, and upon his brow that purple vein leaped forth like the brand of Cain.

"Do I need you to tell me that?" he thundered. "I tell you I know nothing of her and her vagaries—nothing!"

Driscoll's voice was low and distinct, cutting the passion-ladened air like steel. "This," he said, "is a fitting climax to your conduct of late. Would a man who had *acquired* an instinct of honor owe to one woman the debt that you owed, and turn from her to follow like a spaniel at the heels of another? Perhaps I shall hear of your engagement in that quarter," he added, with untempered irony.

Michael was quivering from head to foot. "I love where I choose, and I marry where I choose!" he exclaimed, hotly.

And then Driscoll turned upon him. "I had thought you an honest fanatic," he said, "but now I know you are a damned scoundrel!"

Akershem shivered from the white-heat within him. The lights in the air before him flamed from blue to green and from green to scarlet. His eyes flickered like rusty iron through which a red-hot fire is passing. "I would kill another man for that!" His voice was choked and muffled.

Driscoll laughed sarcastically. Then, with a quick return of his old manner, he took up his pen. As he did so he flinched from a twinge of pain. "Hold on, if you please," he called, for Michael had reached the door. "Allow me to give you this," he continued, with icy courtesy, "and, believe me, it will give me great pleasure to use my influence, now and always, for the advancement of your business interests."

Michael crushed the paper in his hand convulsively. Then he threw it from him. He wished that it had been dynamite, that it might explode, blowing Driscoll, himself, and the room to atoms. "Take that for your influence!" he exclaimed.

As he stood there in his passionate defiance something of the old Michael whom Driscoll had first known and loved shone in him, and the fascination which his dominant nature exerted over all who loved him cast a shadowy spell over John Driscoll again. He softened suddenly. "Shem," he said, with a gesture that was half appealing, "I would have forgiven you anything else."

And—"Damn your forgiveness!" cried Michael, as he rushed out.

The rage within him was so great that it stifled him, and he put up his hand to loosen his collar. A terrible ringing began in his ears. Every bell in New York seemed to burst upon him with an infernal din, ringing him out of the city.

He rushed on, almost oblivious of his way. He saw that he walked upon bricks and they burned his feet. He saw that people were passing about him, and he longed to fall upon them, one and all, to do some terrible damage to mankind or to himself. A newsboy held a paper towards him and he pushed it aside with an oath. A tiny child stumbled and fell at his feet, and he strode over it and went upon his way.

As he ascended the stairs leading to his office an adver-

16

tising agent passed him, and he bit his tongue to keep back a volley of curses.   Upon the landing a young lawyer, who had an office across the hall, was standing, a huge volume under his arm, and Michael put him aside as he would have put a child.

Entering his office, he slammed the door violently.   When he saw that he was not alone, that Kyle sat at his desk, he attacked him vehemently.   "Can I never have my room to myself?" he demanded.   And Kyle turned upon him, and he saw that his rage was equal to his own.

Kyle left the desk, and Akershem crossed over and stood beside it.   They regarded each other in silence, as beasts awaiting a spring.   Michael was breathing so heavily that the labored sound fell harshly upon the stillness of the room.

Kyle spoke first.   "So this is the end of your principles?" he sneered, with a snap of his fingers.

Akershem clinched his hand with such force that the nails grew purple.   A fleck of foam whitened his lips.   "Confound you!" he retorted, "what is it to you?"

"Did you strike a good bargain?"   Kyle's voice rose jeeringly.   "How much was your honor worth?"

With one hand Akershem opened a drawer, closing upon something.   The other he stretched out passionately, as if warding off Kyle.

"Take care, Kyle!" he shouted, hoarsely—"take care!"

"You blackguard!   Can't you name your price?"

There was a sudden flash as of lightning; one report that rang out sharply upon the silence; a tiny cloud of smoke wreathing heavenward like the breath of a prayer.

"Oh!" cried Kyle, sharply.   He coughed a half-choked cough; a clot of blood rose to his lips, oozing slowly down upon his shirt, and from his shirt to the floor—drip, drip, drip.   He reached out, clutching at emptiness, and fell heavily forward.

Akershem threw the revolver from him.   It struck the opposite wall with a dull clank.   Then he knelt beside Kyle, feeling, with white, nerveless fingers, for his heart.

"Kyle! Kyle!" he called. "Speak! You aren't hurt! It can't be! Speak! Call me a blackguard—anything!"

Kyle's eyes stared at him blankly, barren of all reproach; his hand fell limp and relaxed at his side.

In his agony Michael rose, stretching out groping, agonized fingers, clutching, as Kyle had clutched, at emptiness. "Oh, my God!" he cried.

There was a stir at the door; in a moment it opened, and when his eyes had cleared a group surrounded him. They surveyed him curiously.

Suddenly a man coming in pushed them aside. "What is it?" he cried. "What does it mean?"

The lawyer with the volume under his arm turned quickly. "Mean?" he answered, with professional exactness. "Why, it means manslaughter."

THERE was noise and confusion in the depot. A Presidential candidate, after having successfully instilled into the ears of the North the fact of his absolute loyalty to that section, was journeying South for the purpose of convincing the voters below Mason and Dixon's line of the exact opposite. As he strolled along the platform frantic cheers arose from the rabble assembled. Above this jubilant expression of a nation's confidence sounded the mocking whistle of out-going trains, and the shouting of station-hands as they succeeded in demolishing a piece of heavy baggage.

A gentleman standing upon the outskirts of the throng turned to wink at his companion. "Touching tribute of public favor," he remarked; then apologized to some one, who, in leaving the waiting-room, had stumbled against him, thereby knocking him breathless. "Pardon me for existing—" he began, when all irony fled. "John Driscoll, as I'm alive!" he exclaimed. "What! Seek you the clime of eternal sunshine?"

Halting suddenly, Driscoll recognized the speaker and smiled. He looked ill and worn, and acute physical pain had sharpened his features. As he walked he limped slightly.

"You are looking badly, man," continued the first gentleman.

Without replying Driscoll tossed his grip to a porter. "Florida Special," he said. "Section six. Look sharp!" Then he smiled again. "You see, it's this plagued rheumatism," he explained. "I am all but insane! If I can't cut this eternal civilization my mind won't be worth a con-

tinental.   As long as your bones aren't crumbling you can
put up with it, but the devil and civilization at one dose
will prepare any man for bedlam."

"It is annoying," commented the second gentleman,
motioning to the excited crowd.   "Witness some of the
faults of our nervous age.   Now civilization is—"

"Tommy-rot!" interrupted Driscoll, crossly.   "But you
can't get rid of it," he complained, irritably.   "I've tried
every spot upon the known world.   Even Greenland has
its explorers ; and as for Africa, by Jove ! I settled in a jun-
gle once, when who should come along but a missionary
who wanted to convert the apes.   And Florida ! why, when
I bought my place near Key West there wasn't a man in
shooting distance, and now, mind you, a German has put
up a cottage across from me with green window-blinds.   Of
all the abominations of civilization there is not one that I
abhor so utterly as green window-blinds."

"But you return to them."

"Not I !   I am going to buy a little island to myself—
one of those small ones, you know, off Jamaica—and there
I'm going to settle, and I'll shoot the first thing in clothes
that sets foot upon it—"

"Hello!" called a man from behind; "that's Mr. Driscoll,
isn't it ?   I say, John, this is a bad thing about Akershem."

Driscoll scowled silently.

"Why, what has he done now?" demanded the first gentleman.   "I thought he had quieted down of late."

"The mischief !   Why, there's been a row at *The Iconoclast*.   Something between Akershem and—what's his name,
that Irish fellow ?"

Driscoll started.   "What is it ?" he demanded.   "Who
is it ?   When did it happen ?"

"They quarrelled—something about the paper, they say
—and Akershem shot him down.   Shot him in cold—"

"Here, porter !" called Driscoll, excitedly, "stop my baggage; it can't go !   Confound it, let it go if it wants to !"
And he rushed off.

At the door some one stopped him inquiringly. "What's wrong?"

"Oh, Akershem! He's made a fool of himself at last." And he passed on.

"That's a weakness of Driscoll's that I can't understand," remarked the first gentleman, with a shrug of his shoulders.

"Nor I," agreed the second. "I always said Akershem would come to the gallows. It's no surprise to me."

"He was always such a—such a cad, you know," added the third.

In John Driscoll's mind just then there was only room for self-reproach. It seemed to him that his own impetuosity had been the cause of Akershem's overthrow. Knowing Michael's undisciplined nature and his own disciplined one, he told himself that he was a fool to judge him as he judged himself—or any other man. As the result of conflicting circumstances he saw that Michael was but a victim to disregarded but controlling laws—laws that remain ignored for generations, and recoil upon the heads of the children of children. Now that his anger had cooled he saw in him not the man revolting against the system, but the abnormal development revolting against the normal. He beheld in him an expression of the old savage type, beaten out by civilization, and yet recurring here and there in the history of the race, to wage the old savage war against society. And he reproached himself, remembering Michael as he had seen him last, his nature aroused in all its primitive ferocity; the seething passion which he, John Driscoll, had laughed at because he could not understand. It seemed to him that had he reached forth and drawn him back, had he ventured one appeal to that better nature which was overthrown and vanquished, this tragedy might have been averted.

He, the cynic; he, the clear-headed scientist, had been dolt enough to ignore the force of that unreasoning violence because the force was opposed to his own. Dolt! Idiot!

And now, when the key turned in the lock and he stood

face to face with Akershem, he felt constrained from very strength of feeling.

Michael, hearing the opening door, turned from the window of his cell and faced him. The daylight sifting through the bars showed the intensity that hate and wretchedness had graven upon his face.

" Shem !"

He came slowly forward, and for a moment they stood with locked hands.

" Driscoll ! so it is you !"

Driscoll felt something choke in his throat; he coughed. " Shem, old man," he repeated, and it was all that he could say. There was so much to feel and so little to express.

Akershem turned from him as if avoiding an expression of sympathy. He walked restlessly towards the door and restlessly back again. " So you have heard ?" he said.

" Yes."

He went on rapidly. He looked feverish, his face was flushed, and there was suppressed excitement in his voice; his eyes emitted a nervous glare. " To think that it was Kyle !" he said. " If it had been some one else I don't think I should have been so cut up; but Kyle of all men. Why wasn't it Mr. Mushington ? Why wasn't it that beast Van Houne ? Why was it obliged to be anybody ? I never hurt anything in my life. I always hated pain. I could not see a chicken-fight without getting sick. Why did I do it ? Oh, I was mad—mad ! And yet if I was mad, why do I remember it so distinctly ? I see him as he stood there. I see him clutch out. I see the blood that he coughed up, oozing upon his shirt. I see him as he lay there dead—stone-dead."

Driscoll groaned. " Shem," he reasoned, " it was in self-defence. Stop and remember. Surely he would have struck you."

Michael threw back his head impatiently. The fever in his face deepened.

" No ; he only spoke. I remember it well. He held out

his hand, but it was his gesture, and I knew it. He was always dramatic, you know. I tell you he was right; he knew me better than I knew myself—"

"But he raised his hand. Think; your freedom depends upon it. He came towards you, he raised his hand."

"It was a gesture, I tell you, and I knew it. Am I a fool? Do you want to make a liar of me as well as a murderer? Good God!"

Driscoll looked into his excited face and grew angry. Did Akershem realize that he was ruining himself? Was he mad? He felt an impulse to kick somebody — Akershem or himself. Why, after all, should he hold himself responsible for Michael—for his love affairs and his crimes? What had he to do with it?

Akershem was silent, his gaze bent upon the floor. He was wellnigh delirious, and Driscoll, seeing it, was softened.

Suddenly Akershem spoke. "Poor Kyle," he said.

A twinge of rheumatism caused Driscoll to flinch sharply. The physical pain irritated him. He was provoked by Akershem's obstinacy and his own concern.

"Do you know," continued Akershem, "that the only thing I ever killed in my life was a rabbit? I murdered a rabbit once—shot it just as I shot Kyle, in cold blood. I did it for pure devilment—for the pleasure of it. I was a fiend then, as I was a fiend yesterday. I wanted blood. And since I have been sitting here and trying to think of Kyle, I can't believe it. It seems to me that I am a boy and that it is a rabbit. I see it as clearly as I saw it then —the pasture, the sunrise, and the rabbit in the road. I see it all alive, and then I hear the cry it gave; I see the blood on its mouth, and the life has gone out. It is that horrible feeling of having crushed out life. Why is it that I can't get that rabbit out of my head? It was Kyle— Kyle—Kyle. And I was not mad. I was only a devil."

"For God's sake, Shem, be quiet! If money and influence are worth anything you shall be free, but you must help us."

But Akershem paid no heed; he had fallen into a torpor, and was gazing at the bare walls.

"Unless the New York lawyers are bigger fools, or a New York jury honester men than those of any other spot, we will get you off," added Driscoll. Afterwards he wondered why Kyle's death had seemed such a small matter in comparison with Akershem's liberty, and could not say.

On his way out Semple overtook him, and his sympathetic utterances increased Driscoll's ill-humor. He was disgusted with the world, with Semple, with Akershem, with himself. This infernal aching in his limbs—would it never leave off?

"Our counsel," said Semple, with accustomed optimism, "is the best in New York. Akershem will be backed by wealth and influence, two powers which count. If the worst comes to the worst, we must remember that justice is salable. But I wish you'd reason with him, Mr. Driscoll, when he grows quieter. It is out of all question, the stand that he takes. Public opinion was never on his side, and he can't afford to trifle with it. He'll have to fight prejudices enough without adding to them."

A twinge again. "Hang it all!" broke in Driscoll, irritably. "Haven't I reasoned with him until I haven't a grain left for my own use? After getting us into this confounded mess, Akershem sits up and talks his rot. He knows it will depend upon us to get him out."

"It is unfortunate," admitted Semple, his jovial brow clouding. "He has been reckless, far too reckless. I feared evil."

"It is a pity you didn't fear it a little sooner; then you might have refrained from instilling your nonsense into him. He has only lived out the views you play with. Good-evening."

Turning a corner he disappeared, leaving Semple transfixed upon the sidewalk.

Between physical and mental pain Driscoll was wellnigh exhausted. He was tired of humanity in general and

Hedley Semple in particular. He wanted only to be alone and to think. As he opened his door a slight sound from the inside caused him to frown blackly. "More fools," he muttered.

Then he entered, and Rachel Gavin rose and came towards him. She had been sitting before the fire, her brow resting upon her gloved hand, and at his entrance had risen hurriedly, her muff falling to the floor. Despite the pain in her eyes her whole figure was so light and blooming—so vitally alive—that the contrast between it and the jaded man whom he had left in his cell jarred Driscoll painfully. He felt that Rachel and he were at the bottom of the whole tragedy. "Can't you, at least, keep out of this?" he demanded.

Rachel stopped suddenly, a slight, startled figure, before him. Even then he noticed that there was an added dignity in her presence—the dignity of grief. "Oh, you must help me!" she cried. "You don't—you can't—know what it means!"

He felt goaded and harassed. The agony in his arm as he lifted it turned him white. But for these two he would have left this climate and have found relief. The knowledge that for Rachel's sake he had put all the passion of his nature into that last interview—the interview that had driven Michael to his ruin—hardened him. "My ignorance of your meaning I confess," he said, ironically. "As to what you are driving at, I suppose it concerns Akershem."

She grew white; the terror in her eyes was appealing. "Tell me," she pleaded, "how you left him?"

"In excellent health. You can hardly expect his spirits to be above zero; ours are not."

"But you must help me. I must see him. Won't you take me?"

He eyed her with irritated displeasure. "Are you sure that he would wish to see you?" he asked, and felt dully the cruelty of his speech.

She drew back, shivering slightly as one in pain. From her face all trace of color had flown. "That—that is not the question," she faltered.

And then in desperation he spoke, knowing that he alone had the power to save the few shreds that remained of a reputation that had once been as white as driven snow, and that for her at least Akershem would not be worth the sacrifice.

"We would go together, you and I," he said, mockingly. "The world has a sense of humor, and we should afford it an opportunity for gratifying it. It would say that we were beginning to console each other, you and I."

Some demon seemed urging him on. Again she shivered, hiding her face in her hands, and again he felt the brutality of his words.

When she looked up it was with fresh resolve. Her hat had slipped aside, and he saw the anguish upon her face. "But—but you can't understand. It is my fault," she pleaded, the tear-drops falling from her eyes upon her gloved hands—"it is my fault! Oh, how can I bear it!" The last was a cry of agony, wrung from her by the memory of his words. He looked at her, and his eyes softened. "You cannot judge him, nor can I," she said, and his heart hardened. How dare she seek to palliate Michael's guilt to him! "He is all impulse—all emotion. We—"

"Yes, you and I are without feeling," he assented, in grim irony.

"Oh, don't! don't!" she cried, despairingly. "Pity me! —at least pity me!"

"Rachel!"

"I have made so many mistakes," she sobbed, "I have done so much harm. I have ruined him whom I loved. My purest motive has been at fault. But if you knew all you would have mercy!"

"Rachel, don't mind me. Can't you see that I don't

mean it? I only seek to spare you—to spare you a useless sacrifice !"

"Useless !"

"He thinks only of himself and his—his fault. If you went to him the whole world would condemn you. It would spoil all chances of your future life, and—"

"What is that to me? What do I care for my life?"

"And not help him."

"But—but I must go !"

"He has not mentioned you."   ·

"I must see him !"   .

"He does not think of you."

She looked at him, her hands clasped convulsively. "Why—why are you so cruel?" she asked.

The smile that he bent upon her was half sad, half cynical. "Perhaps I *have* a few sensations, after all," he replied, "despite your previous assertion."

She turned from him hopelessly, then back again. "If —if he asks for me, will you take me?" she asked.

He looked down upon her and held out his hand. "Yes," he said.

She went out silently, but in a moment came back. Her eyes, as she looked at him, were luminous. "Forgive me !" she said. "You are a far—far better friend to him than I have been."

"Rachel !" He cried the name sharply. She held out her hands and he took them in his own.

"You made him," she said, with a shadow of her old radiant smile, "and I have unmade him."

For Rachel yesterday he could have killed Michael ; to Rachel to-day he could speak no word.

"Good-bye," she said, and passed out.

Driscoll stood looking after her. He saw her muff lying upon the floor where she had left it, and he calculated the amount of agony that it would cost to stoop and pick it up. The calculation overbalanced his possible powers of endurance, and he decided to let it lie. Then he turned slowly around. A tea-table stood beside him, and for a moment his eyes rested upon the sugar-bowl of Crown Derby. Then with a deliberate gesture he lifted it and hurled it at the opposite wall. It fell with a crash.

"Damn everybody!" he said.

MICHAEL sat in his cell. A single ray of white light entering from above fell across his bowed head, across the table upon which his arm rested, across the cold and uncarpeted floor. Upon the table before him lay a pile of unanswered letters, and at one corner a confused heap of telegrams; but he was thinking neither of them nor of their senders. Even when the words caught his eye—"Sympathy. Wire if I can be of the slightest use"—they seemed an empty form, devoid of significance. He had sorted the letters mechanically, desiring rather to occupy his hands than his mind. He was vaguely surprised at the interest strangers had shown in the trial and its results. He was even annoyed by the tenor of a host of anonymous communications. Those abnormities—half women, half fools—that had plied him, as they plied the wife-murderer next door, with condolence, revolted him. He knew that a print of himself in the Sunday *World* had sufficed to turn some of the sentimentality of the feminine portion of mankind in his direction, and dully he resented it. Near his hand lay a perfumed note with which the nameless sympathizer had sent crimson roses, and the odor of the flowers caused him a sickening sensation. He had placed them as near the door as possible.

Sensibly the strain of the last few weeks had told upon him. His face had grown gray and bloodless, the haggard lines accentuated by his heavy hair. The hand resting, relaxed and nerveless, upon the table had lost its old vigorous grasp. With his impassioned nature retribution had followed swiftly upon crime.

Suddenly the key turned in the lock. He started with a

terror that was childlike in its instinctiveness. As a man entered he stared at him blankly, seeing that it was his senior counsel, but making no motion of recognition.

The man came forward and stopped. He coughed deprecatingly.

"Mr. Akershem."

Michael looked up inquiringly.

"Mr. Akershem"—he paused to rub his hands with affable hesitancy—"you will understand that, considering the prejudices your previous career has inspired in the mind of the public, the verdict was not—er—not unexpected. The fact that it was lighter than was generally looked for (he had assumed the tone he employed to the jury) is due, we believe—if you will allow us to say so—to our personal interest in the case and the tireless efforts of your friends—"

"Yes," interrupted Michael, "but—"

"As you know, there has been a refusal to set aside the verdict."

Michael returned his gaze with blank regard, and, as the lawyer paused, stood crumpling the telegrams between his fingers, his lips twitching slightly. "Cowards, they are afraid of me!" he muttered, passionately.

The other rubbed his hands sympathetically.

"Ah! ahem!" he began, "believe me, you have my sympathy—my deepest sympathy."

"Ten years!" said Michael, slowly, and he paced restlessly up and down his cell. "Ten years!" he repeated.

The lawyer cast a glance of professional compassion upon him and departed. At the door he stumbled against John Driscoll, who was waiting upon the outside.

"Your zeal is commendable, my dear sir," he remarked, and hurried off.

Driscoll entered the cell, and stood for a moment with his eyes upon Michael. Then he came forward, resting one hand upon his arm. "Well, old man?" he said.

Michael looked at him with nervous intensity. "Ten years!" he said, in a half-whisper. "Ten years! Did you hear what that fool said, Driscoll? Somehow I did not take it in before. Ten years! Surely there is some mistake. Driscoll, can't you inquire if there is not a mistake?"

Something stuck in Driscoll's throat; he shook his head without replying.

"Why, ten years is a lifetime!" continued Michael, breathlessly. "I have so much to do, so much to fight for. Take ten years away, and there will be nothing left. I have had only ten years. It was ten years ago that I came to New York and went into your office and demanded work. Do you remember? I was a boy then. I knew as much of life as a baby. Since then I have fought hard. I have worked like a slave, and for what? To do manual labor in Sing Sing. Good God! I tell you it can't be! I have my life to live. What is anything compared to my ambition? I tell you—"

"Shem, be quiet, for God's sake!"

A shudder ran through Driscoll's frame. Something rose before his eyes and blinded him. He threw himself into Akershem's chair, resting his head upon the table. For the first time in his life he could have cried like a child.

He looked at Michael, standing tall and stalwart before him; he saw the haggard brow, the restless limbs, the whole impassioned frame. Over Driscoll a wave of bitterness swept, and at that moment, had it been in his power to redeem that blasted life, he could have struck Akershem dead at his feet. The energetic brow, the flaming eyes, the whole throbbing vitality of the man! Was this their end? O God, the pity of it! In a flash Michael's life passed before him as vivid as the writing on the wall. The good which weighed in the balance with the evil of his blood had been found wanting. The Nemesis of a broken law flamed, a fiery revelation, before his eyes. He saw Akershem, fearless and elated, bearing ever upon him the stamp of genius; saw his strong hands fighting the circumstances which hemmed him in, and, foiled, still fighting in the face of overwhelming odds. He saw Michael as he

had first appeared to him, awing him—cynic as he was—
by that vital and dominant nature ; saw him standing with
upraised hand against an opposing world, victorious by the
unconquerable force of his blood, a force which, recoiling
upon his single head at last, had played into the hands of
the Philistines.

He saw the impress that one man had stamped upon his
surroundings.   He saw himself, satiated with the shams of
life, cleaving unto the one nature which was fearlessly itself, sincere alike in good and evil.   The ruined waste that,
meteor-like, he had wrought in the lives of others blackened
the sketch of his thought ; Rachel, a sacrifice to that force
which draws the aberrant body to its allotted orbit ; Kyle,
a victim to the velocity of the body in its recoil.   All the
terrible penalties that man pays to an outraged nature,
these confronted him.   And lifting his head he looked at
Michael Akershem, and his heart bled with the pity of it.

"Driscoll," said Michael, suddenly.

Driscoll smiled sadly.   "Well?" he asked.

"You—you have stood by me like a brick."   It was the
first sign of gratitude Michael had shown, and it pained
Driscoll.

"Don't, Shem," he pleaded.   Then, with an awkward
struggle for words, he went on : "You know that I would
have given my life to spare you.   Not that it is worth
much," he added with a smile, rubbing his ankle ; "pain is
its essential principle just now.   But for rheumatism I'd
hardly know I was alive."

Michael stopped before him.   "You go to Florida?" he
inquired, with but little show of interest.

"If this confounded thing doesn't go to my heart instead," responded Driscoll.   Then his tone changed.   "But
I haven't given up yet, Shem," he added ; "but for the fact
that several honest men had gotten in the wrong place I'd
have settled it.   As it is, not many weeks shall pass by that
the Governor doesn't hear from me.   He will yield at last
from sheer exasperation."

17

Akershem shook his head impatiently and continued his walk. Then he spoke with an outburst of his old bitterness. Unconsciously his adjustment to conventions had failed; he stood once more at odds with the world. "I am fortunate to have one friend," he said.

Catching a subtle inflection, Driscoll turned quickly. "You have many," he answered; and, "Is there any one in particular whom you wish to see?"

No answer.

"Shem, don't let a woman come between us now."

Akershem smiled. "Nor any man," he added.

"Perhaps—" Driscoll hesitated, but only for a moment; then he began again: "Have you thought of Miss Gavin?"

Michael laughed mirthlessly; the bitterness of his speech stung sharply. "Only that she should congratulate herself," he returned. "Her selection of the proper moment resembles intuition."

"You are wrong, man," said Driscoll, gently; "but—but do you wish to see her?"

A flush rose to Michael's face. With the old passion for sympathy was revivified the old passion for Rachel. It flickered for an instant and went out.

"Could I?" he asked.

Driscoll rose and limped stiffly over to him. "Shem"— he laid one hand upon his arm—"all the women in America could not make me hard on you, but" — he caught his breath—"but is it for love of her? Think what it would mean to her. Do you desire her because you love her or because she loves you?" He waited patiently, but Akershem did not answer.

And the next morning as Rachel worked in her studio the door opened and Driscoll entered. She started slightly, looking up from the colors she was mixing. Since he had last seen her a change had passed over her—something indefinable, blotting out all vivid tints of her youth. She was thinner, and beneath her eyes the purple shadows had deepened; even her lips had lost their scarlet ripeness.

Sitting there with a patience which ill became her, toiling mechanically for the food which she desired not, she appealed to him as she had not done in all her past radiance.

He lifted a paper from the table, examining it idly. It was a colored print of Paris fashions, a chromo-like array of slim-waisted, large-hipped women promenading upon air. He stared at it wonderingly. "What abomination is this?" he inquired.

Taking it from him, she placed it on the table before her, a smile breaking the firm lines of her lips.

"I shall become quite an authority upon fashions," she said, lightly. "Having nothing better to do, I have taken to copying designs."

He looked at her in dismay. "And you do this?" he asked.

At his horror-struck tones she laughed a little, and then went on with her work, her head sinking lower over the table. "One must live, you know," she answered.

"Where is your painting?"

"Behind you are the remains," she replied, with a pitiful attempt at her old animation. "Somehow it isn't bread and meat." Then she added : "I work upon it at odd times. Some day I shall get back my old power."

With the words a sudden flush overspread her face, and he saw that the lingering embers of a great ambition were still warm.

He pointed to the fashion-sheet in disgust. "And who pays you for that filth?" he asked.

"Madame Estelle."

"The modiste?"

She nodded.

"But you loathe it?" he said.

"No," she smiled; "far from it. Indeed, I am growing rather fond of it; it is so expressionless. I always loved colors, and here there are colors and nothing else. My painting sickens me; it is all emotion."

He glanced at the veiled "Magdalen" and sighed. Then

he walked to the fireplace and stood looking into the empty grate. He remembered that she disliked steam-heat, and the thought of her poverty smote him. That she was making a struggle to retain these, her old rooms, to which she had returned, he knew at a glance. One cannot let one's hand lie idle for a couple of years without paying the price.

"You see, I am a cabbage," continued Rachel, with a humorous smile. "All my animal vitality has become exhausted, and I shall stagnate for the balance of my life. When one only eats and sleeps and breathes and loses one's combativeness one becomes a plant, and when one grows to enjoy it one becomes a cabbage. I used to hate cabbages," she added, slowly.

"Rachel!" She looked up and smiled upon him—her old bewildering smile. "Is there not some one down South to look after you?"

An expression of pain crossed her face; she shook her head. "Down there they are all dead," she answered. And added, quietly, "And here I am dead."

He laid his hand upon the back of her chair. "I—I am a poor party to mother anybody," he said, "but I can't leave you like this."

She smiled again. "It is the only kindness you can do me," she answered.

"But you are so lonely."

Her lip trembled for an instant and was firm. "You can hardly have come to tell me that," she responded.

"No," he said, "no. I came to tell you that—that he had rather not see you."

For a moment her busy hands lay still. She looked up at him with dazed eyes that caused him to put out his hand in pained protest. Then she took up her knife again.

"He had rather not?" she repeated, mechanically, and went on with her work.

He stood over her an instant, and then held out his hand. "Good-bye!" he said.

She took it idly. "Good-bye," she echoed.

He went to the door, looked back at her, moved a step forward, looked back again, and passed out. But as he descended the stairs he heard his name called and lingered. She stood upon the landing looking after him, her hands outstretched. He went up to her, clasping them in his own.

"Little soldier," he said, "the fight is not over."

Like a flame her old iridescence enveloped her. She grew vivid.

"You must not go until—until"—her hands closed more firmly over his—"until I have thanked you for your goodness."

Misunderstanding her, he winced.

"Akershem is my friend," he replied. "I should have been a cad not to stand by him."

A hot flush rose to her brow; the tears shone in her eyes, making them luminous.

"I—I did not mean that," she faltered. "I should not presume to thank you for your faithfulness to your—your friends." And she left him.

When the door had closed upon her he turned slowly and descended the stairs, passing from Rachel and from Rachel's life.

INTO the Academy a flood of sunshine drifted, illumining the canvases upon the wall with a golden shimmer dazzling to the eye of the beholder. It was opening day, and a suppressed excitement weighted the atmosphere, emanating probably from the natural possessors of the illumined canvases. Here and there the spring bonnets of the ladies showed amidst the sombre-toned gathering like early blossoms cleaving brown soil, while the light-hued gowns belonging to the wearers of the bonnets lent variegated dashes of color to the nondescript assembly.

In the corners and about the entrances small groups clustered, talking in half-whispers, their voices rising in frequent interjections.

"Oh, do find Clara's picture!" cried a girl in brown, breaking suddenly away from her companions. "Somebody please tell me the name of it. She said it was splendidly hung." No attention being paid to her, she went rapidly on: "Do you know Geoff Lorrilard sold his 'Antigone' for nine hundred? He painted it from the same model that I am using for 'Cleopatra.' Oh, there is a beauty of Bruce Crane's! Look at it! The exhibition is finer this year than it has ever been, they say. Dupont says American art is looking up, and Dupont despises all but the French, you know."

"I hear he has hung a picture which is making a row," broke in a young man with a note-book. "The painter is unknown; I am inclined to think it is Dupont himself. It savors of the French School decidedly."

"Dupont could not do anything so strong as that," remarked another of the group; "it is a new hand. That brush has never dabbled in milk-and-water. What! you haven't seen it?" And they passed out.

An elderly gentleman with a very young lady entered suddenly and paused before an effect in blue.

"Hello!" exclaimed the gentleman, "here's one of Nevins's." And, glancing up, he caught the eye of that artist through a gold-rimmed eye-glass. "How are you, Nevins?" he inquired. "Still producing babies, I see."

Mr. Nevins sauntered over to them. "Well, yes," he admitted; "but you will notice they are no longer at the breast. It has taken me ten years to wean them, and in ten more I expect to have them adults."

The gentleman laughed, and the young lady colored and looked hastily for a number in her catalogue.

"I should think that a grown-up, clothed and in his right mind, would be a pleasant novelty," commented the gentleman. "I'm not a baby-fancier myself."

Mr. Nevins spread out his hands deprecatingly and shrugged his shoulders. "Nor I," he protested. "I never see a baby off canvas without wanting to smash it. It is by severe self-restraint that I keep my hands off my models. But the public must be gratified, you know, and a good half the public are mothers. Babies sell. Nothing else does. I have tried landscapes, portraits, figures, nude and draped, and I return to the inevitable baby. I bring out a baby as regularly as the Season comes." Then he smiled broadly. "John Driscoll used to call me the All-Father," he added.

The young lady looked up quickly. "Oh, do tell me something about Mr. Driscoll," she said. "We used to be such friends, but it has been six—no, eight—years—how time does fly!—since he went away."

"Eight," said Mr. Nevins. "It was shortly after that Akershem affair, but he has been back several times since then. He has been working to get Akershem out; the only job he has ever undertaken in which I could not wish him success."

"Poor fellow!" sighed the young lady, and was silent. Then she held out her hand to an acquaintance. "Why, Mrs. Van Dam," she said, "this is a pleasure! We may always count upon Mrs. Van Dam as a patron of true art, mayn't we, Mr. Nevins?"

Mr. Nevins thought that upon the whole we might, and a pale young man in Mrs. Van Dam's train was convinced of it.

Mrs. Van Dam had raised her veil, and was levelling her lorgnettes at the canvases within her line of vision.

"I am with my daughter," she explained. "She has lived South since her marriage, you know, but she is so fond of art. Cornelia, my dear, I want you to know— Why, where is Cornelia?', she added. Cornelia not being forthcoming, she went placidly on. "You must come into the next room," she said, "and tell me what you think of that large painting, 'Mary of Magdala.' It is the success of the Season. Dupont exhibits it, you know, and he is simply wild about it. So is Mr. McDonough, who is an enthusiast over American art. He proposes presenting it to the Metropolitan, I hear."

They passed into the next room, pausing suddenly before a canvas which hung facing them. At first one noticed à deep-toned richness that suggested a Leonardo, and then from the perspective of gray and green loomed the Magdalen. There was a boldness in the drawing which might have been startling, but was only impressive. In the whole strong-limbed figure, of which the mud-stained drapery seemed to accentuate the sensuous curves, a living woman moved and breathed. In the mire at her feet lay a single rose. Above her head a full moon was rising, casting a pale-lemon light upon her garments, falling like a halo about the head of one scapegoat for the sins of men.

"The painter is a realist," muttered the pale young man. "I don't like realism."

The young lady rustled her catalogue. "How beautiful," she murmured, "and how strange! Why, those eyes are marvellous. There is every emotion in them of which the human heart is capable—every emotion except remorse."

Then she looked for the name. "Merely 'Mary of Magdala,'" she said. "But who is the artist?"

"That is Dupont's secret," said some one from behind. "He is pledged to silence, he says."

"It would be interesting," remarked Mrs. Van Dam, "to know the artist."

"What! you haven't heard?" cried a new-comer, with an air implying the immensity of his own information upon the subject. "It is an open secret. Dupont won't tell, but he'll hint."

The young lady interrupted him eagerly. "Why, who is it?" she asked.

"Well, there can be no harm in saying, I suppose, that it is a Miss Gavin. You remember she did some fine work years ago, but she got under a cloud and was lost sight of."

"Oh," sighed the young lady, "how brilliantly she has reappeared!"

Mrs. Van Dam put up her lorgnettes and surveyed her disapprovingly. "Do you think so?" she said, in an intended undertone. "For my part, I consider that it is adding impertinence to infamy."

The young lady colored and looked down.

"My dear Mrs. Van Dam," reasoned Mr. Nevins, with his usual disregard of danger, "remember that the voice of this democratic people of ours is the voice of God. When it proclaims 'famous' it drowns our 'infamous.'"

The descendant of the Byrds of Westover turned her gaze upon him.

"One may expect anything of democracies," she said.

With a deprecatory shrug, Mr. Nevins spread out his hands. "But the Voice," he insisted.

"I agree with Mrs. Van Dam," declared the pale young man. "After all, the potent voice is the voice of Society."

Mr. Nevins's shrug was still more deprecatory. "What! is Society curtailing vice?" he asked.

"Why, mamma"—a young matron with the face of an angel slipped her arm through Mrs. Van Dam's—"Mr. Lorrilard is saying that the 'Magdalen' is Rachel Gavin's. Can it be? How did you hear that Rachel was dead?"

Mrs. Van Dam stiffened. "From the best authority," she replied, haughtily.

"But she isn't. It was all a mistake, and just look at her work. Why, it is so like Rachel! It makes one think that Christ saw holiness when our blind eyes beheld only crime."

"Why, Cornelia!"

"From the mouths of babes," remarked Mr. Nevins, in an audible aside.

The young matron turned back as she was drawn away. "It is as beautiful as Rachel," she said, "and as brave."

And in her studio, shut in by four walls from the tumult of the outside city, sat Rachel herself. She had grown thin and colorless. It was as if the brush of Nature had blotted out her bloom with a single stroke as she blotted out the colors upon her canvas. The air of close rooms and the strain of overwork had destroyed the vividness of her youth. She was Rachel still—a Rachel that awoke at odd moments in laugh and voice that chased across her worn face in fleeting gleams, like the gleams from a sun that has set.

"So you tell me that I must go to Paris?" she said. She was speaking to Dupont as he stood beside her, having taken the brush from her hand.

"Leave this dirty work," he answered. "Let Madame Estelle and her gowns go to Hades."

Rachel laughed a little bitterly. "This dirty work," she answered, "has fed me when I was hungry and clothed me when I was naked. My painting has not done that."

"It is your fault," he answered. "You have been faithless. I tell you your 'Magdalen' will make you—make you, do you hear?"

" If the making is more satisfactory than Providence's, I shall not complain," she answered, with a touch of cynicism. Then she smiled at him, the smile radiating across her sharpened features. " Dear master," she said, " when one has earned one's bread by copying dressmaker's designs, with a little wood-engraving thrown in, one feels like eating that bread and digesting it without any special saying of grace."

He stamped his foot. " Only a fool or a woman would have bartered such a talent for a mess of sour pottage," he answered.

She flushed, and then, rising, faced him. " I am no longer young," she said. " I am very tired. Art either maddens or wearies me. When it maddens me I do great things— a 'Magdalen'; when it wearies me I do dirty work. If I might only go on copying designs." Then her tone changed. " I will do all you wish," she said.

He looked into her white and wasted face, and beneath his gaze a slow flush rose, tingeing her cheeks.

" I have won you back to art," he said.

An infusion of vitality seemed to surge through her veins.

" I will do you honor," she answered.

THROUGH the crowd which thronged Broadway at six o'clock a man passed. Amidst the congregate mass of moving atoms his outline was all but imperceptible, presenting to an observer from a distant height as indistinct an individuality as is presented to us by the individual in a writhing army of ants. He was an entity, but, surrounded by a host of greater and lesser entities, the fact of his personal existence was not conducive to philosophic reflection in another than himself.

There was a sharp edge to the air as biting as a mid-winter's frost. If one could have swept aside all visual impediments one might have seen an April sunset dyeing the broken west, a track left by the sun as he ploughed his bloody way across golden furrows.

Above the city the smoke hovered low in a neutral-toned cloud, obscuring what was still day in the open country.

The crowd in the street moved rapidly, dividing in two dark lines that passed in opposite directions. As the man walked he pushed aside with a feverish impatience those that came within his reach, moving as if indifferent to the human stream around him. He stooped slightly, as one who is old or in pain or both, sometimes staggering from loss of breath consequent upon his haste.

He was of medium height, with a frame that might once have seemed of iron, the skeleton of which still resisted the disease that was wasting the flesh away. His features were rendered larger than their wont by the hollows of cheek and brow, and the skin drawn loosely over them was dry and colorless—the burned-out fuel of a hectic fire. Upon his temples the heavy hair was matted and dashed with

gray, and the hand that he raised impatiently to brush aside
an imaginary lock trembled like the hand of one palsied.
It was as if a gigantic statue, formed for power and for endurance, were making a struggle against some insidious
enemy feeding upon flesh and blood. Reaching the corner,
the man paused for a moment, strangling back a fit of
coughing which broke control at last. For the first time he
looked up and glanced about him. It was the corner of
Fourteenth Street, and across the way the words "The
Iconoclast" stared him in the eyes. He remembered that
he had stood at this same corner eighteen years ago, and
had read that sign idly and with ignorance of the part it
would play in the fulfilling of his life. It was new then,
and shiny; now it showed battered and weather-beaten.
It had breasted the years as he had breasted them. Behind him was the warehouse upon which he had seen the
notice of "Men Wanted." He remembered its oblong
shape, the size of the letters, and the effect of the white
tracing upon the blackboard, and instinctively he felt in his
pocket for the phial of laudanum. Could that really have
been eighteen years ago? Why, it seemed only yesterday.
He glanced up at the office window of *The Iconoclast's* city
editor—Driscoll's window it had been then, and he almost
expected to find those shrewd eyes looking at him from behind closed blinds. The thought made him nervous, and
he moved a few feet away.

For the last week, since the hospital doctor had signed
a certificate that secured him his freedom and he had left
the prison behind him, he had been consumed with the
dread of encountering old associations. Driscoll was
South, he supposed, and he was glad of it. Before facing
Driscoll again he must face the world and become rein-
stated in his old Championship of liberty. Through his
wasted limbs his unwasted energy vibrated. He was not
beaten yet.

A policeman touched his arm and motioned him not to
obstruct the crossing. The policeman looked at him as he

would have looked at any respectable but obtruding citizen, but Michael resented the look, and, with a defiant retort, moved onward.   He hated those pugilistic protectors of the peace.

For days he had roamed the streets as feverishly as he had done in his youth, drawn as by some impelling force to his old surroundings, and yet dreading the sight of a familiar face, shrinking from the casual glance of the passer-by.   Before he returned to do battle with the world he must rally his broken forces, must clothe this protruding skeleton with flesh.   Freedom and good food would manage it, but he must give them time.   He remembered the stains upon his handkerchief yesterday.   Pshaw! was he the man to die from the loss of a drop of blood?   There was vitality in him yet.

At Eighteenth Street he turned as from habit, and paused as he found himself facing the Templeton.   From the first floor to the eighth lights shone in the windows, in the very rooms that he had once occupied.   The sight startled him. It was with a certain wonderment that he found the world unaltered.   He had been in hell for eight years and more, and not one laugh the less was heard upon the streets, not one smile the less crossed the faces in the crowd, not one shadow the more fell over his familiar haunts.   It was as it had been, and as it would be though he perished.   How fleeting is the effect that one man produces upon his time! An idol is exalted in the market-place; it falls, and upon its crumbling ruins another is raised towards heaven.   For men there are many divinities, and for a fallen idol there is the mire.

Upon the sidewalk he loitered, glancing into the cheerful interiors.   Vaguely he wondered if these people knew that he—Michael Akershem—stood without.   In one, a room suffused with lamplight, a mother sat singing to the young child upon her breast.   The placidity of her expression annoyed him.   He knew that though poverty and misery stalked in the night at her door she would not awaken the sleeping child or cease her soothing lullaby. In another a woman sat alone. She was lithe and young, and something in the curve of her shapely head brought Rachel to his mind. In such warm and soft firelight had Rachel waited for him in the old days when he was worth waiting for. Now Rachel had gone back to her art and was doing great things—things such as she had always meant to do. One evening in the elevated road he had heard two artists speaking of her and her future. In his embittered mind the praise had inspired an aggrieved jealousy. She, whom he had loved to his own undoing, was gathering her meed of fame, for the crumbs of which he was famishing.

The shapely woman in the firelit room warmed him with memory of the time when a woman had thought the world well lost for the sake of him. Whatever came to her hereafter, once every vibration of her heart-strings had been his—his, a homeless vagrant, with his bones crumbling to dust.

An acute pain in his chest caused him to start suddenly. He remembered such a pain in that illness two years ago, when his breath had been like the agony of travail. Then, in the madness of delirium, he had called upon Rachel, and called in vain. Well, that was over and done with.

He turned away from the ruddy interiors and stood upon the corner, watching the straggling stream of passers-by— a laborer with a tin pail jingling noisily from his hand, a woman with crimson roses upon her breast and crimson marks upon her cheeks, another woman, a man, a child, a man again, a newsboy, a policeman. And then a woman in a fur coat passed him, turned suddenly, hesitated, and came back. Beneath the small hat her eyes looked out inquiringly; under her arm she carried a long roll.

With a tremor he recognized her and drew away. In the haggard face he turned from her only a woman's eyes could have seen Michael Akershem. He cowered into the shadow, but she came on.

" Michael !"

Her voice thrilled him, and he put out his hand, warding her off.

"Michael !"

She had reached him, her light touch was almost upon his arm.

" I am not Michael," he answered, hoarsely.

But as he lifted his head the electric light fell full upon him, and they stood in silence regarding each other. In that silence each looked across the years, and saw the past and the future drawing as to a point—and that point was the present.

She saw pain and misery and wasted strength ; she saw a dread of her and yet a need of her, a desire for solitude, like the desire of an animal that seeks the covert, and yet the longing for a ministering touch ; she saw the hand of Death looming above his face, and the sight made her bold, as would not the hand of Life.

He saw a woman from whom youth but not usefulness had fallen ; he saw shoulders that had borne strong burdens and might bear stronger ; he saw eyes that had looked upon life and found it futile, but that burned with his image as fervently as they had burned in the heat of the passionate past, and looking into them he saw constancy made manifest ; he saw the love that after years of wrong and wandering may lead us home at last.

"Michael, I am so glad !" Her hand was upon his arm, her gaze upon his face.

"Let me go !" he answered. "Oh, Rachel ! Rachel !"

Again he strove to strangle that grating cough, but it broke loose.

"No, no," she said, for he would have passed on. " You have come to me to be nursed and made quite strong again !" She tried to speak lightly, but her voice faltered. "Oh, my beloved, is it not so ?" she asked.

He spoke hoarsely ; his arm trembled from the weight of her detaining hand.

"It is nothing," he answered, but he no longer withstood her; "it is only a cold—it is chronic."

"I will cure it," she said.   A leaping of his pulses that was not the leaping of fear stimulated him.   At that moment the memory of the time when Rachel had craved his love and it had failed her was blotted out.   He remembered only the exuberant passion of his youth.

"Do you care, Rachel?   I am not worth it."

Still clinging to him, she led him on, talking in those light tones which came at will, drawing him from himself and to her.

They entered the Templeton, and, because he shrank from the elevator, mounted the stairs.   Her voice was clear and strong, the result of a nervous tension, warning her that to pause would be to break down, to discharge her swollen heart.

"I have been to the baker's," she said, as lightly as if they had parted the day before—"to the baker's to buy a loaf of bread.   I have supper in my studio now.   I am tired of restaurants and French cooking.   So, like Old Mother Hubbard, I have my little cupboard, to which I resort, and I have also, not a dog, but a cat—a nice gray cat."

His labored breathing caused her to pause for a moment, stooping to fasten the lace of her boot.   It took some little time, and then she resumed her slow ascent, slipping her hand through his arm.

"I have supper all by myself," she continued, "and you shall share it—you and the cat.   I have become quite a good cook, as you shall see.   My oysters are the pride of my life.   I haven't any one to appreciate them except, now and then, Dupont, because, you see, there isn't a soul here now that I care about.   The little mother with the twins moved out West, and Madame Laroque—didn't I tell you? —Madame's husband died and left her property in France, and his brother came over to see her about it.   But Madame declared that she could not survive the sight of a Frenchman, so she locked herself in her room.   Oh, it was

18

so funny! There was the brother-in-law besieging and Madame relentless. It went on for a couple of weeks, when, finally, Madame came down, and one day he met her upon the street, and in a week they were married and sailed to France." She paused, and the tears rose to her eyes.

They had reached her landing, and with an energetic movement she threw open the door of her studio.

"Here we are," she said, "and the tea is brewing, and the fire burning, and the cat waiting." She drew an arm-chair to the hearth-rug, laid his hat and coat aside, and piled a heap of downy cushions at his head. Then she took off her wrap and set about preparing her supper, talking as she might have talked ten years ago. It was all so natural, so much as it used to be—the room, the firelight, the shaded lamp, the casts, the hangings, the canvases—that the years seemed but shapeless spectres and his agony a dream unfulfilled.

He lay back among the cushions and looked at her, his brilliant eyes flaming from between the twitching lids like a slow fire consuming his shrunken features.

Over Rachel herself a radiance that was more than the radiance of the dancing firelight had fallen. Excitement crimsoned her cheeks, irradiating across brow and lips. In her eyes the lustre of her youth shone with its old splendors. All the vivid and evanescent charm that had once been hers returned for one fleeting moment to envelop her. He looked at her wonderingly.

"Why, Rachel," he said, and his tone was querulous, "you have not changed!"

She smiled upon him. "No," she answered, simply, "I have not changed."

She brought the little table and placed it before him, watching him with anxious eyes as he ate his oysters, and pretending to eat, herself.

The cat left the hearth-rug and leaped upon his knee, and he stroked it with a pitiable pleasure in the instinctive confidence animals had always felt in him. Broken and

ill as he was, the little things which he had disregarded in
his strength appealed to him in his weakness. Crushed by
the great things of life, he saw that the little things were good.

Rachel watched him with enraptured eyes. That buoyant interest in the minutiæ of life which had once irritated,
now soothed him. It was pleasant to be cared for, to have
some one care whether one ate or went hungry, whether one
coughed or was silent. He accepted her services apatheti-
cally, feeling not gratitude but contentment.

When he had finished she pushed the table aside, placed
the dishes upon a tray in the hall, and, drawing a stool to
his feet, sat beside him, resting her cheek upon his dry and
fevered hand.

He spoke pettishly. " I am a wreck," he said—" a broken
wreck. Look at that wrist ; the muscle is almost through
the flesh." And he added : " I am a cur that the stones
of mankind have beaten to death. Yes, I am beaten."

Rachel looked up at him. "You are and have always
been my hero," she answered. " From the night in that
little French restaurant when I looked up and found your
eyes upon me I have had no hero but you."

" A poor hero," he said, faintly, choking back the cough
in his throat.

He lay still for a while, so still that she fancied him exhausted and asleep. With a passionate tenderness she allowed her eyes to rest upon him, upon the drawn face and
the whole ruined length of him. And then—

" He is mine," she thought, exultingly—" mine for all
time !"

The broken and wasted remains of a great vitality, the
decay of a towering ambition, querulous complaints in place
of an impassioned reserve, death in place of life—these were
hers. Hers the scattered crumbs from the bread of life,
hers the stagnant slime left of an all-powerful passion.

She moved gently, loosening her hold upon his hand,
fearing to disturb his rest by an emotion which defied control. He stirred and turned towards her.

"Rachel," he said, "don't let go!"

Leaning above him, she kissed his brow, his eyes, his lips.

"You want me?" she asked, with passionate compassion.

He strove to raise himself, but she held him back.

"I always wanted you," he answered, "except when I was sure I had you." And he added, slowly: "You are so steadfast."

She kissed his burning hand. It was her reward.

He struggled up, a light flashing in his eyes, his dominant nature, undaunted by failure and death, asserting itself again.

"Rachel," he said, breathlessly, "would you fight the world for me?"

Her eyes caressed him.

"I would fight God for you!" she answered.

With a sudden energy he pushed back his chair and rose to his feet. As he did so a cord within his chest seemed to strain and snap asunder, loosening the foundations of life. He put up his hand to force back the paroxysm of coughing, but it broke forth with a strangled violence, and with it a thin line of blood rose to his lips, oozing upon the handkerchief with which he strove to stanch it.

He fell back in the chair, letting the scarlet stream pass between his lips, and putting aside the arms Rachel had cast about him.

Then in a moment it was over, and he lay looking up at her, his face carved in the marble whiteness of pain, his brilliant eyes unclouded. There was a harder battle to fight before the end would find him.

In his face the old fearless spirit which could be quenched but by dust shone brightly.

"Give me half a chance," he said, "and I will be even with the world at last!"

But upon his lips was set the blood-red seal of fate.

THE END

www.ingramcontent.com/pod-product-compliance
Lightning Source LLC
Chambersburg PA
CBHW060608030726
47498CB00005B/1600